is a perfect balance of romantic tension, well meaning friends, love on the rise. Add to that a sexy hot guy and a leading lady with important decisions to make about her career and her heart and I couldn't stop reading. I can't wait for the next book in this series.

— AUTHOR, D.W. MARSHALL

I0542166

ALSO FROM MIA HEINTZELMAN

THE ALL MIXED UP SERIES

(Each book can be read as a standalone)

Mixed Signals

Mixed Match

Mixed Emotions

All mixed up series boxset

STANDALONES

It's Got A Ring To It - Releasing Fall 2020

Wrapped up in beau

DARK ROMANCE

Devastated: Wastelands academy book 1

The Stack w/a Emmaline Zanthi

PRAISE FOR ALL MIXED UP SERIES

— PRAISE FOR MIXED SIGNALS

Mixed Signals is funny, snarky, and heart warming romance that I couldn't put down. I can't wait for the next book in the series.

— AUTHOR D.W. MARSHALL

I also liked the humor in the book, and the author's writing style was enjoyable.

— AMAZON REVIEWER, CRZYJEEVES

There's no mixed feelings on this one, I'm glad I read it.

— AMAZON REVIEWER, KATHERINE C.

Cute. Cute. Cute. This sent me into a tailspin. Think zombie but instead of brains, I wanted more books like this one. Cute with a bit of spice, and all things naughty and nice.

— GOODREADS REVIEWER, NICOLE

Mixed Signals was an unexpected surprise for me.

— GOODREADS REVIEWER, DESPINA

Enemies to lovers is my favorite troupe and this one just rocks it! If you like hate at first site books with convincing plot, great characters, hilarious banter, an uptight heroine, a swoon worthy hero, then please go for it. It was an enjoyable read and I like it a lot!

— GOODREADS REVIEWER, BOOKREVIEWER_98

— **PRAISE FOR MIXED MATCH**

This story had humor, heart, and heat and also made me hungry =).

— AMAZON REVIEWER, JESSICA C.

This is classic chick-lit with beautiful poetic passages and a hero and heroine you can root for. I highly recommend it.

— AMAZON REVIEWER, CASSANDRA

You know from the very beginning; this is a recipe for disaster without recovery and wonder these two can come out of this unscathed. I enjoyed the premise of this story and the journey to forgiveness and healing.

— MIDNIGHTACE BOOK BAR

I couldn't wait for this book to go live! I had the opportunity to read an ARC of Mixed Match and I loved it. There

ACKNOWLEDGMENTS

Here we are! Thank you for choosing my book and loving it (hopefully, since you've read all the way to the acknowledgements).

This book was so fun to write. I'm so fortunate to be able to venture down the path of writing, thanks to my favorite book boyfriend and husband, Daniel Heintzelman, who has allowed me to leap because he's my net, supporting me. And also, for understanding when I'm up to the tiny hours of the morning while the house is a mess.

On with the shout-outs!

Thank you to my critique group and writing family, my Thursday Night Therves. Margo Hendricks, Kristina Mull, Dionne Marshall, Diane Clough, and Beth Spaur, you are my fellow introverts and unleashed wild side. I know if you guys love it, I'm doing something right. Thanks for your invaluable, crazy, fun, and hashtaggable critique sessions.

To my editors, Danielle and Danylle of The Author's Assistant, I'm indebted to your polishing skills. You make my work shine. Thank you for your clear eyes and encouraging feedback.

A huge thank you to my Facebook group, the Miamors, my ARC team, and my newsletter subscribers. You are awesome. I love and appreciate your answers to my random questions and honest feedback you give. To librarians, bloggers, bookstagrammers, and reviewers, my sincerest thanks. You are the unspoken heroes who spread the word like wildfire about stories, which feed the mind and nourish the soul.

To my future agent, you, my vision board, and the universe know exactly who you are. I can't wait for you to read my books and know immediately you want to represent my fun, pulse-racing, contemporary romance experiences.

Big hugs and smoochie kisses to my family and friends. You are the petals on my flowering tree and the frame holding up my house. You understand and support me even though I'm always with my nose stuck in a book or with my fingers glued to a keyboard spinning tales.

Mommy and Daddy, I love that I'm equally both parts of your (semi-) social butterfly (okay, sometimes, anti-) and bookworm because you've given me a hungry mind and wings to soar.

My sister, Melissa DeGrazia, we're basically the same person in two bodies fighting with our reflections, but who better to have in my corner to support and uplift me? Thank you. Cheers to leaping in faith!

Finally, to my two daughters and my nieces and nephews, I hope my daring pursuit of greatness is inspiration and wind beneath your wings.

MIXED EMOTIONS

MIA HEINTZELMAN

LeviLynn

First Levi Lynn Books edition April 2020.

Levi Lynn Books can bring authors to your live event. For more information or to book an event, visit our website at www.miaheintzelman.com.

Editing by Danielle Acee and Danylle Salinas

Cover design and Formatting by Tangled Covers

Manufactured in the United States of America

Cataloguing-in-Publication Data
ASIN: B0863HJVYR
Name: Heintzelman, Mia, author.
Title: Mixed Emotions / Mia Heintzelman
Description: Mia Heintzelman | Las Vegas: Mia Heintzelman, 2020.
Subjects: Romance | Humorous fiction.

For Daniel and my crazy mixed up family.
Thank you for believing in my dream.

Mixed
Emotions

CHAPTER 1

ZORA

Z ora Monroe rubbed her arms as she looked up at the old building wishing she had taken one more shot of tequila before she left the house. "Brr. I'm freakin' freezing." Her top lip curled as she sighed. "Tell me again why we couldn't meet somewhere else…indoors, brighter, maybe less sketchy-looking."

She and her best friend, Olivia, were at some place a few blocks off Burnside Street near the concert hall, but she'd never been to this particular spot. From the outside, it looked like any other ancient gray, unmarked hole in the wall—nothing fancy that would have caught her attention otherwise. If not for the glare of the neon lights from the Portland sign, Zora's guard might have been raised higher than it already was.

The skimpy blue dress Oli had forced her into certainly wasn't keeping her warm, but just the look of the building had the hairs on the back of her bare neck standing taller than the spikes of her pixie cut.

"Try to remember this is a night for celebration and not

some deranged plot to get you out the house," Oli said with a straight face. Her eyes twinkled the tiniest bit, though.

"That's what you keep telling me." Zora peeked at her phone. Three little irritating dots were still sitting there baiting her.

"We're going to toast to you getting the best agent out there for your cookbook, and then we're all going to dance and drink way too much, and, hopefully, we won't remember any of it in the morning."

Ah, yes. The foolproof plan.

Though she was still feigning irritation, a smile crept across Zora's face because all of it did sound amazing. Well, except for the whole "drink way too much" part of it. She and alcohol were a slightly less greasy version of oil and vinegar: they did not mix.

"Wait a minute. Who is 'we all?'" she asked.

To this, Oli grinned and moved forward in the line before she turned her gaze back.

"Well, Sophia's scared about her little baby bump, and Everett goes where she goes, so they won't make it, but…" She dragged the word out. "Kara, Steph, Remi, and Lexi said they should make it…" Her brows danced and she bit back a shit-eating grin like she was going to burst if she held in the rest too long.

"And?" Zora slowly lowered her chin to her chest, waiting for the other shoe to drop. The crisp air shimmied up her arms, causing a shiver to vibrate through her, but she maintained her focus on Oli.

"And…you'll finally get to meet Andre."

Zora sighed, and her arms slumped at her sides. Disappointment hummed through her body.

Andre. The dude Oli met at a concert a few months back,

smashed, friend-zoned, and was apparently the perfect leftover to regift to her best friend.

Yay, me!

"Yeah, no thanks. I'm good. Who else?"

"Oh, do you mean Mike?" She pursed her lips and lightly tugged her earlobe—a surefire sign she was lying. "No. I didn't invite him."

Zora squinted her eyes at Oli, reading her.

"So, Mike *is* coming? I saw that little lippy earlobe thing you always do."

"No. He…was not invited." She shrugged and pivoted back toward the front of the line.

Zora stared for a few more seconds hoping to break her. Her friend was hell-bent on keeping whatever scheme she was up to under wraps.

The only problem was, when Zora allowed herself to be talked into this skanky dress, she imagined Mike's tongue falling to the floor when he saw her in it. If he wasn't going to be at the club…well, that just sucked. She was going to be stuck in a skimpy getup that highlighted every one of her physical insecurities. The skintight blue dress, the clear five-inch heels, and the pancake makeup were all part of a costume, hand-picked by her best friend, to supposedly boost her confidence and make her look fierce. As it turned out, it was all a big charade so she could meet a hand-me-down guy.

Perfect.

The thing was, Mike wasn't just any guy. He was her brother's best friend. Or, rather, her brother's older, disarmingly scrumptious best friend who'd been her "pedestal guy" for years. Over those years, no one had measured up because her fun-sized kid crush had developed into an insanely good-looking, green-eyed stunner with a lean build and broad shoulders.

"So, who else, then?" Zora snapped then immediately bit her tongue because the irritation in her voice was too telling and needed to be stopped. She tried not to let her shoulders slump.

"I've got a few surprises up my sleeves." Oli tossed a mischievous look over her shoulder before looking away. She knew Zora could read her better than anyone.

Again, why on earth did I let Oli talk me out of staying in?

"I'll have you know I'm missing an eighties movie marathon for this. You know, they're starting with *Weird Science*."

"Oh 'you know, your basic high school orgy type of thing.' 'It's a mindscrambler.' 'Hurts so good,'" Oli said in her best British accent. She was mocking Kelly LeBrock. Her thick brows dropped into a deep V, and beneath them, her brown eyes skewed into beady lasers. Everything about Oli fit the bill of sex goddess—her blunt-cut black bob, her olive-toned skin, and her full pout.

Blush pink bandage dresses worked for Oli because she had a banging body with normal-sized breasts and killer calves. She was perfection science couldn't manufacture, but a terrible actress, nevertheless.

A sex goddess, Zora was not.

Even with her best friend's fashion advice and styling, aside from the shimmery blue nails, none of her getup made her feel like herself. She'd tried to help Oli see that playing someone else's cards would only leave her lost in the shuffle.

She wanted no part of losing herself for a man.

She hugged her arms to her chest and bit back the chattering of her teeth.

"Whatever, Buttwad. The fact that you quoted the movie proves my point."

"Oh, you might miss it!" Oli put the back of her hand to her forehead in distress. "It's been out for like thirty-five years. I'm sure you already own it, along with every other movie released that decade, so just be present and enjoy yourself, for once."

In the midst of all the shivering and merriment, Zora's phone pinged, and now she really was excited.

It was her turn.

After a couple of minutes, she bit her bottom lip and thought for a second before tapping out a message rapid-fire on her phone. Her thumb hovered over the small green vertical arrow while she considered whether to send it.

Zora:
1. Haggis burgers are going to be the secret weapon for my cookbook.
2. I'm home with Oli on the couch binge-watching the second season of *Stranger Things*.
3. I've been forced to listen to Ev and Soph have sex for the fifth time today.

Ugh, this is too easy.

Zora could feel a serious case of side-eye coming from Oli's general direction. Together they inched forward along the black velvet ropes. Before she could second-guess it, she pressed send. Almost instantly, the phone pinged again.

Her smile was too wide to suppress.

"You're about to meet a fine-ass man, and while you should be practicing your stale flirting skills, you're seriously playing two truths and a lie with Mike?"

"Relax. I'm just—"

"Keeping tabs on him? Whipped? In denial that you're in love with him and have been since forever?"

Zora ignored Oli and read Mike's message as a second one popped up on the screen.

Mike: #2 You suck at lying. lol

Mike: First off, if you ever plan on beating
me at this game, the two truths should
not be glaringly obvious. lol. Your life
and your career are food, so I already
knew number one was true. But, for the
record, haggis is disgusting. No clue
how you're going to mix Scottish and
Creole food into one book. Second, if Ev
and Soph weren't screwing like rabbits,
I'd be worried they were calling off the
engagement. Where are you?

Oli grabbed for the phone, but Zora yanked it back. "What did he say?"

"Mind your own business. Go back to sending *your* little mysterious texts." Zora giggled and attempted to unscrew the lines of her face to give Oli a pointed look, but it did not deter the woman with balls of steel.

"Seriously, what did he say?"

Zora bit the inside of her cheek because she was dying to show Oli, but she liked to see her sweat, too. After a few seconds, Zora flashed the screen to her and Oli burst out laughing. "I love you Zo, but he's right. You really can't lie for shit."

"What?"

"Dummmmb," she dragged out the word. "Even if he did think the haggis thing was a lie, why did you include me in it? Literally, my motto...my mission...my *mantra* is to never be home on a Friday night. The day I cuddle up on your couch on a Friday night fantasizing about the Upside Down is the day I'm officially old."

Dammit, I knew that was too easy.

6

Zora yanked the phone back.

"And don't tell him where you are. Why does he care?" Oli asked.

As if to underscore Oli's rant and rub it in, the phone pinged yet again. Almost word for word, Mike reiterated the point about Oli's Friday night motto then listed his own three truth-lie options before sending another message.

> **Mike:** BTW, congrats on the lit agent. I'll buy you a round when I see you.

> **Zora:** Thanks!!! I still can't even believe it.

Beaming, Zora went back to check out his latest three truth-lie options. She could feel the heat of Oli's eyes blazing down on the screen as she tried to read.

"Shhh." She waved her away. "I can't hear myself think with you hovering like that."

"When you make your choice, will you please put the phone away before you ruin the whole night?" Oli folded her arms. Now, her tone was more serious than playfully pissed.

Why is she being so touchy about the phone?

Zora had no clue, but just when she was about to delve deeper into it, the corner of Oli's mouth lifted. "I want you to have some bubbly, get loose, and maybe try Andre on for size… pun intended."

"Gross."

"You have a book agent and a hot guy chilling on ice waiting for you to uncork him." A squeal escaped her lips as she held up her hand for a high five.

Reluctantly, Zora slapped her hand, but Oli held onto it for a second.

"Besides, I swear you and Mike act like freaking two-year-

7

olds—truth, lies. It's all the same thing. I just wish you guys would go ahead and smash again. Then you can decide whether he's worth all this torment and angst you've been putting yourself through. Or, *maybe* give someone else a chance. You're adults now. It's safe to stop playing games."

"I'm not listening to you." A giggle spilled out, but Zora only shook her head.

"Fine. Don't admit it, but Andre does kind of remind me of Mike. He's also a light skinned, baby faced, full-lipped brother, but less cerebral and brooding and more swaggalicious. He's a little bit taller...and a *doctor*," she said as if she was waiting for applause.

Zora peeked up over her brows. "Not following..."

"Think of the role playing you could do!" She swooned. "Plus, you are so fierce tonight. You're like a sleek, tall, Amazon bombshell dipped in bronze. Seriously, that dress never looked as good on me."

Zora snickered. "'Fierce' isn't exactly the word I'd use. Between this tight dress and these heels, I don't even know what to say." She shook her head in disbelief through a fit of giggles. "If Andre is so fine, why aren't *you* still with him?"

Come on, tequila, kick in.

Before Oli could answer, Zora dropped her gaze back to her phone and typed the number three followed by a long-nosed liar emoji.

"You know he's way more your type than mine." Oli grunted. "Anyway, you can't stop texting Mike for a night? The only lie is the one you guys keep telling yourselves. You've been holding each other at arms' length for I don't know how long. Why can't you just tell him how you feel and see what happens? It can't be that bad."

"Because I don't know if that's how I feel." They'd been over this. Innocent flirting and hanging out was one thing.

Going after him, being vulnerable... That was another thing completely.

Anxiety and irritation were affecting her words.

"I just...I like what we have. It's fun and comfortable and uncomplicated." *And perfect. He's perfect.* "I don't want to mess it up, and I don't want all that awkward insecurity and second-guessing. We're friends...practically family." The inflection in her voice rose to a high-pitched squeak when she said "family."

Oli covered her mouth with a fist and pointed at her. "Ooh, now there's a lie—a bold-faced lie."

Zora sighed and shrugged, but Oli's gaze narrowed.

"Yeah. Uh-huh. Keep telling yourself that. I have an eye for this sort of thing. The way you act around each other? I should snap a picture to let you both in on it."

Shit.

The thing about falling for a guy before hitting puberty is it has a way of ruining it for everyone else down the line. Oli knew it. Whether Zora wanted to admit it or not, she knew it, too. It certainly didn't make matters any better he was her brother's best friend.

"Look, let us be. We're good the way we are. We're just... having fun together. I don't want or need a man."

"Is that the story you're sticking with?"

"Yes, and anyway, I don't need any distractions. My agent —" Zora giggled at the way it sounded so surreal on her tongue. "She gave me twelve weeks to get this book ready. She wants me to find my niche and come up with a new title to go along with the pictures, recipes, and personal stories. I *really* don't need a man right now."

Well, maybe for a few things that didn't require her to buy batteries in bulk at Costco, but, no, really, she didn't want a man at the moment. *Especially, if it isn't Mike.*

Oli turned and grabbed Zora's hands, squeezing as she

deepened her gaze. "Fine. Whatever, but just for tonight, let's *lose* ourselves."

Oh, just...lose ourselves. No big deal. Nothing to write home about.

Except that it was for Zora.

Ever since she was four, her singular goal in life had been to *avoid* losing herself and to stay true to the woman her grandmother raised her to be—strong against the odds. It was exhausting but worth it when she knew what being weak did to a woman. *Mom.* Every day that she looked in the mirror, she was reminded.

For one night and for the friends who were coming to celebrate with her, though, she could afford to let loose. Heck, she was already dressed the part.

Zora put on her game face. "Fine."

Oli did a bouncy, happy dance and stepped forward as they reached the door. She opened her purse for the beefy doorman, then stopped to give him a sultry, batted lash look before she turned back and waggled her eyebrows at Zora.

"Work and play don't have to be mutually exclusive," she purred.

Zora was pretty sure that last bit wasn't meant solely for her benefit, considering the fine specimen of man her friend was flirting with.

Zora opened her small clutch, smiling awkwardly at the bouncer. "Thanks. *Anyway,*" she said to Oli. "Mike and I are friends. That's it. I'm fine by myself. Plus, he's with Kate, and, he's not here."

Oli snickered. "I'm just going to mind my own business, sit back, and watch what happens."

CHAPTER 2

MIKE

Michael Kennedy sat on the edge of a wooden stool with his elbows propped on the long, sleek black bar and his chin resting on his clasped hands. While he knew he should be looking around the silent disco for Olivia and Zora, he wasn't exactly in any hurry to find them, considering Kate's prickly mood.

"Do you see them yet?" she asked for about the fifth time since they'd arrived.

"Relax."

He wrapped his hand around Kate's and flashed her a reassuring smile. Within a few minutes, a young bartender with a full beard and two sleeves of tattoos nodded in his direction.

"I'll have a jack and Coke and a vodka cranberry for the lady," Mike called out over the hum of the crowd.

"You'd think they'd be here before anyone else."

The impatience in Kates's voice ripped through Mike's thoughts. It irritated the shit out of him, but at the moment, he was picking his battles. Really, he didn't know what to expect.

Would Kate and Zora resort to that female tendency to hate,

then judge, before looking closer to see if they liked one another?

Mike blew out a breath to try to take the edge off. It wasn't Zora he was worried about. He'd known her since she was a kid. The girl was laid-back, even-tempered, and fun-loving. But Kate was territorial and unpredictable—always on defense. This meant he was going to have to spend the rest of the night convincing Kate she had nothing to worry about.

He and Zora were friends.

How many times do I have to say it?

Mike scanned the sea of faces and swaying bodies. The silence was baiting his nerves. Maybe if he saw Zora first, he'd have a small advantage. Be able to gauge the situation and see where her head was at…warn her. But, still no sign of them.

Kate released an audible sighed.

"Chill. We just got here, too. They'll be here soon."

She whipped her head around to face and scrutinize him as if there was more to this night out. "I'm just a little confused. Tell me again why *you* have to be here?" Her tone was laced with accusation. "You're Everett's friend, not Zora's."

In a divine act, the bartender placed their order on the edge of the bar, saving him. Mike made a mental note to leave a generous tip.

"Thanks, man."

For a few seconds, he pinched the bridge of his nose. Then he grabbed both of their drinks. At this point, Kate seemed to sense his annoyance and shimmied between his legs, appealing to a lower power. Mike's hands betrayed him as he set his drink down again and let his hands wander down the thin fabric of her black mini dress.

He sighed.

Sadly, and far too cliché for his liking, if there was one thing that he was a sucker for, it was a tight dress.

Kate ran her fingers through his hair and waited for him to meet her gaze.

"I told you," Mike began. "With the high-risk pregnancy, Everett and Sophia didn't want to be out. Plus, Zora got a book agent and everyone is going to be here to celebrate. She's like a sister to me. I've known her forever." He exhaled and began again slow and measured. "You wanted to come. I could've just as easily dropped in by myself. I just want to tell her congratulations, so we only have to be here for a little while."

Mike laid two twenties on the bar, picked up his drink, and stood. "Tell you what. Why don't we put these headphones on and enjoy ourselves—have a good time while we wait for them?"

Kate shrugged and forced a tight smile. Her eyes were a frigid shade of iced marble.

"Drink up. Let's dance. I want to see you how you move in this dress." Mike winked, ignoring her attitude, and polished off his cocktail. As he waited for Kate to finish hers, he checked his phone one more time and pulled his headphones over his ears.

Before long, he and Kate were vibing to the hard beat of a rap mix, courtesy of the deejay on the right. Their headsets illuminated with blue lights, and bass pounded in their ears. Mike preferred the green station, but Kate kept urging him toward the upbeat sounds of some new mumble rapper.

Beat for beat, she matched Mike's moves, their bodies molded together as they grinded up against one another, groping and kissing.

Inarguably, Kate was *fine*. Physically, she could make any red-blooded, heterosexual male drool. She had wild, curly, blonde hair, cool ivory skin, and, usually, a pair of sunny blue eyes. Her face was *Cosmo*, her body was *Sports Illustrated Swim-*

suit Edition, and if that weren't enough, she was a Trailblazers cheerleader, to boot.

For the life of him, he couldn't understand how a woman with all the goods could be so insecure.

Zora wasn't his girlfriend. She was his bounce-ideas-off-her, call-when-you-need-a-friend, gets-me-on-a-different-level person, but that was just because they'd known each other for almost two decades. Kate should understand that. The fact that Zora had grown up from a scrawny, ashy-kneed kid into a woman was beside the point. It was bound to happen.

Mike lifted his chin and his eyes darted into the dark corners of the club, searching for Zora.

Still nothing.

"Turn to the green," Kate moaned, closing her eyes. Her hips were winding as she threw her hands up in the air.

"Gotcha." He forced a smile as he pushed the button.

As far as Mike was concerned, awkward introductions like the one about to happen tonight were further reason he kept his romantic life separate from his friends and family, especially Zora. It just seemed cleaner and neater that way.

Which was why *he* hadn't mentioned Zora's party to Kate.

When Olivia called out of the blue the week before, he'd only answered because he thought it might have been an emergency—that, and sheer curiosity since she never called him. During the few interactions they did have during game nights, he got the distinct impression Olivia hated him. So, he couldn't imagine why she was calling.

Unfortunately, once he was on the phone and Olivia got to talking about a celebration for Zora's book deal, he had a hell of a time trying to get her to pump the brakes. Not only was he busy working on the building purchase proposal that could tip the scales toward making him partner, but Kate was only a few feet away in the shower. Still, Olivia pressed on, insisting he take the details, and by the time he'd jotted them down, it was too late. Kate was already out of the shower, wondering where "we" were going.

"I can't wait to finally meet your friends."

For three days, the party was all Kate talked about *until* she found out the celebration was for Zora. So, Mike had been both looking forward to this day and dreading it.

Mike kept the drinks and the music flowing, and soon he'd loosened up and lost track of the time.

A flush crept over Kate's skin and she peeled her hair off her neck and pulled it into a ponytail. "I'm going to run to the restroom. I'll be right back." She was winded and smiling as she walked toward the back of the club. She seemed like she was finally having a good time.

In her wake, Mike didn't leave the dance floor. He closed his eyes and fell into the rhythm of the music. At the change of the song, he checked his phone to see there were still no updates on Olivia and Zora's whereabouts, but, as he lifted his chin and scanned the room, he spotted a couple of Zora's friends, Remi and Steph. They were dancing off to the side with some other girls he'd met once or twice but whose names he couldn't quite remember.

Mike waved.

When they saw him alone, they all rushed over to dance with him.

"Hey guys, how are you?" he asked, noticing the slight slur to his voice.

One by one, the girls greeted him with a hug.

"Oh my gosh. We thought you weren't coming." Remi's brows furrowed in question. "Zo is going to be so stoked."

"Yeah. Olivia invited me. I wouldn't have missed it for the world. I know how hard she's been working toward publishing her book. Where is she?" Mike lifted his chin above the crowd on the dance floor.

"You know how she is. She's over there by the bar pretending to have a good time. She's doing a good job of it tonight. Zo is fierce. *You* might not even recognize her."

"Oh, yeah?" He cocked his head to the side, unsure about what Remi meant.

Why wouldn't I recognize Zora?

"Uh…" His lips twitched as he bit back a laugh. He forgot exactly what he was about to say. For some reason he couldn't explain, a mixture of curiosity and disbelief flooded his insides. He needed to know what Remi was talking about. Whatever it was, it was enough to give him pause.

He hated change.

More to the point, he hated the idea of Zora changing.

In the back of his mind, she was sort of the sweet mainstay in his life—untouched by time. To him, she would always be Everett's crazy little sister who kept him tapped in to what was current and cool. She wasn't exactly a millennial, but she definitely had the undistracted drive and leaned into her goals with a fierceness he envied.

"I've, uh…been looking for her. Will you take me to her?"

Mike looked over his shoulder toward the restrooms for Kate before weaving himself into the crowd behind Remi and the other girls. As he worked his way around, the dimly lit wall framing the sleek bar came into view, and he felt a vibration in his pocket. He fished his phone out just as a notification dropped down from the top of the screen.

Zora had posted something.

Or, rather, Olivia tagged her in a picture.

As the image filled the screen, it did take Mike a second to recognize Zora. His gaze raked lazily over her. Usually, she wore loose jeans and T-shirts or some casual bohemian getup.

He wasn't blind, he'd seen her in shorts, so he knew she had great legs. Every once in a while, she'd show off some midriff, but not much else. Tonight, though, she was wearing a tight, sexy blue dress that gave him a good idea of what she was working with underneath it.

Every nerve ending in his body stirred and tingled as he scrutinized her.

This Zora wasn't the friend he hung out with sometimes and played games with since they were kids. That sleek body didn't belong to Everett's cute little sister, either. Nor the endless legs extended by a pair of clear heels or the delicate column of her neck or the pink-tinted pouty lips…

Mike bit his own lip remembering how he once got to taste her mouth so long ago. The memory took him aback. He hadn't thought about it in years. That was intentional. He wouldn't let himself.

He was breathless.

And apparently, losing his mind.

It's the same Zora. Nothing has changed, he tried telling himself.

But as he dissected every one of her lean, svelte curves, Mike felt the change by the tightening of his cock. He couldn't unsee the woman. He zoomed in on the image. Her smooth, tawny skin and slightly flushed pink cheeks. Her expressive almond-shaped eyes still held the promise of joy, a summer sunset, and all of their inside jokes.

What am I doing?

In the picture, the room was dark and crowded, but Zora was on the side of the bar where he'd been sitting earlier with Kate. Below the image there were no comments, only three hashtags. #Silentdisco #Zoragothergrooveback #Mikewho

Mike who?

Am I the surprise? Is this why Olivia invited me?

At the moment, he didn't know whether to hug or strangle Zora's friend. His heartbeat raced as warmth flooded his body. His eyes darted over to the bar as he pushed passed people. He was breathless as he made his way to the edge of the dance floor. Then he spotted her.

Zora.

She was leaning on a barstool with her arms wrapped around some guy's neck and her lips pressed to his.

Mike's heart dropped into his stomach. He felt like he'd been sucker punched. A burning sensation took root in his chest, and his stomach hardened. He felt the heat rise to his face as anger and humiliation washed over him. His breaths were coming coarser and faster.

What the fuck, Olivia?

He definitely wanted to strangle her. He was pissed— mostly at himself.

Where is all this coming from? Why do I want to pummel that guy?

Mike tore his gaze away, tasting the bitterness on his tongue. He couldn't watch.

It was then Mike noticed the pinched expression on Remi's face, but she wasn't looking at him. Mike turned to find Kate beside him and it didn't take a genius to register the sullen look on her face. Tears welled at her red-rimmed eyes and she swiped them one by one from her cheeks.

"Nothing to worry about, huh?"

Kate had seen the way he watched Zora. He assumed it was probably the way she wanted him to look at her.

It wouldn't make Kate feel any better, but Zora transforming into a fine ass woman and having this effect on him was new to him, too.

CHAPTER 3

ZORA

Game night rotated houses every other Saturday. Tonight, it was at Everett and Sophia's, Zora's current digs while her house was under construction. She cursed this situation most days—like when her brother's lovemaking came through the walls in surround sound. At the moment though, she couldn't be happier. She was in fluffy socks and sweats and curled up on the couch getting ready to play board games. More importantly, she was not in the sticky, hot silent disco where she'd apparently lost her mind along with her inhibitions.

"I vaguely remember wiping my mouth with the back of my hand." Zora held her hands to her throat and opened her mouth like she might wretch at the memory then fell back in a fit of laughter.

Oli's top lip curled. "Ew, that is *so* nasty."

"Don't act innocent like you didn't try to pass Andre off on me after you got dog-slobbered, too. That was no kiss."

Lord, if Oli ever accused her of never losing herself in the name of fun, Zora would hurl on her…projectile vomit.

Zora had literally allowed a man to deflower her mouth with his slippery snake tongue—not fun.

They were giggling uncontrollably now.

"I hear you guys starting without me," Sophia hollered from the kitchen. "Don't talk about the guy at the club yet. I'm not ready. We need snacks and drinks for this kind of juicy gossip."

"Fine," Zora and Oli both muttered in unison, but given the magic Sophia made in the kitchen, Zora was more than happy to wait for her snacks.

By the back door, Blue whimpered as his tail slapped against the tile. "Honey, let the dog out for me!" Sophia yelled.

She was always hollering about something, but it sort of went with the territory with a loud crazy family, which Zora was beginning to love. For too long, it was only Zora and Everett after their grandmother, Babs died. Then there was a lot of silence. Having a brother was great, but Sophia already felt like the sister Zora never knew she wanted.

There was something to be said for having a fierce, loud woman in your corner—especially a kickass chef who could throw together five-star appetizers for impromptu pre-game girl talk.

Zora puckered her lips at Blue, her brother's chocolate lab, who seemed to be wincing at a combination of Sophia's healthy, prenatal pill-fueled lungs and his own heavy bladder. She got up to open the door for him. "I know, buddy. I'm going to be in the same boat after I eat all your mommy's food and drink way too much," she said as he scurried out.

Sophia walked slowly into the living room balancing a fancy gold-trimmed tray in her hands. Her loose auburn waves were piled on top of her head in a messy bun and she was wearing black yoga pants and a loose-fitting blush pink shirt, effortlessly looking A Pea in the Pod flawless.

"Now, what do we have here?" Zora's brows bounced with

excitement. She licked her lips and rubbed her hands together at the scent of warm bread and rosemary wafting through the air.

"Just a little something to munch on."

Sophia gently set the tray down on the coffee table beside a stack of board games. The tray was filled with two wine glasses, a cup of juice, cheese, grapes, and the mouthwatering little pita crackers she made from scratch. Sophia was careful not to knock over the tiny Faberge egg given to her by her mother. It was one of many knickknacks Helen had scattered around, insisting it would make Patton Place feel like a home.

She passed the wine to Zora and Oli before taking her juice. Then she settled into the cushy chair beside the couch and propped her feet up on the table. "Now, I'm ready. Start right after you noticed this guy in the back, and don't leave out any of the details."

"So, I had just flipped to the green station and I was starting to feel the music. It was like the perfect mix of verse and voice over a slow beat," Zora said remembering the easy ambiance of the club. "As I started to dance, *this* crazy woman," she pointed at Oli, "drags Andre over to me—"

"Stop editorializing." Oli rolled her eyes and flashed Zora a quick smile. She was listening, but as usual, an early morning wedding photo shoot had sapped most of her energy, and now she was nodding off.

"Then what happened?" Sophia sliced a thin layer of brie and spread it over a cracker and popped it in her mouth. She closed her eyes, relishing the flavors.

Zora couldn't help getting sidetracked. Food had a way of always taking her off topic. "Did you get this at the farmer's market at that booth way in the back?" She cut off a small piece and pressed it to her tongue. "Hmmm. Good god, that's amazing."

"I'll give you all the details later," Sophia said. "Now keep going."

"Anyway, by then, the tequila shots were in full effect. At least behind the beer goggles, he was decent looking, so when his hands slid down my sides and around my waist, I got caught up."

As Zora described the guy's bass-filled voice, and the way they danced with their bodies molded together, Sophia took longer sips from her cup. Zora took her time, sparing no detail as she told them how he didn't take his eyes off of her...or his hands. Then those hands slid behind her and palmed the curves of her ass. There was also the delicious goodness she felt dragging her hands over his chest...

Then he kissed her, and everything went south.

"You were probably fantasizing about Mike the whole time," Oli droned.

Zora laughed, but she *had* closed her eyes and imagined Andre was Mike. She imagined they were on the dance floor in between a few dozen people and he slipped his tongue in her mouth like he did when she was eighteen. She was back there—his hands roaming her body, the heat of their skin pressed together as he made love to her in Babs's wine cellar.

A shiver ran down Zora's back. Just then, her phone trembled across the table. She stole a glance at the screen and heat crawled up from her neck to her cheeks as she bit down on her bottom lip. When she looked up again, she could feel the giddy smile return along with the tingles.

"With that goofy grin, it sure as hell isn't Andre." Oli grumbled. Then she curled into a ball and let her eyes close again.

A new bout of giggles bubbled to the surface. Zora touched her fingers to her lips. She and Mike had texted all through the night after she got home from the club. The questions in the game were crazy, and strangely, bordered on flirtatious.

I sleep naked.

It was a truth that had tortured her into the early morning.

Lord have mercy, the images of Mike covered in nothing but her body, were still reeling through her head. She could feel her cheeks flush.

While it sucked lying to Oli and Sophia, Zora loved having this *one thing* to herself.

Oli had said to lose herself.

So what if I did while fantasizing about Mike?

Sophia nearly spilled her juice as she sat up. She cleared her throat and held up a finger. "Okay, so let me get this straight. Not only did you wear a skintight hoochie dress that barely covered your hoo-ha, but you kissed this guy you met the same night?"

Zora winced and peeked over her shoulder toward the kitchen to see if Everett was within earshot, but she couldn't stifle the smile spreading across her face. "Something like that." She fell back onto the couch and covered her face with a pillow.

"You did!" Sophia accused. Her mouth fell open as she shook her head.

"I told her that dress was magic." Oli high-fived Sophia who was apparently still in shock because they were locked in a weird staring contest. "I can't tell you how helpful it was. It worked all kinds of magic."

Zora leaned back and propped her hands behind her head then immediately jolted back up when Oli asked her next question.

"Did I tell you guys what kind of doctor he is?" She paused for a few excruciatingly long seconds. "He's a gynecologist."

Zora and Sophia gasped, their eyes wide with shock.

"Besides the horrible fact he kisses like a fish, now I know I'm never going to see him again," Zora said. "I don't want to have sex with someone who'll probably take notes and compare my 'hoo-ha' to every other 'hoo-ha' he's pried open with that duckbill speculum thingy."

The three of them burst into loud, contagious laughs.

In the front of the house, Zora heard the alarm chime and the front door open. Everett was talking to someone. When she heard the bass-filled voice, she figured it was probably Mike. She wondered if he'd brought Kate, the woman he was dating, who he still had yet to bring around. Or maybe it was Jason, Mike's friend who loved to play games but happened to be the biggest sour loser ever.

"Hey." Mike walked into the living room with a red game box tucked under one arm and a bottle of champagne in his hand, ripping and ready to go. Even in loose navy sweats and a plain, white tee with a scruffy goatee, the man was a sun-baked god among peons. He flashed the girls a cocky, lopsided grin, slowly blinking his adorable lashes at them, giving them a glimpse of his piercing green eyes.

Zora sighed.

He didn't even look at me.

Zora craned her neck to look behind him. No Kate. No Jason. *Hmm.* His head was down, and he still hadn't looked at her. She was pretty sure it was by design.

"You get my text?" she asked, sounding far too anxious. The content had been way beyond PG-13.

"Uh, yeah. I was driving, though." He went to set the champagne bottle down on the table but missed the edge and scrambled to catch it.

"You okay?"

Mike finally met her gaze and that's when she saw it. Was that heat in his eyes? It couldn't be. She cocked her head and blinked.

No. Uh-uh.

They were flirting last night, but she'd figured it was one-sided and that Mike was humoring her.

She wanted to look over her shoulder because surely someone behind her was the recipient of the panty-dropping, half smile hinged on his chiseled jaw.

Zora's mouth watered as he licked his lips, and her heart did a little flip. She only realized it because in that moment, she stopped breathing.

Oh, yeah. I'm losing it, all right. Hallucinate much?

No question about it, she was definitely going to keep her little dance floor fantasy to herself.

CHAPTER 4

MIKE

M ike placed the board game on top of the stack already sitting on the wooden coffee table. He took a deep breath and hugged Sophia preparing to take the seat beside Zora when he met Olivia's eyes. He could already feel his body tensing as he clenched his teeth.

"Olivia." He didn't smile or hug her because he was not happy to see her. He was still trying to figure how he was going to make it through game night when a war was being waged inside him.

Between the urge to lash out at Olivia and the battle with his body not to physically respond to Zora, Mike wasn't sure how to act. He only came to game tonight to confront Olivia, but now…his emotions were all over the place instead of neatly tucked away where they belonged.

One emotion in particular stood out.

Anger.

The second he sat down beside Zora, their thighs touched, and the memory of her kissing some random dude shot fire through his veins.

He'd been played.

Hard.

Mike studied Zora's friend, if one could call her that. *What kind of person secretly invites you to a setup under the pretense of a celebration?* What Olivia did was foul. Dirty. And it was burning him up inside.

His clenched teeth couldn't hide the tightness in his expression. He was glaring at Olivia and itching to confront her, but he wouldn't do it front of Zora.

Olivia was apparently feeling the weight of his stare because she abruptly got up off the chair. "I'm going to be right b—"

"Can I chat with you for a second?" Mike cut her off, getting to his feet, too.

She sighed. "I have to pee." Then she looked at him, pursed her lips, and gave a light tug of her earlobe as she looked off to the left.

"That's fine. I'll wait in the kitchen. Everett said he needed help with a few things, anyway." The words seethed from his mouth. At his temple, a vein twitched and his muscles quivered.

Why am I so angry?

All night, he'd tried to convince himself he was only irritated because Olivia had deceived him. Zora didn't even know he was there, and he was all cocksure, assuming he was her surprise. *What a fool!* What did he even think was going to happen when he walked over? Either way, he was with Kate, so what right did he have to be mad or jealous?

I am not jealous.

Mike stalked off toward the kitchen where he grabbed a beer from the fridge and leaned up against the counter with his arms folded. Was he pouting now, too?

Everett jumped headlong into talk about the upcoming purchase of the Chessington building the following week. Mike had been trying to convince him he could handle the deal. It was a great time to really drill down on the reasons he was the man for the job. Even though the investment would take the commercial end of the company to the next business tier, at the moment, he could not focus on work..

He was only halfway listening.

His mind was stuck in the same place it had been since the night before: back at the club watching Zora kiss a man who was not good enough for her.

"What the fuck is wrong with you?" Everett asked, snapping Mike out of his trance.

"Nothing." He *was* pouting. "I just have a bone to pick with Olivia, that's all. She's in the bathroom. I'm waiting on her to come out."

Everett swiped Mike's beer from his hand and took a swallow before posting himself up beside his friend. With the bottle, he pointed at Mike then toward the bathroom door, his face twisted into a question.

"No, fool. I would never do that." Even the insinuation that he would hook up with one of Zora's friends felt dirty to Mike. He let his head fall into his hands. "I don't even know why I'm so upset."

"I do." Olivia sashayed into the kitchen with her blood-red lips curved into a smirk. "You know what they say, denial is more than just a river in Africa."

Mike stood taller now. "What the fuck was all that about last night? What was your plan…to make me jealous?"

"Are you?" Olivia and Everett barked in unison.

Suddenly, he felt like he was on the defensive, but against what? This whole thing was for the birds. He wanted to go back to seeing Zora as the sweet, untainted girl he knew.

He let his head fall into his hands as he slid onto the barstool at the massive granite island. "I don't know what I am.

All I know is...that I hated seeing her kiss that dude. He's not nearly good enough for her."

All this time, Mike told himself he wasn't waiting for Zora, but watching her in that dress with *that guy*... She was most definitely grown up. It was no longer a question of whether she rejected him all those years ago because she wasn't ready. Maybe she just didn't want him.

His shoulders slumped as the air inside him slowly leaked out.

"Mike, you don't even know him. Besides, why do you care?" Olivia asked.

"Wait, who are we talking about here? Kate?" Everett asked.

Olivia took one look at Everett and rolled her eyes. "Oh, lord. I think it's time we start the games."

Mike realized he shouldn't have come. He threw his hands up in the air and glared at Olivia as he walked back to the living room and planted himself beside Zora on the couch.

"What's going on with you guys? What did Oli do now?" Zora cocked her head toward him, appearing to sense his mood. "What happened?"

He met her gaze as Everett and Olivia filed into the room, plopping down on the leather armchairs. "Is it okay if we don't talk about it right now?"

"Yeah." Zora searched his face for a brief moment. Her eyes were the color of whiskey imbued with light, so they appeared amber with flecks of gold. They were wide and pleading the way they were when Mike wanted nothing more than to give her the world. That was back when he knew the only way to keep her safe was to keep his distance. He'd wanted to wait until she was ready.

She gathered him into a side hug, and he did his best not to linger. "We can talk whenever you're ready," she whispered.

Relief flooded his body. How was he going to do this? How

was he going to pretend like something hadn't shifted between them?

Sophia tilted her head sideways reading the spines of the board games. "What should we play first?"

"I vote for Apples to Apples or Taboo," Zora said, tucking her legs beneath her on the couch. "Do you have the Midnight version?"

"I don't know what that is, but I say we go with a classic—either Monopoly, Scattergories, Clue, Sorry, Scrabble, or Battleship," Everett suggested. "I'm probably going to win, anyway. You pick, Soph."

Before she could select a game, Olivia chimed in. "I've got a better idea." Mike didn't miss the sly wink she gave him. "Since Mike and Zo are always on their phones playing games, why don't we go with their favorite? How about we play Two Truths and a Lie?"

She slouched into the chair pressing a pillow to her chest looking rather pleased with herself.

"Fine by me," he said, lifting his chin with a confidence he didn't feel.

While Sophia and Olivia helped Everett hunt down pens, paper, plastic cups, and more drinks, Mike took the moment to swipe the champagne he'd brought from the table.

"This was for you, by the way." He leaned over to hand Zora the bottle. As he did, he smelled her light floral scent with hints of coconut. Something roared to life inside him and he stifled a growl. It took every fiber of his being to ward off the flashes of her body in the blue dress as it blurred into a night so long ago when he'd crossed the line.

No.

He didn't want to go there. He couldn't. Those feelings had washed away, but now all at once, they threatened to come rushing back. He was caught in the undertow. He could deny a lot of things, but he couldn't deny the temptation to be with Zora was always lying dormant.

It was never this strong, though.

Mike didn't want to feel it. He didn't want to *want* her. Zora deserved someone she could trust with her heart, someone who could protect her.

That night years ago, he'd swallowed hard over the lump in his throat as heat crawled under his skin and settled there. He could still see the hurt in her eyes, the agony, and he couldn't have left her…even if she was his best friend's sister.

She was *his* friend, too.

The memory of their night stirred in his groin and he adjusted himself, shifting closer to the armrest. "Congratulations, again. I uh…know the cookbook is going to be amazing."

He was staring straight ahead and hating the stilted tone to his voice. Their normal banter was replaced by an awkwardness he hated even more.

"Thanks for the champagne." She fingered the bold red script lettering on the bottle, biting down on her lip. It drove Mike crazy. He knew the sweet taste of her swollen lips. He could still feel the memory of them on his aching skin.

His cock hardened and understanding washed over him. He blew out a cleansing breath.

That's what this is. It's not emotional, it's just physical—one body reacting to another. I'm driving myself crazy for nothing.

Mike almost sighed with relief.

I'm just horny.

He pressed his fist over his mouth to hide his grin. This was the same Zora in a new dress, which just so happened to highlight every curve of her tight little frame.

New. This was his body telling him it was tired of fucking the same woman. All he needed was a good lay. A new lay.

He was so happy he could almost kiss her.

"I'm going to go grab some water." He sprang to his feet. "Want anything?"

"How about a glass for this stuff?" She held up the bottle.

His grin spanned from ear to ear as he let the words fall from his mouth. "Anything for my friend."

Just friends.

Yes. This was just his body talking. He might not be able to undo the texts he'd sent last night, but he was only going to be thinking with one head from now on.

Mike made his way to the kitchen where he found the "three amigos" conspiring in hushed whispers. As soon as he walked in, they all scurried like roaches in the light. He had to laugh because he knew they were plotting something, but at the moment he didn't have one fuck to give.

He wasn't nuts, he was just horny.

The game started off just as Mike expected. Olivia's truths, of course, were centered on photography and weddings, while her lie was predictably about how much she loathed guys with beards. Considering the last two guys she dated looked like lumberjacks, it was pretty easy to spot.

Mike had also easily spotted Everett's lie about wanting to be a football coach back in high school and Zora's about hating *Ferris Bueller's Day Off*. At the moment, he was winning the game 3–0, when Sophia's turn came up.

Sophia flashed him a tight smile as she scooted to the edge of the chair. "Okay, Mike. Let's see if you can get this one." She straightened the lines of her face and gave him a deadpan stare.

"Let me have it."

"One. I've been put on light activity to avoid putting the baby at risk , so we're going on a month-long vacation to Bali. Two. Patton Place has dry rot and termites, so we need to vacate the property for fumigation and repairs. Three. I only watch *Game of Thrones* for the nudity.

Mike slid his finger over his top lip as he pondered the options. They were oddly specific and some were kind of personal. It was classic Sophia to go for the jugular right off the bat.

"Let's see. That's pretty specific," he said out loud.

"But you don't even like *Game of Thrones*," Zora added.

Zora and Olivia were both studying Sophia and Everett, waiting for the news hiding between the lines. They could all hear it in what Sophia wasn't saying.

Mike felt his own body stiffen.

"Are you guys trying to tell us something?" he asked.

His heartbeat pounded in his ears. Everett had told him before he met Sophia, she gave birth to a stillborn, which was why he was so worried, particularly the first three months. He said Sophia was about nine weeks and that most miscarriages occurred in the first trimester, so that had to be true. They would never joke about something so serious. Otherwise, why would they have been so worried about going out to celebrate?

Why would they choose the middle of a game to disclose something so personal?

"So the house has termites and dry—" Mike was still working out her angle when Zora cut him off.

"Is the baby okay? What happened?"

There was a catch in Everett's throat as he responded. He squeezed Sophia's hand, pulling her in tight against him. Both of them were glassy-eyed, but they held it together. By the way his upper lip stiffened and hers trembled, Mike could tell that they'd been suffering in silence with this news. Having to say it aloud was only reopening the wound.

Immediately, Zo and Olivia stood and rushed to them, murmuring their sympathy and apologies. Mike was the only one who wasn't crying. His tears were all dried up by now. He knew too well what the pain of losing a child…or sibling, did to a person.

In the back of his mind, Mike saw his younger brother Lucas. His face was always falling. Mike knew there was nothing he could have done to help. Still, deep down, he knew he would never allow himself to be responsible for another person's life.

While he should have offered sympathy and shared Everett and Sophia's burden now, friend or not, Mike couldn't help but watch Zora.

"I'm so sorry. I know how much the baby means to you," she cried. The way she so freely gave of herself and was both gentle and strong at the same time—she was everyone's rock and reprieve wrapped in one. The sight of her tears always stirred something in Mike and left him unsettled.

"We've scheduled the fumigation," Everett began. "In a week, we're going to have to be out. My gorgeous fiancée and I are going to take a long overdue, stress-free vacation." He gazed at her so endearingly, tenderly. "I'm thinking lots of time in the bed."

"Ev," Sophia playfully slapped his shoulder, beaming despite the unfortunate circumstances.

Mike couldn't imagine a better couple to be parents. "Whatever you need. I'm here for you," he said.

Both Zo and Olivia offered their help, too.

"You know you can count on me for anything," Zora added. "This whole trip seems awesome. You guys deserve this so much. Except…I hate to have to talk about this in light of everything…but I've got nowhere to live." Zora shrugged.

Sophia and Everett eyed each other then turned to Olivia with expectant eyes.

With the bomb Sophia dropped, Mike didn't think about this aspect of the sudden turn of events. He sucked in a breath, anxious to know the plan, and then he saw Sophia and Everett exchange a meaningful glance.

"This is where the three of you come in."

The way Everett's tone dropped, Mike should have expected the worst, but what came next, he could never have prepared for.

CHAPTER 5

ZORA

Tuesday morning, Zora and Oli stood in front of their respective burners at Zora's favorite commercial kitchen, Cuisinette. They already had a dozen or so small glass bowls of seasonings and ingredients lined at their stations, so they spent the remainder of the prep time picking from a selection of neon pink aprons. Each was embroidered with a bold print and had a sassy slogan scrawled across the pocket. For Zora, who was going to be homeless by the end of the week, something as simple as having the choice to pick the perfect cooking accessory gave a sense of dignity.

Zora swallowed back her worries and turned to Oli, holding out the hem of an apron that said, "Nothing beats a good rub" on the front.

"Isn't this perfect? It's like it's reading my mind."

The way her week was shaping up, she needed a massage in the worst way.

Oli was still struggling to tie her strings in the back.

"Here, let me," Zora said, whipping them into a wide bow. "Turn around. What's yours say?"

Oli pivoted, and Zora immediately bit back a grin. "Really? I don't know what I'm going to do with you." Given her friend's affinity for thick, beefy, defensive lineman types, it was perfect that hers read, "I like big cooks and I cannot lie."

"What?" Oli smirked.

"Um…I'll have to keep that in mind when I find a guy to return the favor for Andre," Zora said. "Just give me a little time. As soon as I get my life back in order, you've got it coming, sister."

Never one to veer off course, Oli threw the ball Zora had been dodging for days back in her court. "Speaking of… What *are* you going to do?"

"Nope. I don't want to think about being homeless. I'm stressed enough as it is thinking about Sophia and the baby." They'd been over this a dozen times since game night.

Oli threw her body onto the counter of a nearby station with a delayed cackle, and began heaving.

"Wow. Dramatic much?" Oli stood back up. "It's fumigation and a few repairs, so relax. You are not without a place to stay. I mean I would totally let you stay with me if my cousins weren't coming into town. Oh, and, FYI, you're not going to a hotel—they won't take Blue, anyway."

They ambled back over to their stations, still giggling every time they looked at each other.

"Anyway, I thought you and Mike were *friends*," Oli drawled. "He volunteered his place, and I think you should take it. You've got, what, another month until you close on your house? Think of it is as a sleepover. A slumber party for hard-headed, stubborn, sexually-frustrated adults."

Zora ignored most of what Oli said, but she still couldn't get past the word, "friends" and the nearly audible air quotes thrown around it. It stuck her like a thorn in her ass.

Friends.

She couldn't even begin to explain why it bothered her so much,. Technically, she and Mike *were* friends. They had gone down the romantic road before and agreed not to ruin their friendship, but then the way he had looked at her at game night... Her heart flipped at the memory of the heat darkening his mossy green eyes. He was inches away from her, but she'd felt the fire radiating between them. She sucked in a stark breath as electricity coursed through her veins.

I'm completely losing my shit.

"I'm not going to impose on Mike. I'm not staying at his house." Zora refused to look at Oli. "I've already checked out two apartments, and I have two more to see this Wednesday and Thursday with immediate move-in options, so I'll figure out my living situation later."

"Ugh."

"Right now, I just want to cook and not think. You might remember, there's a little cookbook I'm working on..." Zora sighed.

Before her grandmother passed, she was showing Zora how to perfect a rich, delicious, dark roux the way Monroe women had been doing for generations. In the process, Zora had burned her fair share of the thick stew, trying, but never quite getting it just right. So the second Zora heard that shrimp étouffée was on the menu for this cooking class, she'd jumped at the chance and decided to drag Oli along for moral support in case she burned the place down.

Still, it felt like a sign.

This was her chance to add something rooted in family, love, and tradition to her book. It was the edge she needed. Shrimp étouffée was what she should focus on, not libido-teasing living arrangements and awkward friendships.

"It's going to be nasty." Oli sucked her teeth loudly. For a second, Zora thought she was talking about the dish, but then she went on. "Probably some cheap little place out in the boondocks without running water. Oh, and an outhouse for a bathroom if you still want to close on time."

"Now who's being dramatic?"

"Seriously, Zo. You have to provide bank statements or canceled checks for all large purchases when you're buying a house. It could delay the whole process another month otherwise."

Zora sighed. "Thank you for the CliffsNotes on home-buying."

"Well, if you're not going to take advantage of Mike's totally state-of-the-art, *free*, appliances, why don't you cook here?" Oli asked. "This place is gorgeous and chic. I could totally see you *Top Chef*-ing up some masterpiece in this space."

Those were Zora's thoughts exactly—the one bright spot, other than her apron, in her suddenly cloudy life was the possibility of getting in at a commercial kitchen. She bit her lip and squinted at the whiteboard in the back of the room with bold writing on it. It looked like they were subletting the kitchen on Tuesdays, Wednesdays, and Thursdays.

This place would be perfect, actually.

With all the space and upgraded commercial appliances, she could work on the final tweaks for her recipes for the cookbook here—after she got her living arrangements settled.

"I think I'll stop by the front desk on the way out." Zora was still nodding at herself when she looked over at Oli, who seemed to be fully entertained by the setup on the counter.

"His place is *free*," Oli repeated, shaking her head. "Anyway, I thought you already picked all of your recipes for the book. I was just suggesting a place to cook for the blog." She opened the jar of clam juice and sniffed. Her brows dipped in question.

"That's for the roux," Zora explained. "Now put it back, before you spill it. They're going to start in a few minutes."

Oli set the jar back down and picked up the mix of Cajun seasoning, wrinkling her nose. "Rue, as in a street in Paris? Or, as in deeply regretting the day you didn't hook up with Mike? Either way, what has that got to do with this fish water?" She inhaled before sneezing loudly, barely missing the mix.

Zora gingerly removed the bowl from Oli's hand and replaced it on the counter. "Bless you. Good Lord, stop touching stuff. You need all of this for the roux. That's the gorgeous, thick, dark, flavorful stew used to smother rice and meat."

When the jar and the bowls were neatly lined up the way they'd found them when they arrived, Zora explained. "Grandma Babs tried to teach me, but if I can master it in time, it'll be just the personal touch I need for the book."

There was movement out of the corner of Zora's eye. The instructor had arrived and the other students hurried to their stations.

"I want you to grab your saucepans." The instructor said, calling the class to order. She was a homely woman with shoulder-length red hair and smooth skin dappled with happy freckles. Loud clanks echoed and bounced off the glossy walls as all four rows of people struggled to lift the cast iron cookware.

"It's heavy, isn't it? The last thing you want is a lightweight pan. It'll only burn your roux, and *poof!* You're back at square one. This is where we start—the bare minimum. Bare."

I sleep naked.

Ugh. There was no way it would work. She was not staying with Mike even if they were friends.

41

Anything for my friend.

Double ugh.

Following the instructions, Oli set the fire to medium-low heat. After adding the flour and vegetable oil into the pan, Zora slowly stirred.

A faint ping sounded from the phone in Zora's back pocket and she fought the urge to pull it out. She wasn't in the mood for truths and lies. He was so hot and cold. One minute he was sharing flirty lies, setting off fireflies in her stomach, and the next they were fizzling back into Platonicville.

She hated the way her hopes got up, but he was right.

They were never going to be anything more than friends. So, whatever her heart was feeling, she needed to just get him out of her head.

Oli flitted a glance her way then back to the heavy pan. She spoke under her breath. "Let me say this in a language you can understand, since you only speak cliché eighties movie lingo. This is basically the same as *Some Kind of Wonderful*, only you're not Amanda Jones. You're Keith Nelson, the idiot totally ignoring the good thing in front of you, which is Watts, who clearly wants to be more than friends but only realizes it when it's too late."

Zora screwed her face up. "Are you saying Mike is Watts in this lovely little scenario you've cooked up—and botched, by the way?"

"You get the gist." Oli checked for the instructor before continuing. "Did you notice Kate wasn't at game night? They broke up."

Zora almost knocked over her saucepan. "What?" She tried to whisper, but it came out as a yell.

The instructor glared over at them.

"Shhh. Oh my gosh."

Zora's gaze locked on her roux as she stirred vigorously,

putting as much elbow grease as she could into it the way Babs had shown her. Meanwhile, her heartbeat was a bass drum in her ears.

The air warmed with the robust scent of Creole country with hints of...*burnt toast?*

She flicked a glance over at Oli's roux. "Pay attention. You're burning it." *And not telling me anything.*

Zora chewed on the fact Mike was now a single man. Of all the times in the world, Oli chose now to be tight-lipped. Zora stirred intently, making sure *her* mix didn't stick to the bottom of the pan.

"So...Mike and Kate are over?" she asked.

"Yep. I heard Everett tell Sophia last night." Oli waggled her brows.

Zora sighed and stared down at her roux. Her mind was spinning out of control. *Mike was single...*and quite possibly about to be her roommate if the last two apartments on her list were equally as shitty as the first two. She zoned in on all the implications of living with the only guy who could get under her skin—in every way.

Her heart pounded in her ears as she swallowed back a wave of panic. Her stomach was tied up in knots. It was one thing to be in the house with Mike and know that he was in a relationship with Kate and off limits, but knowing he was available gave her a strange sense of uncertainty.

"Earth to Zora."

She blinked a few times, hoping that she didn't look as flustered as she felt.

"What are you over there thinking about?"

"Ugh. Turn your heat down. It's burning again. Stir all the way to the edges and don't stay in one spot too long." Zora dismissed the laughter pulling at the corner of Oli's mouth.

She was seizing up. Frozen.

43

Cooking with Oli was not doing the trick of getting her mind off of the living situation chaos or Mike. If anything, all this talk about shacking up with her very *single,* friend who liked to sleep naked put him squarely in her thoughts. It was a disaster. She needed to find *anywhere* else to live.

CHAPTER 6

MIKE

Ever since Everett and Sophia dropped the news about their trip last weekend, Mike found himself still hard up and knee-deep in the paperwork for the Chessington building purchase. Yes, they worked together, but Mike and Everett were more. They were friends—family—before anything else. Although he couldn't see himself hacking away at happily ever after, Mike believed a man deserved to be there for his family in an emergency without worrying about all the walls at work crashing down. He needed Everett to know he could depend on him to share the burdens at work...and at home.

His home.

For fuck safe, he'd volunteered his house to Zora for a month.

A month.

It wasn't the smartest idea. It was probably the opposite, given their history and his hormones, but it was what any friend would do for one another. This was his chance to be there when someone needed him.

After all, he and Zora were friends.

He'd made sure it was the only thing they were.

Then he'd offered his house up on Saturday night.

It was now Thursday and he still had no clue whether or not she was going to actually take him up on it. He'd given her plenty of space—not even a single text. The least she could do was let him know one way or the other.

Her silence was both annoying and rude. He had a mind to retract the offer altogether. If Mike was being honest with himself, though, the suspense was what was killing him.

He didn't know if he should grocery shop, put sheets on the guest bed, stock his place with emergency survival kits…who knew? How was he supposed to focus on getting properly laid with all this hanging over his head?

Right after I review this contract one more time, I'll just…send her a text.

No big deal.

"Kendra," he called out to Everett's assistant down the hall. "When you get a chance, can you *please* bring me the purchase contract? I need to see one more thing." He heard her grunt in the distance. "Thank you."

He let his head fall back to crack his neck, then drew in a breath and released it with a heavy sigh before it morphed into a theatrical groan. *Stop thinking about Zora.* He needed to get the image of her in that tight blue dress out of his system, and get himself into someone else's if he was going to get anything done today.

Mike slammed his desk drawer just as Everett twirled into his office. He was beaming. All week, he'd been unbearable, gloating about his Balinese vacation. Today, he was dressed in jeans and a turquoise, short-sleeved, Hawaiian button down—his fourth of the week. The others had been light green, lavender, pale yellow—each was as loud and obnoxious as his happy, carefree attitude.

He strode by then stopped at the wall length window to strike his pose. "What do you think? Is the turquoise too much?"

"Go ahead. Rub it in," Mike said, biting back a grin. "Are you sure you should even be going? Isn't Soph supposed to be on bed rest or something?"

"Light activity, not bed rest. As in no heavy lifting or strenuous activity. Although, I have every intention of propping her feet up."

Everett was a cheesy fool. Then again, if a month of sandy beach days and bedded bliss lay ahead of him, Mike would probably be flashing a goofy smile, too,.

Mike lowered his gaze back to the folder in front of him, shaking his head. "Please take all of that sunshine and rainbow stuff with you as you exit."

"Don't be salty. Sophia and I need this vacation." Everett pressed his hands down the front of the shirt smoothing the light fabric.

"Yeah, I know. I'm just giving you a hard time."

"Plus, you and Zo are the ones who said you wanted more responsibility." He mocked Mike in a low baritone. "'I need more challenge. Let me handle Arnold and the Chessington building.'" Then, Everett's voice went up six or seven octaves as he imitated his sister. "'Don't worry about it, Sophia, the restaurant will be in good hands. I can do this job with my eyes closed.'"

They both guffawed at his animated impressions.

"Really? Is that how Zo and I sound to you?" Mike said, struggling to compose himself. The sound of her name on his tongue was sobering and dragged his mind back to his offer—still floating out there, unanswered.

"In all seriousness, though, I know you guys can hold things down here and at Bite-Sized," Everett said. "Sophia's done pretty much everything to get the restaurant ready, but are you really good with Zo coming to stay with you?"

No. "Yeah. Why wouldn't I be?"

"Two reasons." Everett held up two fingers. "I know how you get in your savior mode trying to rescue everyone, and you beat yourself up thinking the worst will happen if you're not right there acting as a human safety net. It's okay, because I know why you're like that, but this is nothing like what happened with your brother."

Mike lifted his chin, but he couldn't control the way his arms hung loose by his sides. "Can we not go there? I just want to be available if she needs me, that's it. What's the second reason?"

Everett seemed to hesitate as if he was contemplating whether or not to continue pressing Mike on the first reason. To Mike's relief, he shrugged and continued.

"All right, man, whatever you say. The other reason I'm wondering about my sister staying with you is because you just ended things with Kate. We both know you like to go sow your royal oats after you've been tied down too long. Is my sister going to get in the way with the ladies?" He averted his gaze like he wasn't sure he wanted to hear the answer.

Mike had never told Everett about what he'd shared with Zora in the cellar, though, from time to time, he suspected he knew.

"Nah. It's cool. I probably won't be home much anyway, not that it matters since she still hasn't let me know one way or the other." The bitterness he'd been holding at bay weaved its way into his words.

Everett stared at him just a little too long.

This time, it was Mike who looked away.

48

Leave well enough alone, Ev.

When the lecture he awaited didn't come, Mike blew out a frustrated breath. "Stop worrying. You guys just go and relax. Enjoy each other. Take in the sites. We'll be fine here."

"Uh-huh."

Mike could feel the weight of Everett's stare. He sensed this conversation still wasn't over, and it was going to be up to him to end it.

"No matter where she ends up staying, I'll look out for her. And I'll be fine as soon as you get me the zoning and land use reports I asked for an hour ago." Mike snapped his fingers playfully, recalling the last items on his mental checklist. "Oh, and the commercial survey, too."

But Everett didn't move. He seemed to refocus as a smile played on his lips. "Oh, I'm not worried about her. What I want to know is why you're all bent out of shape?"

"What? What are you talking about?"

"Is it my sister or the business because if it's the business you don't need to worry. I told you Arnold is a long-time family friend. Dealings between the Monroes and Arnolds go way back to my grandfather, so this meeting tomorrow is just a formality. He already accepted the terms of the offer, the comparative market analysis has been done, and we've agreed on a fair number."

"It's not about Zora. What else has been done to prepare for this meeting with Arnold?"

Everett paused, appearing to sense Mike's reservations. "That's it. What else do we need?"

"Are the Arnolds anything like the Harmans? Do we have to take them down, too?"

The past year or so, Everett and Sophia worked tirelessly to tie up all the loose ends after the Harmans tried to steal Patton Place. It was a perfect example as far as Mike was concerned.

He didn't believe in under the table, back room handshake deals based off of old loyalties. It didn't stop Everett from trying to convince him , nor did it stop Mike from listing the merits of getting all their ducks in a row legally.

"It's just due diligence," Mike said. "It's what I do—checks and balances. Cuts out all the back-end work, so indulge me. If everything is on the up and up…"

Everett threw his hands up in the air. "Have you always been this anal?"

"Yes."

"Every item that you put on your little checklist is complete. All you have to do is show up, make sure he signs in the right places, and file them with the county."

Ev, you're losing your edge.

A thin, tight smile pulled at the corners of Mike's mouth as he reclined in his chair. He steepled his fingers, tapping them against one another as he scrutinized Everett. Mike had successfully thrown him off his scent. He wasn't worried about the business. If there was anything to be found, he would find it. Zora on the other hand, she *was* the reason he was bent out of shape.

The blue dress swam across his mind again. "Then that's what I'll do," he said.

"Good."

"Right after I run a fine-tooth comb over the contract." *And jerk off in the restroom.*

CHAPTER 7

ZORA

"Arrived."

"Thanks, Baby," Zora said to her GPS unit. It had a perky female voice, so she named after her favorite eighties movie character from *Dirty Dancing*. Also, she would never put Zora in the corner.

She tapped the screen to end the route and looked over at the split-level home converted to a duplex in Centennial. It was within walking distance of the nature park. From the outside, it wasn't half bad. It looked fairly decent. Based on curb appeal—well-maintained lawn, no shingles hanging from the roof, no weathered side panels from jousting the elements. It *was* booger green, though.

Lord knows I should learn not to be so picky. No pun intended. Zora snorted. After she'd seen the house of horrors, the teensy she-shed, and the condemned shack earlier in the week, she just needed the last one to be livable enough to keep her out of Mike's house.

On the sidewalk, Zora took in the tree-lined street with its single-family homes, heavy traffic, and high noise levels. The app said it was a mix of urban living and suburban quiet, but it pulsed with activity—a crazy amount of activity—even on a Thursday afternoon. Out of the side of her eye, she caught site of a tall guy with black hair, tons of tattoos, and rumpled clothes striding toward her.

She tightened her key between her middle and ring fingers as she flashed him a tentative smile. She held her breath. Her heart raced as she fought the urge to run.

"Hi," she managed. Her voice was as shaky as she felt.

He kept on walking, albeit with a rather creepy, lecherous look in his eyes. Zora swallowed back her panic. The guy could not have cared less about her. Freaking Oli with all of her "heads-up" information.

This was her fault.

"Ooh, Centennial," she'd said. "I don't think that's such a good idea for a single woman living by herself. The crime rates out there are off the charts. And the noise levels... Please."

Zora shook it off and exhaled as she made her way to the door on the bottom level.

The realtor Sophia recommended said she would be there early. With a deep breath, Zora placed her hand on the door-knob, which was...jiggly. And apparently, missing a screw or two.

Ugh.

Still determined to make this house work, she twisted it, opening the door, and immediately breathed a sigh of relief.

"Thank. Goodness."

The place wasn't exactly her taste, but it was clean and roomy. There were windows on every wall with light shining in from every direction, hardwood floors, granite countertops, a decent-sized kitchen, and a nook for her precious TV.

She broke out into spirit fingers and was about to do her

happy dance when she heard movement toward the back of the house.

"Is that you, Zora?" her realtor asked.

"Hi, Ellen." Zora was still beaming. "If this place is as great as it looks, I'm going to owe you big time. I mean it's not in the best area, but I think I can make it work for a month or so."

Ellen came out to greet Zora with a tight smile that failed to reach her eyes. "Okay, then. Let me show you around." Ellen had hot pink rimmed glasses and leopard flats. She was a cute, trim little thing, but her soft-spoken, uptight demeanor didn't seem to match her fashion sense.

Zora thought she might have been a little more bubbly. It took spunk to pull of pink and leopard. But she wasn't here for Ellen, she was here to find a place to hole up until her house was finished.

It wasn't forever.

She winced at a crack in the ceiling with a small brownish, watery stain in the center, likely from a leak.

It's fine. Everything is going to work out.

Determined to find the good in the quaint little duplex, Zora forced a smile and reminded herself of all its pros. Granted, it wasn't the best house, but she could make it work. It was one of very few places with a month-to-month payment, so she wouldn't be locked into a six-month or year-long lease requirement.

So what if the doorknob is loose?

Zora had a tool kit. Or, maybe she could change the locks if it was allowed. There was street parking and a washer/dryer, for goodness sake. If she felt unsafe, she could get some of those alarm system stickers.

This was fine. Everything was going to be fine, and best of all, she wouldn't have to stay with Mike.

"It's smoke-free and pet-friendly." Ellen swiveled around

when she noticed Zora hadn't followed her. The plastered-on smile was back in full force. "The owner already pre-wired for an alarm system, which I recommend."

Zora nodded, taking her cue to follow along.

The bedroom wasn't huge, but it could fit her queen bed and one nightstand. The living area pretty much had her at the built-ins.

So far so good.

Ellen led her down the hall for a quick peek at the closet with the stacked washer and dryer before they got to the sole bathroom. Since only one of them could fit inside at a time, Zora sidestepped her way in and did a small turn toward the shower. The basin was kind of dingy and the caulking was cracked in several spots. She leaned in closer, squinting.

"Is that—"

"Bleach. All you need is a little bleach and it'll be…fine."

Zora righted herself and met Ellen's gaze. "It's mold. Black mold." She sighed and ran her fingers over her hair. "Bleach? I thought mold could make you very ill…ruin your lungs."

The realtor's brows bounced, and, magically, the tight smile made its way back onto her face. Ellen didn't disagree with her or try to deny that spores of a micro fungus that could shut down organs, incapacitate the immune system, or leave someone brain-dead were growing freely where she was supposed to bathe.

Wow. What a selling point.

Zora blew out a breath and shook her head. Okay, so that was one major setback.

Maybe I can just get one of Ev's contractors out here to take a look. It might not be that big a deal.

Zora pivoted toward the toilet and flushed.

"You just have to hold it down," Ellen offered helpfully.

When she did, the water went down quickly then made a gurgling noise as it struggled to refill itself.

From there, the showing continued going downhill. The water came out of the faucet in temperatures ranging from iceberg to inferno. In the cabinet beneath the sink, there was a small leak along with five half-dead, twitching roaches and an intricate spider web that appeared to be in active use.

Yay.

As if the black mold, sketchy plumbing, jiggly doorknobs, and insect menagerie weren't enough, her helpful realtor saved the kitchen for last.

Not only did the stove gas line look like it was hotwired with red and green duct tape adhering it to the wall like a bomb waiting to go off, but a foul stench oozed from the malfunctioning refrigerator. Sadly, that wasn't the worst of it. Zora practically hyperventilated when she discovered the rat's nest inside the pantry closet.

Under no circumstances was she going to pay one red cent to live in this death trap when an equally dangerous but *free* option was available.

It took mere seconds for Zora to get out of that house, into her car, and head back home. She had just enough time to say goodbye to Everett and Sophia before they left for their trip later that evening.

When Zora arrived, she found Sophia upstairs repacking her suitcase, and, apparently, waiting for her.

"I'll bet Mike's house is looking really good right about now." Sophia's brows waggled as she rolled a pair of jeans and set it in her empty suitcase. Beside it, piled on top of the comforter was about a month's worth of clothes.

While she sifted through outfit options, Sophia explained that Ellen wasn't just her realtor, she was also her very chatty friend. She'd already given Sophia the lowdown on the black mold hole. In fact, Ellen had kept Sophia and Everett abreast of all the properties Zora viewed. Given scarcity of suitable living options, they were right to assume she wouldn't find a decent place on such short notice.

So, Sophia took it upon herself to prepare strict instructions for Zora and Mike to refer to in her absence.

"It's over there on the dresser." Sophia pointed across from the bed.

"Right on top of that, Rose!" Zora joked, quoting *Don't Tell Mom the Babysitter's Dead*. She walked over and grabbed the list from beneath Sophia's passport. Then something neon orange on the bed caught her attention. She pinched the fabric between her thumb and forefinger, lifting it up. "And what the heck is this?"

"A bathing suit."

"Isn't it the rainy season in Bali?" Zora's brows braided together. "Plus, Soph, this is really skimpy."

Sophia paled, averted her gaze, and rubbed her belly. "Why don't you just focus on the list?" she stammered, growing flustered.

"I'm just saying." Zora waved it off, deciding not to push the issue. She dropped her attention to the list.

Number one was pretty fair. Sophia's and Everett's phones would be in the hotel safe, and Zora and Mike were not to call unless someone was dying. Numbers two and three were the hotel information and the fumigation and repair schedules. The process was to begin Saturday, leaving Zora only one day to get everything she needed out of the house. Number four was all of Blue's emergency contacts and feeding info.

"I'll put it right on Mike's refrigerator, front and center," Zora assured Sophia, tossing her a firm *you betcha* nod.

Though Zora was poking fun, the last thing she wanted for Sophia was stress over stupid stuff—especially not anything concerning her and Mike. Sophia had already suffered the loss of one child. Zora couldn't bear the thought of anything happening to this one.

Zora briefly skimmed over the final three items on the list. There was something about her restaurant *Bite-Sized* and real estate development. Then, Sophia had added a plea for Zora to unwind, enjoy Mike's company, and get her cookbook under-way. Zora didn't read everything thoroughly, mostly because all she could think about was her impending doom.

What's Mike going to say? How will he act around me?

Was it going to be as excruciatingly weird and awkward as game night? What if he ended up getting back with Kate? What was his kitchen like? The questions wouldn't stop. Her head was exploding with a million "what ifs" and "hows." Then, she landed on the worst question of all.

Where am I going to sleep?

While she was mentally breaking down, Sophia was still rambling on.

The paper was shaking in her hands, so she set it back down on the dresser. She nodded a lot and tried to keep her breathing steady though she was literally freaking out. She was feeling so much like a teenager again, she wouldn't be surprised if tomorrow morning she woke up with an acne breakout.

"Is everything okay?" Sophia asked.

"Yeah, you don't look so good," Everett said walking into the room. Of course, he wouldn't miss a chance to give her crap when her life was going to hell in a handbasket.

"Okay, well, guys, don't worry. We'll take care of everything around here and you go and enjoy and relax and take care of our baby, and…" Zora was babbling, but she couldn't stop herself. If she let them in on everything erupting inside of her, they'd never leave, and she needed them to *go*.

She still had to pack, find some kind of matronly pajamas,

and think about how to tell Mike she was going to have to take him up on his offer, after all.

Zora kissed Sophia on the cheek and hugged Everett then edged out of the room into the hallway. All the "truths and lies" she and Mike had shared were getting to her, and now she was having a hard time digesting all the information swimming around in her head.

I sleep naked.

Ugh.

Why had she let herself fantasize about Mike when she was kissing Andre at the club? Between the steamy "truth" texts afterward and the heated gaze he'd flashed her at game night, it was no wonder she couldn't stop thinking about him.

Who am I kidding?

Mike had always starred in her fantasies, but he'd also always been safely at arm's length. Still, somehow imagining him doing all the things she'd let a random guy do to her on the dance floor had left her unhinged and yearning for it to be real.

All it took was one night out, and now she'd gotten lost in the fantasy. Zora knew very well what letting the heart lead did to women, and she was not about to get caught up in the temptation. Even if she was going to be under the same roof, she would keep her distance.

If she and Mike were going into this with eyes wide open, she was going to see it for exactly what it was. They were friends and roommates, nothing more, no matter how much more she wanted.

CHAPTER 8

MIKE

J ust before 6:30, Mike slid the final service contract into a file and into his briefcase. He was set to head home for the evening when his phone vibrated across the desk. He rubbed the back of his neck before he reached for it. His stomach churned as he turned it over and saw yet another message not from Zora.

At least this time it wasn't Kate.

It was a text from Jason Adelstein, a friend of his from law school who he hung out with from time to time but who lived too comfortably for Mike's taste.

> **Jason:** March Madness. I'm having a soiree
> on the water tonight. You in? Heard
> you got rid of your baggage. Hoping to
> get my wingman back.

He was a real fly by the seat of his pants type of guy who was always on the go, jet-setting to St. Tropez and Greece, or

Vegas, his favorite place in The States. Jason was a trust-fund kid, an attorney at one of the best firms in Oregon and bound for partnership. He was well connected and willing to throw his money around to keep it that way.

If there was an exclusive new restaurant, hot club, basketball game, or private event, Jason could get VIP access. Whatever the craving—alcohol, women, mood enhancers—he supplied it in spades because he wanted his name on peoples' minds and the good word of mouth.

Hanging out with Jason meant quite possibly getting laid. He owned a one-hundred-foot yacht and regularly threw crazy, alcohol-fueled ragers complete with a buffet of hot women lined up to help him and his closest friends take a load off.

Shit.

Mike let his thumb hover over the keyboard on his phone.

Most of the time, he ignored Jason's texts or made up some excuse why he couldn't make it out. Tonight, though, his friend made a good point. Mike had gotten rid of his baggage. He was a free man in need of physical release, and it wouldn't hurt getting it with someone new. It wasn't like he had any other standing obligations. At least, not with Zora. He still had yet to hear from her.

Mike loosened his tie and pulled it through his collar, folding it and stuffing it into his pocket. He slid the strap of his briefcase over his shoulder and flicked off the lights before responding. As he stepped into the elevator, he decided.

Mike: I'm in.

Jason's response was almost immediate.

Jason: Wait until you see the honeys I've

got lined up tonight. Might need to play
a little five-on-one with yourself before
you get here.

Mike smirked.

Mike: Already got it handled. I stay ready.

The yacht screamed "daddy's money." It was Jason's
personal cruise ship and pleasure den complete with
lights strung over the pool, pulsing music, courtesy of a live DJ,
and yacht stews making drinks.

True to his word, Jason had invited only the best of the best.

The deck was crawling with fine women. Mike felt over-
dressed and underdressed simultaneously. The men were
wearing fine Italian suits, but the women were dressed in little
more than thongs.

"Bro! You made it!" Jason called out from a lounger where
he was flanked by a topless redhead and a barely clothed
blonde. The man was straight out of a Brooks Brothers catalog
—a strapping young lad, dashing and dapper with a square
jaw, cleft chin, and side-swept blond hair.

He leaned down and suckled the redhead's breast, running
his tongue over her pebbled nipple. "Ah. So sweet. Don't go
anywhere." He licked his lips then the blonde's neck before
getting to his feet to meet his friend.

Mike's brows lifted in amusement, and he released a short
bark of laughter.

"I see you've got yourself a buffet here…and…" He leaned
back. "Are you growing a beard?"

Jason nodded and stroked his stubble before quickly bringing Mike's attention back to his companions.

"Only the best... Get yourself a snack and catch up." He gave Mike a hard slap on the back and pulled him into a hug. "It's so good to see you, man. Thought I'd lost you for a minute there."

"Nah, just putting in the work for the dream, you know?"

Jason gripped Mike's shoulders and held him at a short distance to study him. For a moment, he just stared. Then his brows furrowed.

"What?" Mike asked.

"Which dream are we talking about, here?"

Mike sighed. All he'd ever wanted was to grow his own business. Partnering with his best friend had been awesome. Mike was there every step of the way when Everett had put the business plan together for his family's real estate development company, so he felt a certain loyalty to the company. He wanted to be there to help it go the distance— the setbacks, the challenges, and the celebrations.

Mike also wanted to invest in his own future. Deep down, he wanted to be full partner, not just in-house counsel.

"You know me. I've been trying to get Monroe to make me a partner."

Jason shook his head. "You were top of the class at Berkeley. If this dude doesn't see what he's got, come to Baker & Bronson. I'll make sure they snap you up quickly. You'll probably make partner before I do."

He held his hand up high and Mike slowly reached up to slap it, chuckling at his friend. *Will this guy ever grow up?*

"So, anyway—" Mike was just about to change the subject when Jason beat him to the chase.

He zeroed in on someone behind Mike. "Six o'clock. Blonde.

Tall. Body for days. Giving you total 'fuck-me' eyes." Jason's chin dropped like he was sharing a secret, but it seemed his gaze was still focused on the blonde as he whispered. "A mouth that'll make you cum—"

At the sound of heels drawing near him, Mike pressed his shoulders back and turned.

Kate.

His lips parted as she closed the distance between them. Her sun-kissed curls were loose, untamed, and tousled to one side over the soft pink curve of her cheek. She wore a simple, sleek black dress and she looked as beautiful as ever. She seemed smaller, though. Fragile.

He hoped he hadn't broken her spirit.

"All right, man. I'm going to leave you to it," Jason said, winking then backed away toward his harem.

Kate waited until Jason was out of earshot. "Hey," she said in a low voice. A genuine smile tugged at the corners of her mouth and relief flooded Mike.

The last time he'd talked to Kate was the night of Zora's party. She had stood there with tears in her eyes wanting what he didn't have to give. He'd wanted to apologize, but how could he be sorry for something he had no control over? He'd been telling his heart for years not to want Zora, but that night he'd learned the hard way that the heart wants what it wants.

It was only after that that he'd decided to stop listening to it.

When Kate took off, Mike didn't have it in him to go after her or call her. He did text to make sure she'd made it home safe. Somewhere between *I'm glad you made it, I'm sorry,* and *good night* he couldn't stop himself from texting: *I think we should go our separate ways.*

Having his desire for Zora reflected back at him through Kate's eyes made it glaringly clear. He wouldn't ever be able to give Kate the love she deserved. So, he'd been dodging her calls and texts. It was a weight off his shoulders he wasn't aware he'd been carrying. He was relieved to have the romantic part of their relationship over with, but he deeply regretted hurting her.

Without saying a word, he went in for a hug now and held it a little too long and tight. Through the hug, he tried to convey all the things he couldn't actually say.

Sorry.

I didn't want to hurt you.

You're still important to me.

When they pulled apart, she peered up at him. "I know. I think I'd always known, but I'm happy for you...kind of." She giggled nervously.

Mike shot her a pained expression. "Oh, just kind of?"

"Well she was kissing some other guy, but I'm sure she'll come to her senses soon enough and realize what a *mediocre* catch you are."

They both laughed.

"I see you're a comedian now." He stepped back, enjoying the comfortable feeling between them without any of the expectations and promises. He liked that the sex and pretenses were removed from the equation and seeing that there was still a friendship left worth holding onto.

"No, it's not like that, though." He slipped his hand to the small of Kate's back and guided her over to the bar. A cool, crisp breeze feathered her hair over her shoulder and in the soft glow of the string lights, he felt her reading him.

"Me and Zo, we're...just friends."

His heart squeezed as if challenging his words.

"You don't believe that, do you?" she asked. Her amused smile was genuine.

"Yes, I do. We've known each other since we were kids. Everett is my best friend. We're family." He looked off toward the water.

Mike's mind reeled to the day all those years ago when he and Everett came back from riding bikes and Zora was waiting for them on the porch. She couldn't have been more than eight. It was the first time he'd really seen her as anything other than Everett's sister. Her hair had been freshly pressed and she wore a new purple dress. From there she seemed to blossom overnight, but he kept his distance for over a decade.

Until he couldn't.

It wasn't the day her mother died, but at age eighteen, Zora finally broke down on the day Eva Monroe would have turned fifty. Before her memories were properly cemented, she was a motherless child with no one to talk to but her grandmother about boys and love, periods, and prom. Mike understood Zora finally felt the heartbreak. of knowing the woman who was supposed to love her unconditionally wasn't willing to fight for her—to choose to live for her.

He'd sensed in that moment, Zora needed someone, and he wanted to be there. He'd been waiting because he knew what not being there did to a person. He knew about the shame, guilt, and self-blame.

"I know you don't want to hear this, especially from me," Kate said, snapping him out of the memory. "Mike, I think you're in love with her."

Just then Mike's phone vibrated in his blazer. As soon as he saw the message, it drove Kate's point to his core.

> **Zora:** Hey, I hope it's not too late, but if the
> offer still stands, I'm going to take you
> up on staying at your place. Let me

know and I'll see you after work
tomorrow.

Mike met Kate's gaze. Thank goodness she was gracious enough not to say anything. Once again, her expression reflected his truth back at him.

CHAPTER 9

ZORA

Friday morning, Zora rose at dawn. Well, technically, she just laid in the bed blankly staring at the television with one foot hanging out of the covers, but she was up. She didn't get a wink of sleep thinking about Mike's house and the sleeping arrangements. She'd also spent a good deal of time thinking about the women cycling in and out of his bed now that he was single again.

Coffee.

With a loud, huffy grunt she slipped out the bed, phone in hand, and slogged toward the kitchen. She turned on the coffee maker and slinked onto a barstool. As the machine hissed to life, she called Oli.

"Hey, girl, hey. Bright and early, I see."

Zora groaned in response.

"Oh, so no coffee yet. Want to call me back?" This was why they were friends. The woman knew her too well.

"No," Zora sighed. "I'm just…grumpy."

"Chin up."

"Seriously? That's your pep talk?" Zora slumped lower on the barstool.

Oli's voice squawked into the receiver. "Not you, fool."

Zora pulled the phone away from her ear to make sure they weren't Facetiming. "Thanks? Well then who are you talking to?"

"Tilt your head a little bit more toward me. And now the chin. Perfect." Oli laughed. "I'm at that shoot at the Japanese Garden—the Wellington wedding I was telling you about. I'm finished with the detail shots. You know, rings, dress, shoes, and flowers. I was multitasking, but I'm talking to you, now."

"Oh."

"By the way, she had *the* most gorgeous dress. I'll show you the proofs later." The line was muffled for a second before she continued. "Doing the prep shots now. Anyway, why are you so grumpy?"

The last steaming, hot drip plopped into the coffeemaker and Zora got to her feet to gather the cream and sugar. "Never mind. Go back to work. I'll figure it out."

"Earpods... Multitasking... I'm good, if you don't mind hearing my directions now and then. Does this mood have anything to do with you moving in with a certain somebody?" Her voice took on a velvety tone.

Zora pulled a mug from the cupboard and filled it to the brim then added her personal touches until it was a creamy bisque color. She took her first sip and inhaled the robust, sweet aroma for a second, letting it warm her throat before responding.

"The last house I saw yesterday was disgusting. There's no need to say 'I told you so.' Whether I like it or not, I'm going to have to stay with Mike." She slouched against the kitchen island, sounding hopeless and defeated, which apparently Oli was keen to disregard.

"Yes, girl. I love it. Now you guys are going to be forced to address the old wrinkly-ass elephant that's been in the room for way too long." She paused and Zora heard her tell someone to straighten the train of the dress. "Don't get mad at me, Zo, but I really hope you guys at least have one nasty, dirty night of sex. Or, day of sex. Either would be hot."

"Ugh. This is not funny." Zora kicked her legs and pouted. "What am I going to do? I need to set some ground rules in place otherwise this is not going to work. I haven't even been focusing on the cookbook. I need to pack before Mike gets off work, and now I'm going to be holed up in his guestroom trying to dodge him without looking like a weird hobbit."

By now Oli was cracking up on the other end of the line, which only infuriated Zora more.

"Are you going to help me or not?"

While Zora was waiting for her friend to come to her senses and stop reveling in her torment, her phone chimed with an incoming message. She didn't recognize the number, but it wasn't hard to decipher who it was.

> **Unknown:** Work has been crazy this week since we're expanding the practice, but I want to see you and kiss you again. Olivia couldn't stop raving about you, and I'd like to get to know you even better. Maybe somewhere quiet this time, just the two of us. Any chance you're free this weekend?

As if life weren't complicated enough already, now Andre wanted to crawl out from wherever he'd been hiding for over a week.

"Why do you have to micromanage it?" Oli cut into Zora's

thoughts. She was still arguing her point. "This is Mike, your *friend*. I think you're taking it way too far with rules. If anything happens, let it be organic. Let it happen and stop trying to control everything."

"I did the whole *get lost in the moment* thing last weekend and now I'm... Ugh, forget it. Just help me think this through. I'm not trying to be a burden on him. I cannot have a *thing* with Mike."

Even though it was still piping hot, Zora took a long drink from her mug.

"Why?" Oli whined. "He's free. I told you he ended things with Kate."

Zora re-read the message from Andre. The coffee was kicking in and now a beyond brilliant idea brewed in the back of her mind. She still needed to set the record straight for Oli, though.

"Just because it's over with Kate doesn't mean he's out of the dating cesspool. Let's not forget, it's been well established. We. Are. Friends. Just friends. So why not—" She trailed off.

As she drained the rest of her coffee, an idea rooted itself in her brain. She did a run-walk back to her bedroom.

"Holy macaroni! Why did I not think of this before?" she asked herself. Finally, it was feeling like she might have found a way to deal with the ruins of her childish crush.

"Why not what? Why didn't you think of?" Oli asked.

Zora forgot Oli was still on the line. She was on a mission.

"Hold on a sec."

She plopped onto the bed and scrolled through her book-marked articles until she found the one. Back when she'd worked customer support in that call center for a telemarketing company, she'd sat next to a nice, but rather touchy-feely male coworker who refused to get the hint that they were just friends. She'd gotten zero personal space from spaghetti arms.

There was always a hug that lasted too long, a hair he needed to push out of her face, or his hand on the small of her back.

Right before Zora had been about to give her coworker a potentially job-threatening piece of her mind, the godsend of a woman who sat on the other side of him emailed her an article listing the rules of platonic friendship.

It worked so well Zora saved it for future reference.

Present Zora owed past Zora big time.

For the next twenty minutes, while Oli worked on candid moments of the bridesmaids and groomsmen getting ready, Zora told her the rules she planned to implement over the next month.

The phone went silent.

"Well, what do you think?" she asked.

Finally, Oli materialized with an audible sigh. "You're serious?

"As a heart attack."

"It's not going to work."

"It just makes so much sense. Talk about it in the open. No touching. Only hang out during the day. No sexy clothes. Treat him how you would a same-sex friend. Oli, you have to admit this stuff is brilliant."

The silence resumed, then she heard a muffled Oli excuse herself from the room for a 'small emergency,' which Zora knew was code for, give me a second to knock some sense into my best friend's hard head. When she came back on the line, it was in surround sound.

"You're out of your mind, Zo!" Her voice was shrill and crazy shaky. "I mean, you've literally lost it this time. I get the no Netflix and chilling thing, but what kind of crap is that about it's okay to cook for him but not eat together? That just sounds stupid. Avoid sexual conversation? They act like people just sit around talking about penis and vagina all the time. It's not like you're texting each other about sleeping naked. It's ridiculous."

Zora cringed. She and Mike were having veiled conversations about sex. All the more reason for these rules.

"Whatever. Did you hear the most important one?" She read verbatim from the article. "'Accept the sexual tension for what it is, but having feelings doesn't mean you have to act upon them.' Come on, if that's not me and Mike, I don't know what is. It's there. It's always been there and probably will stay there, but we don't have to act on our attraction. We both know we're better off friends. He told me so himself at game night."

Oli seemed to chew on this new piece of information. "He did?"

"Yes, and that's why... What if...?" Zora rubbed her finger over her top lip.

"Lord have mercy, woman, spit it out. You're killing me. I'm dying. I'm dead."

As Zora hopped off the bed, she began undressing for the shower. A bout of confidence filtered her voice. "The rules said to let him know about your other person, so he knows there's nothing going on between you..." She mulled over the words again, putting all the pieces together. "Mike let me know about Kate. What if he wasn't the only one?"

"Only one what?" Oli scoffed. "You're not making sense. This little 'Aunt Flo emergency' I've conjured is only going to last me so long, so out with it."

Zora thought about Andre's text. She wasn't some unfortunate-looking, housebound, shrew. People compared her to Nia Long, for goodness sake. She had options too. Even if she weren't particularly interested in sucking face with a slobber hound, a date *would* help set the tone in the house.

"He's not the only one with options," Zora stressed. "He let me know about Kate, so I'll just have to let him know I'm going on a date this weekend."

Without second-guessing it, Zora hung up with Oli, found Andre's message, and confirmed. Saturday night at eight she was going meet him at *Bite-Sized.*

CHAPTER 10

MIKE

M ike arrived at work a half hour before his scheduled meeting with Harrison Arnold and waited in the conference room. He wore a tailored navy blue suit paired with a white button-down, a striped red and navy necktie, and a matching pocket square. His files were meticulously tabbed in the designated signature sections and he brought extra pens for the occasion. Though he was only assigned this meeting a week ago, Mike felt like he'd been waiting for this opportunity to prove himself to Everett for years.

With a deep breath, he checked his watch for the tenth time, but the minutes seemed to tick by like hours. He was always early to give himself a chance to let his nerves settle.

You've got this.

He was scribbling with the third pen to make sure it didn't dry out when the glass door opened with a whoosh and Kendra entered. Her braids were pulled back into a neat ponytail. She wore light makeup on her ebony skin and her usual casual dress was replaced with a serious black skirt suit. She was all business today, and her folded arms and rigid posture seemed guarded and territorial.

Not until the door clicked shut did she meet his gaze.

She lifted a thick brow at him.

"Is he here?" Mike asked, adjusting his blazer, glancing at the closed door.

Her lips pursed. "I'm glad you're sitting down. He's not coming today. The guy rescheduled."

"Did he say why? What exactly did he say?"

Mike pushed back from the table and crossed his arms, too. He could feel his face twisting in annoyance. With a deep inhale, he breathed out slowly. His teeth clenched, and his jaw tightened. Even though the air conditioning was on full blast, he was hot.

Kendra wiggled her fingers over the documents on the table. "Listen, I don't usually get into the details about all this, but something seems *really* fishy. It wasn't him on the phone. It was my girl, Ellie, who works for Arnold Corporation. She knows everything going on even though she's just the front line."

"Like what?"

"She said Arnold told her to reschedule for a week from today, next Friday. But that's not all of it. She said he has an appointment with Easton Investments LLC *this* afternoon—a company that basically does what we do." She pursed her lips. "If you ask me, I think they're our competition, and he's switching teams."

Mike considered this. He scrubbed a hand over his face and loosened his tie as he blew out a heavy breath.

"How is he still vetting deals when we were supposed to sign today? This was supposed to be a done deal, a formality." In the back of his mind, Mike wasn't completely surprised.

He'd warned Everett about getting all their ducks in a row before making plans. "Fuck. This is some bullshit. He's basically hedging his bets. He'll meet with them today and see what they offer then use our deal to ensure he maxes out. Shady."

Kendra cocked her head. "Ellie said he knew Everett was going out of town. So he planned this shit."

The woman was hot-headed, but he was right there with her.

Mike got to his feet and paced the length of the conference room, turning on his heel as he figured his next move.

This was not going to happen on his watch.

Monroe Properties needed this deal too much. They passed on so many other prospects that were just as good if not better, but Everett insisted on going with Arnold due to their family ties. There was no way Mike was going to do nothing. He wouldn't let the company fall.

He was hot just thinking about it.

He clenched his teeth. *Keep your head together.*

"Okay, even if they do sign today." He nodded, mentally running over the logistics. "It takes three to five business days for the filing to process. At the earliest, it would be Wednesday, but more likely Thursday or Friday, which is why he rescheduled for Friday."

"That snake."

Mike pulled his bottom lip between his teeth and squinted as he met Kendra's gaze. She looked like she was seeing red. Like Mike, she might tell Arnold exactly where he could stick his secondhand deal. Most days she was a feisty back-talker who put her nose in places where it didn't belong. Today, he needed that, though. Because of her fierce loyalty and nose for details, she'd sniffed out this problem.

Now Mike might be able to do something about it.

Still standing, Kendra whipped a notepad and pen out of nowhere and held them at the ready. She seemed to be waiting for him to let her in on their course of action.

"Ellie fucking hates this dude," Kendra said. "She said he's an asshole and a dictator, and she knows he's up to no good."

"We're not sitting ducks. We have a little time. Not much, but enough to do some digging." Mike lifted his chin as Kendra rounded the table and sat down in the seat facing the door. "In the meantime, get me everything you can find on Easton Investments. If you don't mind, see if your friend is willing to do a little more snooping around. Find out what number they're coming in at. I'll be wracking my brain all weekend, but I'll come up with something by Monday. Maybe we can match whatever Easton is offering, so we don't lose out on this deal."

Mike fell into to the seat across from Kendra. Suddenly, he felt exhausted. There was no escape. He glanced at his phone again. All this shit was going on at work, and he doubted he would find any solace at home. In a few hours, he'd be moving in a new roommate.

He tugged his tie off and cracked his neck.

Zora was still heavy on his mind. After what Kate said on the yacht, it was getting harder and harder to deny how he felt about Zora. That his mind was on her when he was in the middle of a crisis at work meant there had to be some weight to Kate's words.

Am I in love with Zora? Wouldn't I know?

The silence in the room ripped him from his thoughts, and he lifted his chin to find Kendra watching him.

"Is it this, or is something else bothering you because I noticed you looked a little tighter around the collar this morning." Kendra's pen was down and her body was angled to him. She seemed to scrutinize his every movement.

Is it that obvious?

"Come on, now," she said. "Out with it because I need you thinking clearly about Arnold and the Chessington Building. A deal like this will do a lot for this company, and I could use a raise."

She grinned, but Mike sensed her prying had less to do with the growth of the company, and more to do with her affinity for juicy gossip. Plus, she was itching to insert herself into someone's relationship. Ever since Sophia locked Everett down, Kendra had been hinting at finding Mike a match.

She looked at him with questioning eyes.

If he was in love with Zora, and he seriously doubted it, why was he holding out? What was the worst that could happen?

He never felt about any other woman the way he did about Zora. She was kind, free-spirited, and a firecracker— blazing and beautiful, but just out of reach. They'd gone down this road before and decided to turn back, but what if she was it for him? What if they were wasting away the best years they could be spending together?

There was so much at risk. Although, if he really thought about it, there was even more to gain.

Mike eyed Kendra thinking of the benefits of getting a woman's point view for a change. He could use her as a sounding board before he did anything stupid like tell Zora exactly how much he'd held back all these years. Against his steely nature, he parted his lips and let everything spill out...in a roundabout way.

"So this guy...a friend of mine, he's known this girl for almost their whole lives," Mike began.

"Uh-huh. Ooh, I love this kind of story," Kendra murmured adjusting in her seat to get comfortable. She hugged her shoulders close to her and rubbed her hands together.

"She's beautiful, sweet, motivated, and a good friend who's

stood by him even though he's basically been avoiding her by dating as many women as possible to keep himself from getting hurt or causing her more hurt than she's already been through."

Kendra nodded. "Okay. I get it."

"So she deserves so much better, and he knows it," Mike went on. "But it doesn't stop him from feeling like he needs her —even if they've gone down this road and he got rejected once. I don't know what to tell him, but it's like his life is magnified ten-fold when he's with her. Everything just feels right, you know?"

"Yes."

"They laugh together, play together, and they are more themselves when they're together than when they're apart."

Kendra pressed her hand over her heart for a second like she really got it, but then she scooted her chair close to the table and squared her body to Mike like she was about to school him.

"Let me guess. They're both broken?"

Mike nodded, but Kendra was not done yet.

"Her pain is about her parents, who were two amazing people. The mother lost herself somewhere along the way. The dad stepped out on their marriage and replaced their family, so she thought the grandmother could take care of the kids and everyone would be better off without her. This girl, the one your friend loves, she's scared of repeating history, right?"

Mike's eyes went wide, and his mouth fell open.

"How long did it take you to figure out I was talking about Zora?"

Kendra smiled and tilted her head forward. "When you said, 'so this guy.'" She laughed. "Please give me *some* credit. How long have I been working here? How long have I known this family? I'm required to keep my mouth closed, not my ears."

Mike bit back a grin.

"You're in love with Zora." It wasn't a question.

"No," he shot back too quickly.

Kendra dipped her chin and gave him a "who do you think you're fooling" look.

"I mean, I know Zora owns part of the company but..." Mike was dumbfounded. "She's more of a silent partner. She's not around enough for you to draw that kind of a conclusion. What makes you say that?"

"I'm not blind," Kendra said in her sassiest voice.

Panic coursed through Mike. Why was everyone telling him he was in love with Zora?

What am I missing?

It was always the missing pieces that scared him the most.

His mind drifted to Lucas. He wished when he thought about his little brother he remembered the happy times. The joy on Lucas' face when he found Mike's hiding place, his chubby toothless smile in their family pictures. He wanted to remember all the firsts and beginnings. They were still there, but the image always at the top of Mike's mind wasn't a happy one. It was Lucas' ending.

Every time Mike ventured to imagine a new beginning, it scared him. What if he was five minutes late? What if the stars were already aligned and fate decided before he took his position? What if he couldn't save her like he couldn't save Lucas?

Mike couldn't imagine any type of ending with Zora.

"I think this has little to do with her and more to do with you," Kendra said in tune with his thoughts.

"Have you ever missed being there to help when something bad happens? I just want to be there for her, but I don't want to add to her pain. Does that make sense?"

"Completely."

Mike felt validated in his thinking.

For about two seconds.

"Let me tell you one thing my mother said it to me," Kendra said. "If you're always looking in the rearview mirror, you'll never see the beautiful view in front of you. Do you know what *that* means?"

Mike nodded slowly but he didn't want to forget about Lucas and he couldn't forget what losing her mother had done to Zora.

"What you're talking about is not this. Love can be either an explosion or an implosion. You can tell the person how you feel and risk all the falling, breaking, and gooey good stuff about gluing each other back together into one piece, or you can fall apart inside. It's that simple, but it's always your choice."

Mike dropped his head and wringed his fingers as he considered her advice. A sense of urgency flooded his insides and he was suffused with warmth and a fresh energy. He was weightless and floating on air.

But he was also desperate.

She was right. All this time, he'd been falling apart inside.

Kendra cleared her throat and Mike snapped his eyes to hers. "You know their grandmother, Barbara, used to tell me about all of you guys," she said. "She'd really hoped you two would end up together." Her features and tone softened. "Barbara said you guys were made for each other, but neither of you would ever admit it. As far as I can see, she wasn't wrong."

"She said that?"

"What have you got to lose?"

Mike drummed his fingers across the glass tabletop. "I've actually thought about it." He laughed, holding up a hand to list the risks. "Let me think—the only family I've ever known, my best friend, possibly my job, and my only chance at love. How's that for a gamble?"

Kendra flashed him a full, proud grin as she stood and

smoothed her skirt. She ambled over to the door then turned to look at him. "Sounds like you're making the right choice. It's only ever worth it when all your chips are in."

His spirits soared. In his heart, it was settled. Over the next month, he was going to up his ante and call Zora's bluff.

CHAPTER 11

ZORA

Later that afternoon, armed with her new tools of salvation, Zora finished her packing in a breeze. She was weightless and carefree and ready to go into her new living arrangement feet first. Mike usually left work late, which meant there was plenty of time for her to kick back, relax, and take a load off before packing up her car for the move.

Besides, it was five o'clock somewhere. Wasn't it?

She'd earned a drink after finally making a decision. She'd made a choice, even if it was to maintain solely a platonic relationship with Mike. It was definitely cause for celebration.

The weight of the world was off her shoulders.

Today, she would meet with him, acknowledge her feelings for him—remembering to keep it brief to maintain her sanity—then cut them off before they could do any more damage and before she moved onto his territory.

It was the only solution—complete and brutal honesty.

Once she and Mike were solidly comfortable in their conversation, Zora would tell Mike about her date with Andre.

Really, the whole thing is genius.

"Why am I even sweating it? I should have done this a long time ago."

This deserved a toast to her own brilliant, empowering decision to let her past go. She poured herself a glass of Prosecco and lifted it before taking a long swig. The bubbles were contagious. She *felt* lifted. Overjoyed. She was positively buoyant with having the weight of her crush off her shoulders for good.

"Cheers!"

Sip after sip, elation suffused her being, and by her second glass, Zora was cozied up on the living room sofa, deep into the movie *Coming to America*. Akeem had just stood on the subway dressed in all his princely garb and renounced his thrown. He was professing his love for Lisa McDowell when Zora's phone vibrated.

With her buzz fully going by now, she labored to press pause and reach for her phone on the coffee table. It was only a few inches away, but she was starting to feel heavy and relaxed.

> **Mike:** Sophia texted and asked if we could stop by the restaurant to check the inventory. *Headed over there now.* Starting the weekend early. Why don't you meet me there, we'll grab a to-go box, then get the moving under way. After, maybe we can catch a movie on Netflix and just chill???

Zora glazed over most of the message. Her focus centered on the three question marks then the four words that preceded them. Was she drunk? Was Michael Dwayne Kennedy really asking to Netflix and chill?

"That's some good ass wine."

Her head bobbed slightly as she leaned in way too close to look at the label. Her mouth was dry, and the air was a little stuffy, but she had to be drunk. It was the only way to explain this kind of hallucination. She and Mike never Netflix and chilled.

Did anyone over twenty-one really hook up on the couch under the pretense of watching some lame, non-eighties movie? No, they most certainly did not.

"Snap out of it."

Zora slapped her cheek then pinched the bridge of her nose. She was not in the right state of mind to deal with this kind of proposition.

The trusty rules of her plan streamed through her head.

I need to start establishing the rules now. What was it? What is it? Rule number one…talk about it out in the open.

Squinting, she held the phone at a distance before pulling it within an inch of her nose. She squeezed her eyes shut then blinked as she tried to sit up, only to be forced to lie back down again from light-headedness.

What is Mike doing? Where is this coming from and why can't I put two words together?

Wiggling onto her side, she glanced at the message again. It blurred in front of her as her head bobbed. Spittle dribbled from her lips.

> **Zora:** Can we tell me something you? I'm so straddling. I think I need to start masturbating again.

Ease into it.

For good measure, she sent the emoji with the parted lips because it seemed like it just inhaled a deep breath, which at the moment, seemed like a good thing. Then, she added the quiet face emoji for fun.

Relief flooded her chest. It felt good to be so honest with him. This was exactly why she needed the rules. It was basically color by numbers for the friend-zoned and dating-challenged.

Talk about it out in the open.

Yes.

Zora blew out a slow breath. She was taking the necessary steps to get there. Start with something simple then get to the crux of it.

> **Mike:** Wow.

The three text dots popped up. He was typing again. Even Mike could appreciate how good it felt to have a friend to confide all the crazy things life throws at you. Lazily, she glanced back at the message. The ellipses disappeared and reappeared and then disappeared again.

"Wow" was the only response he could come up with after a friend confides that they're stressed? *Come on Mike, even you can do better than that.*

What did he have to think about?

> **Mike:** I don't know what to say. I'm
> flattered you're over-sharing this
> with me?

Zora squeezed her eyes then opened them wide. *Over-sharing?* She scrolled back to the green text bubble with her message and almost fell off the couch.

Oh my god. Oh my god. Oh my god.

"Holy…" *Fuck.* "Fuuuck. This is not happening to me."

Her head pounded, and she looked over at the empty wine

bottle. Heat blazed from her neck to her cheeks, and even through her woozy haze, she was mortified.

"Holy shit, I'm never drinking again." Fumbling, she gripped the phone with two hands, stabbing at the keys. Her legs were restless, ticking to a rapid, wired craze.

"Fucking autocorrect!"

> **Zora:** OMG. I'm so fleakign sorry sorry. Autocorrect did it. The message was supposed to say: I'm so STRESSED, not straddling. I think I need to start MEDITATING again, not masturbating.

Mike's reply was quick.

> **Mike:** lmfao. I'm dying. I was not quite sure what was happening, but I was entertained. Lol

I cannot believe I just told Mike I think I need to start masturbating again.

Her fingers were moving but she was not in control of them at the moment. Her heart raced as she fought a losing battle to steady her nerves. How was she ever going to live this down?

> **Zora:** As you can tell, I might have have hd one too many glasses of wine. I'm going to bury myself in the covers. Can we do the restaurant tomoorow?

Zora fell back on the couch and covered her eyes. Her phone vibrated.

> **Mike:** Yep. You're definitely in no shape to
> do any type of inventory. We've got to
> go bright and early because of the
> fumigation schedule, so get some rest.
> I'll meet you at the house
> TOMOOROW.

His last message was followed by a string of laughing-crying emojis punctuated by a ripe eggplant. Perhaps "talking about it out in the open" might not have been the best rule to begin. The sexual tension was out there now. If it wasn't glaringly apparent before, there was no escaping the fact Zora needed to come back strong with her resolve.

Start again in the morning.

Fresh.

Clean slate.

Maybe she would try a simpler rule, like "no touching" or "no date-like outings." And definitely less alcohol.

CHAPTER 12

MIKE

The following morning, Mike showed up early to Patton Place. The scent of pine and freshly cut grass wafted in the morning breeze. The sun was still hiding amid the grayish blue sky. It was "tomoorow," as Zora had typed it. He chuckled to himself. It was a little sooner than he really needed to be there, but he was still high on his decision. Whether or not Zora knew it, he was ready to face this challenge head on and see where things went between them.

He rang the doorbell three times before he resorted to knocking on the window. When Zora finally opened the door, it appeared he might be way too early.

"Hey. No Blue?"

Zora flashed him a heavy-lidded glare before she covered her mouth to sneeze. "Dog hotel. I'll pick him up tomorrow. Why are you here at this ungodly hour?" Her voice was thick with sleep as she coughed to clear her throat.

"Good morning...sunshine!" he sang.

Maybe a little overkill. Easy, boy.

"Allergies are getting the best of me today." She grimaced

then winced. Maybe she was remembering their text conversation yesterday.

Mike pulled his bottom lip between his teeth to keep from laughing at her.

She blinked a few times. "Whatever. Nine or ten would have been good. Don't ask me to look at you. My head isn't right yet. I need coffee." She groaned then turned on her heel and padded toward the kitchen leaving Mike in the doorway.

He followed behind her amused by the combination of her embarrassment and evident hangover.

"I thought the guys would be setting up for the fumigation." Mike pulled out his phone to double-check the email as they entered the kitchen. He scrolled past a new one from Jason with the subject line, "Easton Investments LLC."

The whole weekend was still ahead of him. He had time to dig up dirt on Arnold's plans. He kept scrolling.

"See, right here. If they're starting at nine o'clock, there should be trucks and equipment outside. Where's the big tent thingy?"

"Coffee first, then I do the things. Not a second sooner," Zora grunted.

They sat in silence while she brewed a fresh pot. Only after she took the first sip and moaned with satisfaction did she nod for Mike to continue speaking. Unfortunately, he was still reeling from the lustful sound she'd made. His cock twitched and he cleared his throat.

It was the sound he imagined she would make when masturbating.

His insides flooded with warmth. "So, uh, where are all your boxes...the stuff you're taking to my house?"

Zora met his gaze then quickly averted her eyes. "They're in the car in the garage ready to go. I thought I was going to be able to do this last night, but I was held up by a bottle of Prosecco."

She bit her lip and refused to look at him. It was amusing, but Mike didn't want to revel in her discomfort.

"I can go move the car around while you get ready, if you want," he said, way too quickly. Mostly, he wanted the chance to do anything other than stand there awkwardly ogling her. Just because he'd decided to see where things would go between them, he wasn't going to profess his undying love outright. He thought he'd take it slow, put out some feelers, and see where her head was at.

It seemed his "other head" was moving way faster than he wanted, though.

What is going on with me?

It wasn't like he and Zora didn't ever hang out. They were together all the time at Everett's house, the farmer's market, and bars. Those were all safe places, with food and crowds, where he could trust himself to remember that she was his best friend's younger sister and not the woman in the tight blue dress...the woman whose body starred in his wet dream last night.

Mike pinched the bridge of his nose and turned on his heel.

It took him about ten minutes to move a few of her boxes around in the car and squeeze out of the garage. He parked on the street in front of the house and scanned the perimeter. There were still no signs of anyone preparing to fumigate. He considered he might have read the message wrong. As he climbed the steps to the front door, Mike read the pest control company email once more.

He didn't recognize the company, but he knew Everett was pretty picky about the businesses he used. Just below the confirmation and order numbers on the invoice attached was the appointment information.

Saturday, March 14th, 9:00 a.m.

It was the right day and not too far off the right time. They were either late or simply had the wrong address.

Mike was getting the feeling something else was wrong altogether.

The top of the invoice included a phone number, so he dialed them up. After four rings the line cut off, leaving him staring at the screen. It wasn't a call failure and there was no option to leave a voicemail. He needed to tell Zora.

Mike walked back into the house and rushed down the hall, following the sound of her sneezing. He rounded the corner into her bedroom without thinking.

"Hey, something's up," he said, but then he stopped in his tracks.

Through the steam, he saw Zora's naked form in her bathroom mirror. His gaze glided over her tight body. He wanted to run the pads of his fingers over her wet silken brown skin. She was leggy and slender, but with sensual, endless curves. Her breasts were small but full, and her ass was worthy of being endlessly kissed.

He sucked in a stark breath, as electricity coursed through his veins. Then he released a low growl.

He'd thought it was low, anyway.

Zora looked over her shoulder and saw him watching her. As she met his eyes, his mind went blank. She was striking, and he was struggling with the decision to look away or keep staring.

In the meantime, she didn't move to cover herself.

Zora raked a hand through her fringe of dark hair and lifted an accusatory brow at him. It wasn't a wistful glance. Heat flared in her eyes.

"You were saying?" She urged him to continue as she turned off the water.

Mike made a strangled sound.

In turn, his face grew hot and he chided himself for standing there gawking like he'd never seen a naked woman before. While he had many times, he never saw a woman as captivating and disarmingly beautiful as Zora.

Suddenly, he was twenty-two again. A breathless Zora lay beneath him with her breasts and soft curves pressed against him, he hovered over her gently and nervously, thankful she'd chosen him. His darkened gaze had moved over her as a slow and sexy grin crept through her tears. Her eyes were hooded, and she'd whispered his name.

Shaking off the thought without turning away, Mike forced his eyes to meet hers.

"I'm sorry," Mike managed. It didn't sound like an apology, though. It was more like a low whisper full of the angst and desire coursing through him.

The same half grin from years before settled on her face as she stepped slowly and sexily out of the shower and leveled him with a penetrating stare.

There was no towel—just beautifully sculpted flesh and her mouth-watering womanhood.

Fuck me.

He bit his lip, and his breath stuttered. The heat in her eyes seared through Mike, gripping his groin low and tight. Another growl pried its way out of him as he took in the fullness of her lips, the supple swell of her breasts, and, Lord have mercy on him, the delicate curve of her neck.

She'd rattled him. Again.

She was the only one who could.

Mike was breathless as he blinked out of his trance. He'd seen her naked before, but never like this—never when she was so confident and empowered.

"I..." he trailed off, swallowing hard over the lump in his

throat. "I'll just talk to you when you're ready. We'll drop your stuff off at my house first, but we need to get to the restaurant."

He slinked out of the room with his hard-on between his legs.

"Sounds good," she called after him.

They were definitely at an impasse, but it was too late. He was afraid it might be need, not lust, settling in the pit of his stomach.

It shook him to the core.

If he was going to do this, it would need to be slow and well thought out. Most importantly, it would be a decision he made with his head and his heart, not his dick.

CHAPTER 13

ZORA

Zora walked out of the bedroom with her head held considerably higher than it was when Mike first arrived to pick her up. The steamy shower cleared her sinuses and her mind. Mike was waiting for her by the front door reading something on his phone, standing about as far away from her as he could, which was a good thing. The heat on her skin when Mike looked at her naked body had left her horny as hell, and their proximity almost tipped her over the edge. The rules were working, but not exactly in her favor.

She patted her purse to make sure her phone was in it.

"I'm ready. Just let me lock up." She passed by him and waited for him to make his way down the steps before locking the door and following behind him.

The rules were going to try her willpower for sure. They were backfiring by the second. She was completely turned on. Mike's ass was one of the world's greatest testaments to exercise and fitness. She could just sink her teeth into it.

Zora bit the tip of her finger and tried not growl.

Just then her phone vibrated against her hip.

"Hold on a sec. Let me get this," she called ahead to Mike. She fished her phone out of her purse and took the call. "This is Zora."

"It's Leanne. I'm so glad I caught you. Now, find yourself something to hold onto. Have I got news for you!"

Leanne Ramey was not only the best literary agent on the face of the earth for anyone who ever picked up a mixing spoon, but a genuinely happy person. Every single time Zora talked to her, she was at a New Year's Eve level of excitement about everything—a new book tote, a new place to eat with the best fries in town, a cute pen. Don't even get her started on day planners and Washi stickers.

It didn't take much. So, Zora wasn't exactly ready to grab at something to steady herself over Leanne's great new purse or the fact the sun was smiling on Portland this morning.

"Oates Book Group bought your book!" The decibel level of the ear-piercing squeal Leanne let loose was epic.

Maybe I should have taken her advice.

Zora wasn't sure her eardrums would work again, but she matched Leanne's squeal with a masterful scream of her own and danced on the brick walkway. Then she just stood there shaking her head in disbelief. Her heartbeat was off the charts and all of the hair on her body was standing at attention.

She tossed a worried-looking Mike the thumbs-up, waving off his visibly rising panic.

Not until she heard Leanne's faint voice calling her, did she come back down to earth.

"Zora? Zora?"

"Are you kidding me? Please don't be kidding me because I'm dying! I'm dead. I died."

"Don't die," Leanne said. "This is real. When I say they wanted the book, I mean, we were almost about to go into a bidding war with James & Jensen over it. *This is big.*"

Zora sensed a serious undertone in Leanne's remarks. She pressed a hand to knocking heart. "Wait. What are you not telling me?"

"Well, this is where I need you to be on your A game. They want to put it out in early November."

Zora went silent. She blinked, and her heart was still pounding, but now it sounded like slow motion thuds coursing through sludge. "How? What? That's nine months away! I thought you said it would be like a year or so?"

"Normally, but with the demand for blended exotic food, they're rushing it to publishing." She hesitated and Zora could feel the other shoe was about to drop. "We actually don't have until November. They technically need it by the end of May in order to meet the six-month printing deadlines."

Now Zora dropped to the steps and let it all sink in.

Two months. No, less than two months. It was almost April. She had sixty days to work out her niche, think of a catchy title, and decide which recipes to include. Then she needed to figure out the nutritional information for each ingredient. She also needed professional photos, which Oli could do, but, still... This was crazy. Insane.

"I...I don't even..."

Was it going to be impossible? Had she set herself up for the impossible?

"Zora, breathe."

"I'm here, but I think I am dead. How... Just, how?"

Leanne's voice was measured with a calming quality to it, which was uncharacteristic for her. "I want you to breathe. Then, when your heart decides it doesn't want to come out of your chest, sit up, get up off the floor, and get to it. Take the weekend. Gather all the photos and recipes you sent me and decide on the best ones. Then cook. Do this over and again, and don't forget to have fun while you're doing it."

Zora was nodding, but the words were not computing.

"When I talk to you on Tuesday, you'll tell me all of your ideas, and we'll work on the magic for your awesome Creole-Mexican fusion cookbook. Got it?" For all of her usual crazy, bubbly antics, today, Leanne sounded like a badass business woman.

If Leanne believed in Zora, she figured it must be possible.

She wasn't sure how to go about it just yet, but she could cook. Somehow, the cooking would have to get her there.

"Yeah. Got it," Zora said, doing her best to come off as confident.

They disconnected, but Zora was still staring off into the distance. It was the best worst news ever.

In a daze, she stood and dragged her feet toward Mike and the car.

"What's up?"

"A really great publisher bought my book," she droned.

Mike tilted his head to the side. "I thought selling your book was a good thing."

"It is. It's just I only have about forty-five days to put it all together and make it amazing or risk never getting another deal." She was still shaking her head as she spoke, trying to make sense of it all.

This was definitely a "be careful what you ask for" moment.

Mike shuffled toward the car, but then he looked back at Zora with those damn sexy green eyes, and…it was a very good thing he kept walking away.

"Don't worry. You can do this," he said supportively. Then he bit his bottom lip. "You of all people know how to lean in. When you didn't find a seat at the table, you built your own. I'm not worried at all."

That makes one of us.

He was adorably sweet, and she almost lost it. Zora bit back the overwhelming urge to hug him. *Jump his bones.* Joy warmed her from within and it buoyed her spirits. "Thanks. It means a lot that you have faith in me."

Stay strong. He's just being a good friend. Nothing else is happening here.

Except her heart was knocking around in her chest and a tidal wave of emotions washed over her—endearment, irritation, happiness, fear, and worse of all, desire.

"Let's take your car. I've just got to get my wallet out of the driver's seat." Mike patted at his pants pockets. "I'm pretty sure it fell when I moved the car out front earlier."

Zora sneezed and gave herself a mental "attagirl." She hadn't completely imploded yet. Given the shit storm that was her life at the moment, it was a wonder she hadn't broken any of her rules and lunged for his totally kissable, sweet-talking mouth.

They were friends. Plain and simple. Why couldn't she get that through her thick head? They were two people who supported each other with pep talks when the impossible became reality. There was no Netflix and chilling or cozying up in the living room. If anything, she found a rather creative and hot way to accept the sexual tension without acting on her feelings for him.

A smug smile spread on her face.

She crossed into the street to round the car toward the driver's seat. At the same time, a bright yellow sports car sped by, nearly hitting her. Mike, the sexy-ass hero of her supposedly repressed dreams, jumped into action. He pulled her into him and they fell against the hood of the car.

"Are you okay?" he asked scrutinizing every inch of her body.

They were so close.

Too close.

Mike's hazy green eyes bore into her, riddled with worry and…heat.

Physically, she was okay, but her mind was scrambled. With all the excitement over the book and the way her skin blazed wherever Mike's hands touched, she couldn't focus. Her hips were pulled tight against his. Her breasts were pressed into the hard wall of his chest. They were both breathing erratically.

"I think so," she finally said.

He was hard and muscly all over. Zora felt his hand curl into a fist around the thin fabric of her shirt, and a shiver coursed through her. She felt like she might come apart if they were touching much longer. He smelled of a woodsy spice and sweet vanilla. It was so intoxicating, she couldn't help closing her eyes and inhaling.

When she opened them again, his cheeks were flushed, and desire darkened his irises.

Have mercy.

Zora wished he weren't so good-looking. Maybe then she could turn away, and her heart wouldn't flip.

Mike was both familiar and foreign all at once.

"Zora." His voice was a whisper, but its deep timbre burrowed down and settled in the pit of her belly.

The crease between his brow deepened and she was about to pull away but before she could, his mouth was on hers. His strong arms tightened around her waist and she opened her mouth in response, letting him in. His tongue searched her mouth, and she tasted him. It was a kissed steeped with lust, and a little too much time passed.

Zora's stomach was tied up in knots.

A wave of nostalgia washed over her as her mind flickered between the past and present. She was boneless and whimpering for everything she couldn't say—everything she'd waited too long to say.

Mike deepened the kiss, and her moan sounded strained to her own ears as he gently ran the pad of his thumb over her cheek. As she leaned into his touch, the juncture between her thighs tightened.

What are we doing?

This was wrong. They were supposed to be *just friends*. Mike was her brother's best friend. Mike was also the only guy who made Zora risk losing herself.

This broke so many rules.

"What are we doing?" she asked between breaths, desperate to understand how they'd gotten here.

He caressed the back of her head and her neck adoringly. "I'm kissing you." He smiled into her mouth, softly nipping her bottom lip.

In the moment, she wanted him more than ever. With each press of her lips, she was letting go. The thought of losing herself paralyzed Zora. Her shoulders went stiff, and though her mouth was still gloriously attached to Mike's, her heart stopped cold.

When it began to beat again, the spike of adrenaline made it feel like it might explode. All at once she was dizzy and weak in the knees. As they painstakingly pulled apart, Zora got lost in the tug-of- war of her emotions. How could she be begging for the kiss never to end on the inside, and at the same time need it to be over to confirm her feet were still on the ground?

"Mike…" she trailed off as she breathed his name and forced a smile.

How many years had she waited for this to happen again— to feel the soft pressure of his lips and the sweet taste of his tongue as it glided against hers?

His smile widened as he reached for the driver's side door. "Let me get this for you. Or, should I drive?"

His eyes were lit up like the Fourth of July, but how was she to make any sense of it? Over the years, she'd been spectator to the parade of women Mike showcased and discarded. It was silly, insane really, to believe she was an exception to his rule. He was a clever man. How easily she'd walked into the trap—the magic, the spell he put her under, the way he so easily turned on the charm.

"Sure. You can drive."

I'm in no condition.

Zora felt the flickering weight of his stare on her as Mike zigzagged through the streets toward his house to quickly drop of her things before going to Bite-Sized. His comfortable lean and their easy conversation made it apparent Mike was enjoying this new dynamic between them. He was completely oblivious of her growing unease. A few blocks from the house, he shifted from the conversation from the book deal into talk of the Chessington building purchase—something about Arnold rescheduling, and another company, Easton Investments.

As they came to a stop at a red light, he turned to her. "Maybe you can help me tonight, and then we can celebrate you."

With the new expedited timeline for the book, Zora couldn't think of a worse time to go back down this road with Mike. She couldn't afford to waste time on a fleeting fantasy.

Still, it was on the tip of her tongue to nod and tell him, *Yes, of course I'll help you. I'll be and do whatever you want because you're gorgeous and funny, and deep down, I know the real you.*

Instead of spewing her love-starved guts, she peered out the window and watched as a wave of people crossed the street. One of them caught her eye. She was a pretty brown-skinned woman wearing bright red lipstick. She was tall, and her ebony hair fell around her shoulders. She wore a floral sundress and looked at Zora with familiar, kind eyes. Then, the woman smiled, and for a brief moment, Zora saw her mother.

Don't give up on yourself, her expression pleaded.

Zora swallowed and tore her gaze away.

Before she could take it back, the words were out. "Actually, I can't. I have a…date tonight," she said. She tried her best not to notice how Mike stiffened.

CHAPTER 14

MIKE

Mike rolled down the window, and the cool mid-March air rushed into the cabin of Zora's car. It washed over him, cleansing and fresh as he turned down his street, but it did little to clear the new tension wedged between him and Zora. They'd exchanged less than five words since she revealed she was going on a date later in the evening. It was eating him alive, but this was exactly the karma he deserved for showing up to the game a day late and a dollar short.

He'd waited all this time to kiss her, and now it didn't matter.

She'd made her choice and he needed to respect it. All he could do was keep his head down and make it through the next month or so. He'd give her space and concentrate on work. That was all there was to it.

Still, a fire blazed inside him.

His face, neck, and ears were impossibly hot. His jaw tightened under the weight of his clenched teeth, and every time he opened his mouth, his throat burned with the fear of what might come out. He couldn't look at Zora, let alone conjure up the right words.

She sneezed.

"Bless you," he offered.

She sniffled. "Thank you. I promise, it's just allergies."

He pulled the car to a stop in the driveway and put on the emergency break. Why hadn't he done the same with his body earlier?

What was it that made me think crossing this line was a good idea?

"Listen, Mike..." Zora spoke softly and the weight of her stare set his skin afire, but he heard pity in her tone.

"It's fine. Let's just get your stuff into the house." Mike hated his curt tone, but he wasn't in the right headspace to hear her out.

He still had no clue how he was going to do this. Before he'd kissed Zora, there was the unspoken lie they told themselves. They were "friends with a past," but nothing more. Now, after the way they'd kissed, his body dispelled that lie. She had parted her lips and he swore he felt her tremble in his arms. Her heart and body called to him, and he answered back with every inch of his body pulsing and throbbing with the same need.

He hadn't held back.

All of his chips were in the pot, and he'd lost the hand.

The truth would be living in the house with the lie—a loud, uninvited guest they could neither silence nor turn away.

Mike exited the car and went to unlock the front door while Zora pulled out a duffle bag, her purse, and a few small totes. In silence, they passed each other almost a dozen times as they emptied the car and its trunk. Meanwhile, Zora kept swearing she would stay out of his way. Each time she did, Mike gave himself a mental pep talk.

It's only a month—two tops. You can do this.

All he needed to do was focus on something *other* than Zora.

As he returned to the car again for another load, she slammed the trunk shut. "I think that's it." She shot him a reassuring smile.

"Oh, okay. I, uh…haven't really done much to the place yet, but let me show you around, and I'll get out of your hair."

First, he showed her to the guestroom where she would be staying.

"It's a really nice place, Mike."

"It's not much, but it's warm and comfortable. No termites or dry rot." He flashed a smile and moved on to the bathroom, the laundry, and the storage closet for her suitcases, before briefly noting his bedroom was down the hall.

"You've seen the living room, so, really, the only thing left is the kitchen."

"I'm sure it's amazing," Zora said. "Ev and Sophia said it was better than the one at the restaurant."

The instant they weaved into the kitchen Zora just stood there, slack-jawed and wide-eyed. She didn't say anything. Her posture seemed to collapse.

"What?" Mike felt his shoulders tense. "Is it okay?"

"Oh, my god." Her gaze seemed to cloud.

A smirk pulled at the corner of Mike's mouth. Deep down, he'd hoped she would like his kitchen. It was partially the reason he'd offered to let Zora stay with him. She'd been his inspiration when it was being built. Every appliance and surface were top of the line. On some level, he'd imagined her someday making use of it.

"The kitchen is yours if you want to work on your cookbook. I know you said you were going to use the commercial kitchen at Cuisinette, but you're welcome to use anything I have. Do you like it?"

"Like it?" She held her hand to her chest as she scanned the room. "I love it. It's my dream kitchen." She opened her mouth, but nothing came out, and she closed it again, glancing around and blinking rapidly.

Mike folded his arms and nodded.

"You have an 84-inch-tall column, side-by-side stainless steel refrigerator and freezer. That's a seven-burner double oven convection dual fuel range and a wall-mounted range hood." A smile fixed itself on her face. "There's a wine reserve, for heaven's sake."

Her brows knitted together in confusion as if she could not possibly reconcile Mike having top-of-the-line appliances.

"I don't get it." Zora bit her lip and slowly stepped onto the tile. She shook her head slightly. "You don't know anything about food except how to eat as much of it as possible in one sitting. So, tell me why you have this dreamy commercial kitchen?"

Amusement bubbled in his throat and he bit back a smile. He ironed out his expression, then squinted in mock serious-ness as he propped himself up on the wood and steel swivel barstool. He was trying to figure out an answer he thought she would accept.

"It came with the house." He shrugged.

They weren't square yet, but it was the one answer that would set off her fuse, and right now he kind of wanted a little revenge. She looked dazed and wounded, like life was horribly unfair and she might fall out in a tantrum. Her luscious pink bottom lip jutted into an alarmingly sexy pout that made him want to bite it, then suck it. Hard.

He sighed.

"But you don't even cook," she whined. "I'll bet your refrig-erator literally has a pickle jar—sans pickles—an ancient

Chinese food carton, and two ketchup packets. This is just…cruel."

What was cruel was their forced proximity.

How was Mike not supposed to want her when she was adorable, funny, and sexy as hell?

That wasn't fair.

She opened the fridge and confirmed her suspicions. "Yep. See, I knew it."

This time, he allowed himself to laugh. Mike watched a few seconds longer as she sighed and ran her hands seductively over the range.

"Hello, handsome. I'm here now. I'm going to get your fire burning, and you, you sexy, neglected thing…"

Mike tried not to be turned on at the sight of Zora groping the refrigerator. His cock hardened in his slacks, but he reluctantly ignored it and chose to focus on the one thing that could sober him quickly.

"So…where's this 'date' picking you up?" Mike asked without looking at her. He fidgeted with his hands. The thought of her kissing another man the way they'd kissed today tore at his insides.

He couldn't sit back and watch. He needed to do something.

"Oh, uh…right. I didn't want to have him come here, so I gave him the address to the restaurant since we were already set to do inventory." She shot him a wincing, pleading look, which Mike guessed to mean *don't be mad at me*. "I told him I'd meet him there at eight o'clock, so we have plenty of time. Maybe we could leave in an hour?"

Mike nodded, but he didn't say anything.

He turned and silently retreated to his bedroom where he fell onto the bed with his hands propped behind his head and his eyes closed. Outside, he heard cars rushing by, wind chimes in the distance, and a clock ticking. The whole world was in motion, but Mike's had come to a screeching halt with Zora at its center.

The heart of the matter clawed at him.

Who knew if this thing between them would go anywhere this time? There were no guarantees, but it was the *not* knowing, the what-ifs, that bothered him most.

What *if* Zora was the only woman for him? What *if* she pushed him away again?

He could still feel the hollowness in his chest. His body had ached over sleepless nights. He didn't want to lose someone he cared for all over again.

Rolling to his side, Mike stared at the light beneath his bedroom door. Somehow, letting this chance go by before they really gave it a shot felt like a crossroads in his life. If he didn't try, he would always wonder what would have happened between them.

Mike was left with four hours to figure out which way to turn.

CHAPTER 15

ZORA

Zora leaned against the closed guest room door and sighed. The silence between her and Mike was brutal. Today was a ruthless reminder of what she already knew. This living arrangement wasn't a good idea. How were they going to make it through a month, or more, if they could barely stand to be in the same room without giving each other the silent treatment, or resorting to knee-weakening kisses?

What had that been about?

All it did was confuse her even more, and now she was supposed to forget it happened then primp and preen for a date with a guy who kissed like a Venus flytrap?

Now that she knew the feel of Mike's soft lips, she wanted nothing more than to stalk down the hall to his bedroom and press her lips to his again.

Zora's breath hitched in her throat at the memory and the fantasy. She scrubbed her hands over her face.

"What am I doing?" she groaned.

On the roof, the sound of rain spattering mixed with the

hum of the heater, and the muffled sounds of the city in the distance tore her from her thoughts.

She drew a deep breath and released it, looking around the room for the first time. It smelled of new paint, old books, and Fabuloso cleaner.

A giggle escaped her.

Neat freak Mike had probably been on his hands and knees scrubbing the place clean. It was so him to try and make the room as comfortable and welcoming as possible. Warmth flooded her heart at his thoughtfulness.

There was a twin bed dressed neatly in varying shades of navy cotton sheets and blankets tucked into the corner with a crocheted afghan draped over the footboard. Beside it was a small wooden nightstand adorned with a tiny succulent, an unlit Freshwater candle, a box of tissue, and a snow globe from Disneyland.

"So sweet." She smiled.

Zora walked over, swiped a tissue for her nose, picked up the snow globe, and shook it. A flurry of glitter and smiling Mickey Mouse-shaped snowflakes twirled in the watery storm. It was such a sweet little thing to put on the nightstand. She noticed this room appeared to be designated for keepsakes.

Time ticked by as she stood near the closet and stared at a large bookcase filled with old books and more snow globes from different locations and attractions. She dragged her fingers over the spines and lightly onto the globes, reading titles and seeing the world from Mike's souvenirs. Overwhelmingly, they all pulled at her heartstrings.

How could she know Mike and not really care to learn more about what made him tick?

Zora wanted to know the history behind every book and every globe. She wanted to know why all of it was packed away in this room and not on display in the living room, or on his nightstand.

Knowing felt urgent all of a sudden. She was inclined to ask him, when she heard a creaking door, followed by footsteps and jingling keys in the hallway. There was a knock on her door.

"You about ready?" Mike asked. His voice was gentle but stilted.

She sneezed again, this time louder and more forcefully.

Please, let this be just allergies.

"Bless you," he said through the door.

Zora's gaze darted about the room as she replaced the snow globe on the nightstand and picked up her tote with her change of clothes. She needed to get him talking.

"Yep. I'm coming."

L ater on, when they were up to their waists in inventory, about the only icebreaker Zora could come up with to get Mike talking was the subject of food. It was the only topic where both of them were on common ground, given her love of making it and his of consuming it

"I can't believe lasagna is the only thing you know how to make." Zora propped herself up on her tiptoes on the top rung of the ladder.

She heard a muffled snicker at this. "It's lasagna. What else would I need?" Mike was still in the kitchen freezer, reviewing the inventory log against the meat supply.

"It's good in here," he called out. "Fully stocked...but for the sake of cutting out an extra trip, I'll prep an extra order. More chicken and beef. Anyway, back to your assault on my signature dish, now you can educate me about other cuisines, oh master Creole-Mexican chef."

Zora giggled at this. The clock *was* officially ticking on her cookbook. She'd come up with that fusion based on her family roots and the food she most often consumed. She needed no particular day of the week to prompt her to eat tacos.

"What about Mexicole or Crexican? Well not that, but something along those lines for the title?" She tossed the ideas over her shoulder at Mike who laughed robustly.

"What's wrong with Creole and Mexican Food Fusion? It's a title on a cover. Give it a fancy font and a flashy photo of something delicious, and it's fine."

"Ugh, no. I want it to be catchy so people can hashtag it and start a foodie movement." Zora bit her lip and squinted. "Creo-Mex?"

"Hard no on that one."

"It's kind of cute."

Mike grimaced. "So, I take it you've decided against the haggis then?"

"You already knew that was the lie, so stop teasing me."

From the ladder, Zora could see his head bowed over a clipboard poring over the numbers the same way she'd done the paper goods and boxes. Mike sat back on his knees and pulled his bottom lip between his teeth for a few seconds. "Why would she ask us to do the inventory if she stocked the entire kitchen before the trip? This place is overstocked."

"Did you really expect anything less? Bite-Sized is Sophia's baby."

Sophia had created everything from the savory and sweet tapas to the kitschy pastel decor. In only two years, word of mouth had helped her place become a go-to spot for a quick, healthy lunch or a night on the town.

Mike shrugged, got to his feet, and walked out of the freezer to wait while Zora took account of the supplies on the shelves.

"Um, let's add…one more bulk box of napkins just to be safe," Zora said lowering herself one rung at a time as she double-checked each shelf. "We have enough of everything else for at least two or three months. This is overkill, even for Soph."

"I know. It seems off."

"Oh my God. I've got it. CreOlé. As in *olé*." She snapped her middle fingers and thumbs like a flamenco dancer, beaming with excitement. It was all more Spain Spanish than Mexican Spanish but the "*olé*" worked. "I love it!"

She was just about to step down when she noticed an opened box of Styrofoam take-out containers. It was still pretty full, but to be sure she leaned over, stretching her arm to reach and then sneezed—a chest-heaving, full body sneeze, which caused her body to jerk back, tipping the ladder and her along with it.

One second she was free falling and the next, she collided with a solid wall of muscle for the second time that day.

Mike had caught the ladder with his right hand and Zora with his left. His body trembled and his hands were gripped tightly around her. His eyes widened with terror, and his breath came fast and hot like he was hyperventilating.

Her heart was beating a mile a minute, too. Her breathing came faster and harder as she clutched onto him.

"It's okay. I've got you." The bass in his voice thundered against Zora's chest. "You don't sound so good. Are you feeling all right?"

Are you?

"Allergies are evil." Not that she could think about her nose at a time like this.

Every tingling nerve ending in Zora's body danced beneath

the pads of his fingers. She couldn't for the life of her figure out how she was going to let go. He smelled so good.

She breathed him in on a slow tantalizing inhale. She didn't mean to sniff him, but at the moment, her body wasn't exactly listening to her.

"Did you just…smell me?" he asked, giggling.

She had no idea how tight she was holding onto him until she felt the rhythm of their hearts matched beat for beat.

Her voice dragged out dreamily. "What cologne are you wearing? You smell really good." Zora pressed her nose to his neck and took a long whiff. His skin was smooth and warm to the touch.

"Think you can stand on your own two feet?" He was still holding her, and it felt really good to be in his arms again. He was rough and gentle at the same time, like at any minute he might throw her up against the wall and kiss her until her lips were good and swollen.

She pressed her fingers to her lips and smiled at him. "No, seriously." *Sniff.* "What is that?" *Sniff.* "Soap? Cologne?" *Sniff. Sniff.*

Mike leaned back and looked at her with his arresting green eyes. Suddenly, she could not breathe properly. They were both staring at each other with wide-eyes and parted lips as if they were caught somehow.

Please don't put me down.

"I'm going to put you down now, okay?"

"No." As far as Zora knew, her obsession with Mike was always a teenage crush that had gone on too long. It never wavered, but she assumed it was normal not to forget your first. He was her first crush, first kiss, first…lover. Back then, every girl in school who wasn't after Everett was trying to get with Mike. He had always been gorgeous.

How did I miss this?

Whatever it was happening between them, it was way beyond rules.

How on earth was it possible that she could be around him almost daily from the time she was a scrawny knock-kneed kid and not see all this happening before her eyes?

Who was this magnetic man with his heart and his keepsakes tucked away?

Zora cocked her head slightly, scrutinizing every line of his warm honey skin. She inhaled and couldn't seem to let him go. Her right arm was perched on the cliff of his broad shoulders, and with her hand she pressed into the curve of his neck. The man was lean and firm.

"Zo?" Her name came out on a whisper. Mike blinked almost in slow motion. His eyes were twinkling.

See! Right there.

Where did those adorably sexy sweeping eyelashes come from?

Have they always been there?

Now she blinked hard, but, he was still there, and a slow and cocky, beautifully boyish grin began tugging at the corner of his mouth that was lined with the scruff of a trim goatee.

Good lord, his mouth.

He also happened to have delectable, pouty pink lips. They were basically daring her not to kiss them again.

Her sweet spot twitched.

When had he turned into *this* man?

"Zo?"

He was still watching Zora's every move as he lowered her to the ground.

She was on her feet, but it still wasn't clear whether or not her legs were working. The way they sort of wobbled, she felt unsteady and bendy like a flower in the wind. If she broke contact and stopped clinging to him she might somehow wilt away.

Then, he went and did it.

He pulled his bottom lip between his teeth and bit down. Not hard, but enough for his gloriously white teeth to scathe the delicate skin. Zora almost fainted right then. Her insides clenched ,and finally she exhaled.

Holy shit! This man is on another level.

"Are you all right?" he asked.

Zora finally looked away, and the gravity of what she'd just done sunk in. As whatever spell he put her under wore off, she was now mortified for the third or fourth time that day.

Before she couldn't stop looking at him, but now, the thought of meeting his twinkly eyes felt forbidden. If she dared, there would be wicked consequences.

Thankfully, the date she was dreading would take her away.

Rules. Rules are good, she reminded herself.

"Um…I'll go check with Ceci to see if there's anything else she can think to add to the order, then I'm going to go get ready. Just let me…" She trailed off because her voice sounded shaky and guilty as all hell.

Zora did a stuttered run-walk over to the kitchen doors leading to the front of the house. In her haste to actually watch where she was going—because she was physically incapable at the moment of lifting her chin up off her chest—she missed the swinging door flying toward her. George, who was carrying a tray of about a dozen tables worth of bussed dishes and silver-ware, crashed into her.

For a whimsical split second, cups and plates and sparkling forks flew into the air. It was a silent symphony of blurred shapes. Zora was almost mesmerized.

Then, the ear-piercing *crash* as they hit the floor brought the entire restaurant to a standstill.

Several startled eyes, most notably, Mike's, looked on as she turned.

Rather than buckle under the weight of his spring-green eyes, she fell to her knees and rushed to gather up the shards of glass, throwing scattered knives and spoons into the dish tub with a loud clank.

"I guess I'll add dishes to the order," Mike said. The sight of his retreating form jarred something irrevocably loose insider her.

I want Mike.

When he was out of sight, almost immediately Zora's lungs started working again. The scent of buttery, sweet pastries and teriyaki chicken bites filtered through her nose. She inhaled and got back to her feet as the world started turning again.

Everyone seemed to just go back to what they were doing before she'd utterly embarrassed herself.

Zora had no clue what had just happened between her and Mike, but the spark was explosive. The way he looked at her didn't just nudge something inside of her. It felt more like a sucker punch.

CHAPTER 16

MIKE

Zora felt it too.

There wasn't a doubt in Mike's mind. It wasn't just the way she looked at him. It was in the way she'd held him tight—like she didn't want to let go—the tiny, shallow breaths, and the slight pink flush of her cheeks.

Mike noticed, and he felt the tidal wave rushing back.

"What do you think?" Zora asked as she came out of the restroom twirling.

Her short, black, flowy dress billowed from the hem and settled at her toned thigh. She paired it with strappy black heels, light makeup, and gold jewelry. She was stunning, and Mike was *jealous.*

This wasn't just physical.

Look at me, Zo.

Every inch of him needed to see her eyes and feel the same connection he'd felt with her in his arms.

She craned her neck toward the front window. "I think that SUV that just pulled up is him. He said he'd call when he was out front." She checked her phone, letting loose a sneeze before

MIA HEINTZELMAN

she pressed it to her ear. "I thought it was you. Give me a sec, I'm going to grab my umbrella, then I'll be right there."

Mike didn't realize he was holding his breath. He sighed and deflated just a little. The idea of her walking out to another man felt final somehow, and he was desperate.

Say something.

"Uh…"

When she finally looked at him, he knew she was holding back. Did she want him to try harder?

"Okay, well, he's here, so…I'm going to go. You've got everything here under control?"

She teetered on her heel, rubbing her arms.

You're stalling.

He nodded, feeling hopeful and antsy and wired as he watched her sling her purse over her arm. Unconsciously he stepped closer. "What if it's not allergies? You've been sneezing and coughing…might be a cold," he blurted out, desperate to say anything that might keep her from leaving even for a second longer.

"I'm fine."

"Okay, well, uh. Where's he taking you?" He stuttered trying not to sound desperate, but he *was* at the end of his rapidly fraying rope. Nothing he could do or say would convey the toxic emotions stewing inside him. Stopping her took away her right to choose the right man for herself. Letting her go said Mike was indifferent, which was basically the complete opposite of what he was feeling.

At her raised brow, he explained. "Just…in case you need me. Can't be too safe." He was grasping at straws.

Come on. Don't go.

The soft sigh she released appeared to be frustration. "Portland City Grill." She started toward the door, but then she hesitated for the slightest moment.

"Yeah?" he asked.

He was holding his breath again, silently bargaining with her all the things he would do if she just stayed. He would try this thing between them again, even if his heart flashed its scars at him—a blinking beacon of the last time she ripped it open. If she stayed, he'd prove to her he was worth the risk of putting all her chips in.

Over her shoulder, she smiled at him and shrugged with a *better luck next time* pitied expression—his consolation for the whirlwind he'd put himself through today. Damned if he wasn't going do something about it.

Mike watched Zora shuffle over to the shiny gunmetal gray SUV, her umbrella shielding her from the downpour. Instead of this guy getting out and coming around to open the door for her, he made her wait while he unlocked it from his seat.

"Asshole."

He didn't deserve her.

He didn't deserve that dress.

The headlights blinded him as they pulled away from the curb, and Mike was left stewing in frustration until the name Portland City Grill hit him like a sledgehammer.

This guy, Mr. Unoriginal, probably Googled five-star romantic restaurants in Portland. The place would be at the top of the list with its skyline views and upscale white table-cloth fine dining. It was thirty floors up, required reservations, and easily garnered three- or four-dollar-sign pricelists. It was a favorite for the moneyed elite, including trust-fund lawyers who refused to cook. *Jason.* Mike pulled out his phone.

Mike: J. I need a favor.

The three ellipses popped up on his screen almost immediately, which meant Jason was either with someone he'd rather not be, or he was at or on the way to dinner.

> **Jason:** Two times in one week. To what do I
> owe this honor?

For the first time in a long while, Mike was relieved Jason was available.

> **Mike:** Have you eaten yet?

More ellipses.

> *Jason:* About to pull up to my favorite grill
> as we speak. What's up?

Mike mouthed a soft "thank you" heaven-ward and sagged against the wall.

> **Mike:** I don't have time to explain, and I'll
> owe you, but I need you to be my eyes
> while you're at dinner. Everett's
> younger sister Zora will be at the grill
> tonight with some dude and I don't
> trust him.

Okay, so it was lie, but whether he knew the guy or not wasn't relevant. How Zora acted around him was all Mike wanted to know.

Jason stressed his intentions to cash in on this favor soon, which was a little terrifying given the wide realms of his imagination. The way Mike's heart was racing, though, the risk would be well worth it.

Forty-two minutes later, Jason texted that he'd spotted Zora with Mr. Unoriginal, and some fifteen minutes after that, Mike got tired of the third degree via text. Jason seemed doggedly determined to get to the bottom of Mike's obsession with Everett's little sister. Mike decided to skip the paragraph-long messages and call Jason from his car.

"So, you're seriously not hitting that?" Ever tactful, Jason's voice filtered through the car Bluetooth.

Mike let the motor run for a few minutes as he reclined his seat and listened to the spray of raindrops on the windshield.

"No," he said too quickly. His annoyance flared. "I'm just… looking out for her. How many times do I have to tell you? Everett and his fiancée are expecting, and the stress put the baby at risk, so they took off for a month. I'm looking out for the house, the business, and the family. Zora is his family."

Muffled laughter rumbled through the line.

"Okay, okay. Touchy. I'm just asking. Nothing is really happening. They're just eating." Jason paused for a second, but the laughter was still in his tone when he spoke again. "Do you want to know how juicy her lips look around the fork?"

"Fuck you, man."

Mike bit back a laugh. He didn't know exactly what he was looking for or what he wanted his friend to watch for, but he still wanted to know everything, even the small stuff.

"Does she look like she's enjoying herself? Does she seem to like this guy?"

Do I really want to know?

It was nearing nine-thirty by then, and Mike was driving aimlessly toward the Burnside Bridge. He didn't want to go home and see Zora's bags there without her, so he kept driving heading southeast on Grand.

"Not a bit. That I can say with certainty. I mean, the guy isn't ugly, he's actually a good-looking dude—"

"Thank you. I don't need to know about him. Just...what makes you think she's not into him?"

Jason cleared his throat as if he was settling in to school Mike on the female psyche. "I'm sort of an expert when it comes to women and reading their body language."

"Okay, sure." Condescension laced Mike's tone. "I'm listening."

"For one, she's been on her phone the whole time, so no eye contact or laughing or any of the telltale signs that she might think there's a spark. Also, she hasn't touched herself *once*—"

"Fuck—"

"Not in the way you're thinking. I mean, she hasn't played with her hair like women do when they're flirting. She looks kinda sleepy, actually."

At this one, Mike laughed loudly. He was still driving along watching the reflection of the clouds on the river as Grand Ave blended into McLoughlin in a bit of a traffic standstill. "Where do you get this stuff, man?"

"I'm serious. She's slouched in the seat, and her eyes look heavy. I'm not shitting you, she might have nodded off. If that's not disinterest, I don't know what is."

Jason might be a rich asshole and a male chauvinist most of the time, but it was hard to argue with him. Despite his personal life, he was a good lawyer. He paid attention to detail.

Now Mike was paying attention. He couldn't ignore how he'd been feeling since the Friday night at the club and game night. The kiss they'd shared earlier today sure as hell wasn't one-sided. It was obvious Zora wasn't feeling this new guy, and Mike needed to do something soon.

He chewed the inside of his cheek as he sat in traffic. Up ahead, it looked like the rain had gotten the better of someone. He hoped the accident wasn't fatal. "J. Hold on a sec." He swiped his screen then tapped out a message.

Mike:

1. If I was at the table with you, I'd make
   you put away your phone.
2. I swallowed mouthwash just because the
   bottle told me not to.
3. I've been to Disneyland alone.

After he pressed send, Mike asked Jason. "What's she doing now?"

In the background he heard the buzz of conversation and the sound of silverware scraping as Jason mumbled through a mouthful. "She's…smiling, but still looking at her phone. You're good. Nothing to worry about there."

A message ping echoed in the car.

> **Zora:** Hey, there. First of all, how do you
> know I'm not having the time of my
> life?

> **Mike:** You're talking to me instead of Mr.
> Unoriginal. Stop stalling and answer
> the question. You looked really pretty,
> by the way.

"Is she still smiling?" His breath bottled up in his chest and he smiled into his fist.

Jason, who sounded like he was gnawing on a dinosaur leg, swallowed loudly. "Oh, yeah. She finally looked up. Are you texting her? I'm like a proud father over here, helping you make this love connection."

"All right, man. On that note, I'm going to let you go. I appreciate you, and I'll get back to you."

Jason laughed and reminded Mike he was in his debt, then

disconnected. Meanwhile, Mike moved ahead a few inches closer to the fender-bender, and the traffic stalled again, so he checked Zora's reply.

> **Zora:**Who are you and what have you done with my friend who supposedly shares important stuff with me? BTW, you're a rule-follower, so I know the lie is #2.
> This is not the end of this discussion.
> I'm going to pick your brain about your truths.

Without Jason on the phone to narrate, Mike imagined her still smiling at the phone biting on the pad of her finger while she thought about him and not the sorry ass dude across from her.

> **Zora:**
> 1. If you were at the table with me, I'd be thinking about that kiss earlier.
> 2. Your smile gives me butterflies.
> 3. I've been to Disneyland twice.

Right off the bat, Mike knew the lie.

Zora made a bucket list two Christmases ago, and going to The Happiest Place on Earth was at the very top. So, right now, she was with another man reliving their kiss and thinking about his smile whilst butterflies fluttered in her stomach.

Mike was acutely aware of his heart racing and the stir of his nerve endings pulsing with need. His insides flooded with warmth. He wanted to be with her physically right now.

Up ahead, an officer began waving cars through one by one.

Quickly, Mike tapped out a rapid-fire message because it was now or never.

Mike:
1. I was not at the silent disco last Friday.
2. I broke up with Kate.
3. When you left the restaurant, I wished you would have turned around and decided to stay with me, but I didn't know how to say it.

Now the butterflies rolled in his stomach. His muscles twitched and his mouth went dry. What would she say to blatant honesty? He shook out his hands, feeling restless and unsettled. When his phone pinged, he jerked to grab it.

It wasn't Zora.

Jason: Thought you'd want to know. Looks like she's ditching this guy and headed home. You're welcome. Add this to the favors you owe me.

With a sigh of relief, Mike followed the officer's signals and made a U-turn. Home was the only place he wanted to be.

CHAPTER 17

ZORA

Zora couldn't get out of Andre's SUV fast enough.

"Thanks for tonight," she said. "I had a lovely time."

Not.

Andre leaned over the console as if she would let him kiss her after the disaster date. He had a cocky smirk.

Ugh.

"Will I see you again?" he asked.

Not in this lifetime, Mr. Unoriginal.

"Oh, call me." She smiled tightly and turned to open the door. She slipped out, dodging fat raindrops as she ambled toward Mike's house. Hopefully, the dickwad wouldn't choose now to get his lazy ass out of the truck and walk her to the door.

She was doing a shuffle run-walk as she sneezed and waved him off over her shoulder. Before she even reached for the knob, she realized she didn't have a key.

"Shit."

She slid her phone from her purse and prayed Mike was still

awake. Tapping to get to messages, she was a few letters into *let me in* when another message dropped from the top of the screen.

Andre.

She thought maybe he recognized he'd been sort of a narcissistic douche and wanted to redeem himself with a "goodnight" text or possibly a "I don't blame you if you never want to talk to me again" text, but apparently the universe was not done laughing at her this evening.

Much to her shock and horrified dismay, it was a veiny, gnarled dick pic.

Lovely.

"Asshole!" she turned and screamed as the SUV pulled into the road. Her voice was shrill and filled with blood-seeking venom. Her body locked up with rage.

Oh my god.

She was shaking and she could feel heat flushing through her body.

"Fuck you!" she yelled at the top of her lungs to the fading headlights.

"That good of a date, huh?"

Zora turned to find Mike in the doorway biting back a shit-eating grin. While it *was* downright mouth-watering, it did nothing to cool her searing hot blood.

This was what it came down to—dating and dick pics or using games to mask your real feelings? Truths and lies. *What is it all for?* She'd already said too much in the text messages, but at this moment, she couldn't go down that road.

Not tonight.

"It's not funny," she hissed, still fuming at the image of the crooked boner. She chewed on the inside of her cheek, still fidgety and amped up to do something. But what?

Mike sucked in a breath. "It's kind of funny." He was still

134

grinning from ear to ear as he slid Zora's purse from her shoulder and slipped a warm hand on the small of her back to guide her into the house.

At his touch, she shot past him, releasing a trio of sneezes in fast, body-jerking succession. She was neither in the mood to talk nor to find the silver lining when she was likely coming down with a cold and sick to her stomach at the image she'd just received.

"You want to talk about it?" Mike asked between giggles.

She shot him an incredulous look.

Um, no I don't want to talk about why men think it's acceptable to ambush women with pictures of their janky junk.

She paced the foyer, shaking her head.

Just how had this day taken a wrong turn down a shitty road? It had gone from a mind-blowing, *take my breath away* kiss with Mike to a hell date.

She could have stayed home and worked on recipes or gluten-free alternatives. Anything would have been better than forcing herself to spend the rest of her night with a douchebag.

And why had she subjected herself to the date in the first place? To avoid having a serious conversation with Mike about what was going on between them.

Grow some balls, Zo.

"Later," she said, but she didn't move toward the bedroom. She opened her mouth to say something and closed it again, flashing him a weak smile. "No. I don't want to talk about it."

I'll just sleep it off and start fresh in the morning.

Blowing out a heavy breath, she stalked down the hall toward the guest bedroom. The sound of his feet was behind her, but she promptly shut the door in Mike's face. The creak of his movement sounded on the other side.

Then she heard a small knock. "I'm sorry, Zo. I thought you

were playing around. I didn't realize you were really upset. Did he…hurt you?" His voice was strained.

"No."

His slow and measured footsteps picked up again and Zora imagined him pacing. She ambled over to the door and pressed her hands flat against it. She closed her eyes and breathed wishing she would have made a different choice at the start of the evening.

"Okay, well, did he do something to you or hurt your feelings? I'm worried, Zo. Talk to me. I haven't seen you like this since…" He trailed off, but Zora knew what he wasn't saying.

He hadn't seen her so angry since the night they'd made love.

No one had.

Nothing had ever mattered as much.

Afterward, they'd been lying on the cellar floor. Mike held her, studying her like she was a rare, precious gem that needed to be treasured and protected. In that moment, she'd known he would've given up his future for her—law school, traveling, everything. She would have done the same for him. All of their dreams would have been upended in one night, and she couldn't bear to let him throw it all away for a fleeting whirl in the wind. So, she'd been the one who had suggested they just be friends, and when he'd protested, she'd responded with blind fury and a desperate coldness.

It had been a knife to her heart. When he'd left, her throat had thickened with sobs, and pain gripped her chest. She knew what she was risking—her life, real or imagined, one way or the other.

She'd given up on her once in a lifetime.

Now Zora was starting to wonder if maybe once in a lifetimes came around twice. Her voice softened and filled with understanding. She leaned her cheek to the door. "No. He didn't hurt me or my feelings or anything. I just, I wasn't expecting a dick pic tonight."

On the other side of the door, she felt Mike lean against the door and slide down to the floor. She did the same. He giggled. It was comforting to know he was right there with her, back-to-back, with open ears, and no judgments.

"Ouch. I didn't see that coming at all, but now I get why you were foaming at the mouth."

"Yeah. Imagine my shock when I think I'm getting a good-night text and instead it's a close-up of his worthless family jewels."

Zora's shoulders relaxed as she drank in the sound of Mike's low laugh. For a moment, they were quiet as they sunk into their familiar easiness. After holding him at a distance these last couple of weeks, she'd missed the way they were always able to be themselves around each other. She'd had someone to talk to about Oli's wild dates and how crazy it was living back at Patton Place with Everett and Sophia. It wasn't just him listening to her talk about her blog and her dreams of being a published author, either. She missed *him*, his goofy jokes, their movie trivia wars, and the silliness in their game of two truths and a lie.

Oli told her about his breakup with Kate, and today, Zora had seen the longing in Mike's eyes when she walked out of Bite-Sized, which meant he was there at the silent disco last Friday and he hadn't say a word about it.

"For what it's worth, I think that guy is an idiot. He doesn't know how lucky he was to be with you."

The stupid butterflies were back.

Zora's emotions were all over the place. Every nerve ending in her body pulsed with anxiety. Her fingers and toes tingled, and she shook out her hands. Suddenly, sitting there on the floor with the only person who made her heartbeat quicken, she realized she didn't have just one dream anymore.

Somewhere along the way, she'd found another one she'd tucked away decades ago.

Her logic was about as mixed up as her emotions. Taking a chance on Mike could mean losing sight of her quirks, hang-ups, and professional dreams, which made her who she was. But not taking the chance could also mean losing Mike, and with him, her dream of experiencing real love.

Who knew if what they shared was anything even close to love? She wasn't willing to bet against the odds, though.

It scared her out of her mind, but she could take baby steps because she wanted him.

"Mike?"

Would it be the worst thing to fall for a friend who cared about and supported her and kissed like heaven?

"I'm still here." His voice was gentle and patient.

With the rules officially thrown out the window, Zora took her first baby step. On a deep inhale, she stood, and opened the door. Her heart felt like it might come out of her chest. "Just so you know…" She took a deep breath. "I wish I would have turned around and stayed with you tonight, too."

CHAPTER 17

MIKE

M ike couldn't take his eyes off of Zora.

They were standing only inches apart. Without the door between them, it felt like they'd moved mountains and oceans to get back here. But he was so scared of messing up, he didn't move.

"Say something," she breathed. He could see her chest rising and falling in anticipation, but the words wouldn't come to him. "Please."

"I missed you?" He hated how it came out like a question. "I mean, I missed *you*, Zo," he said again with more conviction in his tone. It was the truth—not just her body and her heart, but her wild and overly analytical mind and the way she made him feel.

This was his opportunity to finally tell *his* truth.

Before he could move to say another word, Zora threw her arms around his waist and he was lost in a storm of warmth and her sweet coconut perfume. He let his chin rest in her hair as he drew her in tighter.

When she looked up at him, it took everything inside him not to kiss her.

Not yet.

"Can we talk? There's something I need to know," he said.

Her eyes filled with questions and worry.

Mike met her gaze. "I just don't want to ruin this again."

Reluctantly, he let go of her and took her hands, guiding her toward the twin guest bed. They sat facing the bookshelf with their fingers still intertwined and their backs against the wall and feet hanging off the side. It was quiet and warm like someone set the scene for them to cross this last bridge before they could move closer to the sunset.

"What is it?" Zora asked once they were settled.

Mike swallowed and lifted his chin. "Every time I've tried to talk about this with you, you've either changed the subject or walked away, but we need to clear the air. I've been lying to myself all this time about you and I can't deny it anymore. I want you. Only you, Zo."

She squeezed his hand, and a soft smile spread from her lips to her sparkling eyes, sending warmth coursing through him. She had to know what he was asking.

"I won't even talk. I'll just listen," he said.

With a little shrug, she seemed to resolve herself to get it over with and began. "Four years old is really too young to understand what it means to lose your mother, you know? I mean, I vaguely remember some of the changes in her, like when she stopped reading bedtime stories to me and began sleeping a lot." Zora pressed her fingertip to her lip and shook her head. "I'd beg her to play and make cookies like we used to, but it was like one day she just stopped caring. And then, she was gone."

Emotion clogged in her throat and Mike nodded for her to continue.

"Then Joseph was gone, too. So, all I really knew after she died was Ev and Grandma Babs, which was fine for a while. But as I got older, I saw other girls with their mothers laughing and doing stupid things together," she laughed. "Like bra shopping and eating at ridiculous mall restaurants, and I was jealous."

Zora's eyes were red-rimmed and glossy, but she kept going. "I know this is not what you wanted to know, but it's all part of it." She shrugged and shifted on the bed to cross her legs and face him. "It's all related because by the time I was eighteen, I was too good at wearing the mask. I knew how to joke my way around the hurt, and distance myself from anything or anyone who could jeopardize the person I was becoming. I was so afraid of letting anyone in and standing there while they slowly chipped away at the good parts of me like Joseph did to Mom."

"Yeah."

"What I remember of her had nothing to do with empty pill bottles or seeing her laid out on the bathroom floor through the crack of the door. To me, she was this vibrant, red-lipstick-wearing goddess who was strong, wore bright colors, and spent her quiet moments with her nose stuck in a book. From the stories Babs and Ev told, she was super funny and wild, ran around the house, jumped out from dark corners to scare us, sewed, and she loved so hard it hurt. More and more, I hated the idea someone could strip all of it away because she'd given him access to her heart." Zora finally peeked up at Mike. "So, I built a wall around mine."

He registered the mix of, joy, and anger in her tone. "I know all about them. The problem with walls is they keep everything out, including love trying to get in."

Zora swiped a tear from her cheek.

"She would have turned fifty the day you found me in the

cellar. I'd been thinking about all the moments she and I missed. It broke my heart to know she wouldn't see me find love, make a million mistakes, or get married and have children of my own, and I was falling apart. I wanted to drink away the memories and the emptiness inside of me."

She smiled at Mike as she bit back tears. It was a pleading smile, begging him to understand her on her deepest level.

Mike did. More than she knew.

"You have to understand, I'd wanted you forever, and you were the only one, but I was so scared because I knew what caring too much about another person could do. To me, Mom was proof of it. When you made love to me in the cellar..." Her smile was bright and whimsical and unseeing like she was back there. "I knew you were the only person with the power to strip me down. So, I pushed you away after, and prayed I wouldn't regret it for the rest of my life."

Wow. Did I really read the situation that wrong?

"Zo?"

"So much for that right? I've been reduced to dick pics and drought. Such great choices." She laughed despite her tears.

Mike lifted his hand and caressed the soft curve of her cheek before drawing her into to him, dismissing the war going on in his head. The raw emotion in her voice hit him right in the heart. Gently, he brushed his lips over hers before kissing away her tears. So long ago, he'd done the same.

He only hoped history wouldn't repeat itself.

"Don't cry," he whispered, holding her firmly in his arms. "I'm not going anywhere, Zo. I've always been right here waiting for you."

The hum of the heater whirred to life.

Her head rested on his chest for what seemed like forever until her sobs subsided. They lay in each other's arms—him flat on his back, her nestled between the wall and the crook of his arm. Mike felt no need to fill the silence. There was nothing more to say, nor anywhere else he wanted to be. For once, he wasn't in limbo between the past and the future.

As much as it scared him, he was loving living in the moment with Zora.

When his eyelids were too heavy to keep open, Mike glided his fingers down the delicate nape of her neck and back up into her short hair.

She moaned her satisfaction.

"You want me to leave so you can get some rest? I know you said you needed to work on your book stuff tomorrow." Mike peeked at his watch. It was past two in the morning. "Or rather in a few hours. It's close to three."

Zora shimmied her body closer to his. She was staring off to the side of the bed. "What's the deal with the Disney snow globe? How come it's not on the shelf with the others?"

Mike groaned. "Haven't we gone far enough down memory lane for one day?"

"You started it. I was ready to go straight to sleep." Her chin popped up off of his chest and she looked at him with her determined whiskey-colored eyes and a shaky smile. "It's fine for me to pour my heart out and you get to take yours to the grave? Nope. Not happening. Out with it."

Mike sighed.

He shook his head and rolled his eyes then picked up the snow globe. The smooth glass was cold and soothing in his hands. Maybe it wouldn't be so bad for Zora to know exactly what he was made of.

With another sigh, he closed his eyes and got lost in the watery storm. "I went there once, by myself."

Zora rested her chin on both of her hands on his chest and listened intently.

"My little brother Lucas always wanted to go to Disneyland," Mike said. "He begged to go all the time. He wanted to meet Mickey Mouse, but we didn't have a lot of money, so my parents just kept telling him 'when you're older, when you're older.' Before he ever got to go, he took a fall."

"I'm sorry," Zora said. "I knew he passed away, but I never knew the story. What happened?"

Mike's shoulders tensed and his grip on the globe tightened. *You have to be open if you want to heal.*

Though she never practiced what she preached, Mike's mom said those words to him almost daily after the accident. She heard it from the family therapist and made it her go-to advice. Mike hadn't thought about those words in years, and he didn't know why it came to him now, but lying there under the weight of Zora's expectant stare, it seemed the only way to go.

His eyes were still closed, and the familiar scene reeled across the back of his eyelids. He started to tell Zora one of the two worst moments of his life.

"We were playing tag upstairs." He smiled widely before it slowly faded. "Lucas was running from me and I was right on his heels when he tumbled headfirst, down the staircase. We thought he was going to be fine because he jumped back up ready to play, but it turned out he wasn't fine. There was bleeding on his brain and he died in his sleep the same night."

"Mike."

"When I was old enough, I went to Disneyland by myself... for him. The snow globe was for him."

Mike felt wetness on his shirt. When he opened his eyes, she looked crestfallen and pained, and his own agony reflected back at him. Her bottom lip trembled and her skin was flushed.

"I'm so sorry, Mike. I knew you lost him when you were young, but you never talked about it," she sobbed. "Why didn't you ever say anything?"

He swallowed over the lump in his throat and shook the

snow globe, sending teeny Mickeys swarming in a flurry of iridescent glitter.

"Like you, I didn't want to get close to anyone after Lucas. It hurt too much to even talk about it and relive the pain every time, so I kept it bottled up. I've never told anyone, but I always felt like I let him down…let my parents down—"

"No."

"I lost my brother, but they lost their child, and it broke them. His untouched bedroom with the Mickey Mouse sheets and Legos on the floor where he'd left them…the scent of Play-Doh and crayons in the air… It got to be too much. Two years later, they divorced and they've been fighting over me ever since. Both of them are determined not lose another son, but all it ever did was drive me away. It's why I gravitated to your family. I could just be a kid again."

Zora kissed Mike's hands.

"I'm sure he's looking down on you, smiling. He was there with you at Disneyland—in your heart—every step of the way. That's what Babs used to tell me about Mom when I needed her to be there for me."

"I should have been there for *him*." Mike stressed the word because not being there was what really churned his heart. It was why he often took the designated backseat in life when he should be driving. He needed to be the lookout, always watching for signs of peril ahead. Meanwhile, life was passing him by.

Zora jolted upright, her legs straddling either side of him. Her body was square to his and her expression was deadpan, dire.

"Don't do that. Don't blame yourself. It'll only stop you from healing. Remember, He died dreaming about playing with his big brother who loved him with his whole heart."

At this Mike sat up, too. Their faces were only inches apart.

He could feel Zora's light breath on his neck. He circled his hands gently around her arms.

"Zo, I'd been so determined not to lose anyone again, I shut everyone out. I didn't know if I'd ever be able to open up. I had this great, big gaping hole in my heart. Then...you sort of crawled in and never left, so when I saw you hurting, breaking down over you mother—"

"Don't."

"I panicked because I knew what you were going through and I couldn't bear to sit by and do nothing while you suffered."

She swallowed and ran the back of her hand over his strong jaw.

Mike's breaths came in quick succession and his heart raced. He lowered his voice and leaned in. "I never knew I could feel this way again." He sucked in a stark breath as electricity coursed through his veins at their proximity. He sought out and found the swell of her lips. Lightly, he licked each one before slipping his tongue inside.

She felt like his long-lost friend and the woman he'd been searching for all wrapped up in one. He was falling in love with her all over again, and this time, he wasn't going to let her push him away.

CHAPTER 19

ZORA

Most of Sunday was a blur. Zora was working on virtually no sleep at all—*not* because she and Mike clawed into the mind-blowing sex she'd hoped her braless body in a short black dress would inspire. It was their raw and open talk. They'd had to be vulnerable in a way they'd never allowed themselves to be around each other. With the floodgates finally open, neither of them wanted it to end.

They literally didn't sleep.

After the night rolled into the tiny hours of the morning, the day called. She got up and picked up Blue from the dog hotel. When he saw a familiar face, he was a furry mass of wet kisses and soft nudges. Mike agreed to food shop for the ingredients she needed for her recipes. In between errands, they'd managed to exchange less than a dozen or so sleepy words.

Then again, there wasn't much left to say that their longing expressions didn't already communicate.

With her skin still oozing coffee fumes, Zora moved about

the kitchen to pour food from a gigantic bag into a bowl for Blue.

"Hey," she said to Mike who was quietly sitting at his makeshift desk at the dining table. He looked as scrumptious as ever with a pen propped behind his ear. He was absently biting his lip and showing no signs of their sleepless night—no sign of dark circles under his gorgeous, bright-green eyes.

On the other hand, Zora, who was going for breezy and chipper, only managed to sound like a croaking frog.

"Oh, hey. I didn't hear you walk in. I'm just trying to get a handle on this before Monday."

You've got this. Just be normal.

Just because the rules were officially out the window and butterflies were apparently permanent residents in her stomach, there was no need to cannonball into this. Maybe, just dip her toes in—baby steps.

"No worries. I didn't want to bother you. Have you eaten?" she asked, grabbing a big pot and setting it on the stovetop.

"Nah, I haven't done much besides sit here and wrack my brain over this building nonsense." Mike sighed at the paper in front of him and lifted his gaze to Zora. "Why? What have you got going on over there?"

She'd wanted him to look at her, but she couldn't have prepared herself for the weight of his undivided attention. The way he watched her was all-consuming and heavy. She breathed out slowly, remembering his words from their talk.

I'm not going anywhere, Zo. I've always been right here waiting for you.

"Uh, just a little something to kick this cold. Soup." She flashed him a quick smile before averting her gaze. She dug colorful vegetables and herbs out of the refrigerator and loaded them on the counter. "I'll make you a bowl when it's done."

Zora was still groggy. Her head was stuffy and her body achy and weighed down from the hard mattress of the guest bed. Still, she had yet to come down from the high after everything they'd said to each other the night before…that morning. "Happy" was not a strong enough word to describe her emotions. Floating…no, levitating was more like it.

Her heart had swelled so full she could hardly keep it in her chest.

Today, every time they passed each other she was positively giddy. Earlier that morning, when she'd gone to freshen up in his bathroom, since the one for guests was being retiled, she was instantly swept into a haze of Mike's scent. It had taken her down, literally, to her knees. Actually, she'd been snooping in his medicine cabinet and under his sink to nail down the woodsy, minty fresh aroma. It turned out to be a combination of Old Spice, winter fresh mint mouthwash, and ocean breeze body wash.

This was what being near him did to her. The man was intoxicating, and Zora was drunk on him.

No wonder I'm slurring my words.

A bout of tingles tickled her nose and she held up a finger as she squinted her eyes. *Not now.* Her nostrils flared and her lips quivered. She just knew she looked somewhere between nauseated and dizzy.

Then, a spastic sneeze escaped.

"Whoa! Bless you."

"Thanks." She sniffled. "Shit. I'm going to need something stronger than spicy chicken noodle soup. I need some feel-good food in a bad way." She rubbed her throat as she swallowed before turning to pour in the broth. With the fire on high, she just stood there holding onto to the stove.

"Need any help?"

"No, I'm just stuffy and sneezing. I feel like shit, and I don't have a clue how I'm going to make this deadline if I get any worse."

"Don't worry. I, uh, grabbed you some medicine while I was at the store, just in case. It's in the bathroom on the sink. I kind of heard it in your voice last night."

Mike was still engrossed in his pile of papers, but Zora was shell-shocked. Her eyes went wide as she shot him an incredulous look. For a second, she just watched him, wondering how she'd missed this thoughtful, caring person. Somehow, she always thought he was being nice to her because she was Everett's sister, but this was some heady stuff. She wasn't sure how to be this way with Mike.

She whipped her head back to her pot where a few faint bubbles were beginning to rise. "Thank you."

"No problem."

The room went silent and Zora could feel the awkward tension thickening the air. "It *was* pretty stupid going out in a tiny dress in the rain, wasn't it? Probably only made it worse."

Wow, I'm really on a roll.

"Yeah. You're probably right."

Zora placed the chicken breasts in a pan and began cutting the vegetables, but she was still watching Mike from the corner of her eye. His brows were drawn together as he rested his chin on his steepled fingers. He'd gone back to scouring his table full of documents and was brooding, cerebral-looking, and apparently unaware his small gesture was huge for Zora.

A fresh wave of desire to slammed into her. At that moment, she knew whatever this connection was they shared, she wasn't willing to let it go.

"What's the problem?" Zora asked. She was focused and calm as she measured seasonings, but she was still watching him out of the corner of her eye. "Your silence is so loud."

He teetered back onto the hind legs of the chair with his arms propped behind his head and laughed. "That obvious, huh? It's just, I don't know if you follow what's going on with the real estate end of things, but I'm just trying to figure out where your brother's head was when he decided to do this deal with Arnold."

"Harrison Arnold?" She looked squarely at him now.

Nodding, he seemed to stifle the rest of his laugh. "Yeah, why?"

Why did he just assume she didn't follow the inner workings of the business? He knew she was a partner.

"You do realize Everett has copied me on everything for the past seven years? You assume because I'm not at the office every day I don't pay attention." The corners of her mouth threatened at a smile. "For your information, there's a difference between passion and passive."

"Tell me how you really feel." He chuckled.

"Anyway, Arnold is such a greedy asshole. I've told Everett time and again not to work with him, but he acts like we're indebted to the guy for some reason. What's he done now?"

Mike updated her on the information Kendra sent about Arnold's meeting with Easton Investments, but she still couldn't work out why Everett thought the Chessington building was such a gem. There were at least twenty other buildings out there at a better price with less risk to Monroe Properties.

"If Arnold is willing to play two hands trying to hedge his bets, do we really want to get in bed with him?" Mike asked. "It's a bad investment every way I look at it, but will Everett see it the same way?"

"So, that fool is double dipping?" Zora shook her head as she turned the fire off, then walked over cradling a wooden spoon in her hand. "That doesn't shock me one bit."

"Here, try this. Be my taste-tester while I take a look at what he's up to."

Mike slipped the wooden spoon into his mouth, he let it linger on his lips. He looked mouth-watering.

For the next forty-five minutes, Zora dove into the purchase documents while Mike helped her taste and devour half of the soup. They eventually arrived at the same conclusion: working with Arnold in any capacity was not only a bad idea, it was a risk not worth taking. It wasn't too late to back out of the deal altogether.

"See, Ev needs you," she said matter-of-factly. "He knows construction and the portfolio and how to best utilize it to grow the company, but you know risk analysis. You know how to identify and mitigate potential issues that could negatively impact the business initiatives and projects."

She paused for a brief moment considering whether to say her next thought aloud. "He should have made you partner a long time ago. What would he do without you?"

It was clear as day to her. Mike was just as much a part of Monroe Properties as she was.

"Thanks. It's really nice of you to say."

"It's the truth. You've been here as long as Everett and me. Have you talked to him about partnering?" Zora took their bowls and glasses over to the sink.

They may have only been talking, but the seamless conversation felt way beyond baby steps. Being around Mike was comfortable in a way too easy to notice as it was happening. Over the last twenty-four hours, they'd shared everything from their darkest secrets to their brightest dreams. They were supporting each other, and staring seductively over bowls of soup.

"I, uh, don't know if he's open to the topic..."

"Does he know *you're* open to the idea? I'm pretty sure you mentioned Jason's firm was interested in you. Maybe he's trying to figure out your end goal."

He pulled the corner of his mouth between his teeth and nodded.

"Yeah. I supposed I should talk to him. I just hope he sees this deal for the bad investment it is."

He lowered his chin and scratched the hair at the nape of his neck before getting to his feet. "I'm finished with this for today. Want to watch a movie? I'll be out of your way tomorrow and you can have the kitchen and the house to yourself to work on your book. Oh, and," he paused for effect. "I've got popcorn."

"Hmm." Zora raised a brow and twisted her lips as if this was something she needed to contemplate, when, really, he'd had her at "movie."

She should be working on recipes and inventive ingredients, but her mind was already lost in the fantasy of snuggling up on the couch with Mike watching one of her favorite eighties movies.

Maybe *When Harry Met Sally* or *About Last Night?* No, too much drama. It had to be something sexy to inspire him to kiss her again, but with macho elements so he wouldn't feel stripped of his "man card." If there was one thing Tom Cruise was good for, it was a rom-action movie. *Risky Business, Cocktail, Top Gun...*

Top Gun!

Already, Zora was doing a happy dance in head at her sheer level of brilliance. If Mike kissed her to "You've Lost That Loving Feeling," she might literally die. Deadline or not, she'd waited too long for this fantasy to become reality.

Zora drummed her fingertips on the counter for a few more seconds then met his gaze. "Only if I get to pick the movie."

"Deal."

Monday is a much better day to start working, anyway—bright and early, dive right in and cook up something amazing and worthy of a book deal.

One day was plenty of time to get back to Leanne.

"What do you say, Mike? Do you feel the need for speed?"

CHAPTER 20

MIKE

R ight after Maverick and Goose ejected from the plane and Tom Cruise did his best impersonation of a grief-stricken, not-at-all-narcissistic airman cradling his dead friend, Mike looked over to find Zora lightly snoring on the armrest. He grabbed the remote, turned off the television, and scooped her up into his arms.

He was just about to lay her down onto the guest bed when a sneeze vibrated through him. He froze, hoping he didn't wake her, but Zora's fingers clutched his shirt. Her eyes snapped open, and heat darkened their golden-brown irises.

"Sorry. I didn't mean to wake you."

She sighed. "I hate that I'm getting you sick."

"No, I'm good. That was nothing. Probably just allergies." He smiled, knowing good and well the tiny itch at the back of his throat would be his doom.

She groaned. "Liar."

"Pants on fire." He couldn't fight the smile covering his face as he attempted again to lower her to the bed.

"This mattress is rock hard. Can you please leave me on the couch?"

Mike lifted his chin and smiled. "Yeah, my mom sleeps here when she visits. I got firm for her back." He blew out a breath and considered what to do.

"I swear, it's not a big deal. I don't mind sleeping in the living room."

"I'm not letting you sleep on the couch." He pulled his bottom lip between his teeth and nodded slightly. "How about you take my bed? I'll sleep here."

Zora's lips were slightly parted as she eyed Mike under hooded lids. It was almost like she was in his head. The idea of her sleeping in his bed—with or without him—sparked a small fire inside him.

She had a wistful gaze like she might still be dreaming.

The way she was looking at him, there wasn't a doubt in his mind that going slowly with Zora would be his undoing. Everything about the way she made him feel was urgent. Heat coursed through him, and he leaned in to press his lips to hers gently.

He pulled back and saw the yearning in her eyes. Feeling her warmth against his chest tied his stomach up in knots. He needed to touch Zora—skin to skin—without anything in the way.

There wasn't much he wouldn't give to feel her writhing beneath him as he licked every inch of her, but would it scare her away again?

Mike wasn't willing to take that risk.

"I don't mind lying with you," Zora said in a tentative, tender voice.

At that moment, he dismissed all the questions ringing in his head. He didn't want to think about how it hurt like hell when she'd rejected him. His heart wouldn't let him worry about their history. Right now, the only thing that mattered was getting to lie beside her tonight.

What they shared was real—even if he was the only one who felt it.

Fuck it.

Mike padded down the hall to his bedroom at a glacial pace. There was still time for her to change her mind. He almost hoped she would come to her senses and let him take the couch. He wasn't strong enough anymore to turn her down.

Gently, he laid her in his bed then took his place beside her. They were facing each other, and he matched her slight smile.

"I want you next to me," he said.

She shimmied closer, and he let his hungry mouth crash down onto hers. She moaned, sending a wave of spine-tingling shivers through him. He released a low growl.

How did I ever find the strength to walk away? Why didn't I try harder all those years ago?

Their kiss was deep and full of need as he slipped his tongue into the heat of her mouth, tasting her.

"Mike," she whimpered against his mouth.

"Don't say this is no good," he protested. "I can't think of anything better than you and me. I've been thinking about this all day."

Her breathing was shallow as she arched her back, pressing her pelvis firmly against his. Mike gripped the curve of her waist and pulled her on top of him so her legs straddled him. With one hand he cradled her behind and focused on her heated gaze then slipped his other hand into her pajama bottoms and beneath the thin fabric of her panties.

She released a sharp cry. Her chest was rising and falling so fast and hard.

She squeezed her thighs tightly around his finger and licked her lips as his cock hardened beneath her. Desire pooled in her eyes.

"Are we doing this?" she panted as her hips writhed and rolled over his hardness.

He could never say no to her.

"I want you, but only if this is what you want, too."

Please say we're doing this.

She rolled her pelvis in response, nodding as she pulled her shirt over her head, giving Mike an amazing view of her swollen breasts.

In response, he dipped two fingers inside her wet folds and growled. "Fuck. You feel so good." He watched as she moaned in satisfaction.

She bucked as he thrust them deeper. The sensation seemed to electrify her.

"Yes. God, yes." Her eyes were closed and she let her head hang back. "I want you inside me." Before Mike could say another word, she stood over him and tugged her fleece bottoms and panties off in one motion.

The sight of her beautiful naked body was almost enough to make him come apart at the seams. She was decadent and dizzying with her flawless brown skin and endless curves. She could be his for however long she wanted.

Mike dragged his bottom lip between his teeth and pulled off his pants, exposing his cock. He retrieved a condom from the nightstand, tore it from the foil wrapper, and glided it down his shaft just in time.

When he was finished, she lowered herself down onto his length.

Fuck.

Heat seared through him as he got lost somewhere between the past and the present. The memories of him on top of the innocent girl in the cellar blurred with the vision of the beautiful woman riding him now.

She was at home—controlled and confident.

Together they rocked to a steady rhythm. She rode him slowly and gently, rotating her hips and cupping his hands to her breasts. Her body trembled with need and she moaned, calling out his name.

"I'm close," Mike whispered sounding strained.

She felt too good. Her slick folds clenched around his cock. It was like he fit inside her perfectly.

"Me, too." She bucked, and electric shocks seemed to jolt through her body as she rode the orgasm, taking Mike with her.

Zora rolled off of him onto her side. He tucked her tightly into the gap between his arm and chest. Mike was satisfied he'd made the right decision—she hadn't run or pushed him away.

Within minutes, she fell asleep. It was so cozy and warm, he soon followed suit. After a soft kiss on her forehead, Mike faded into a deep sleep.

He woke in the morning, high from mind-blowing sex and completely happy, until, he noticed Zora wasn't lying beside him.

A rush of emotions overtook him, but rejection was at the top of the list. Memories of Zora pushing him away vibrated to his core.

He listened…deafening silence. It seemed their history was destined to repeat itself.

CHAPTER 21

ZORA

Zora peeled her eyes open and checked her watch. It was nearly ten in the morning. Mike was probably already at work, which meant he'd slept like a baby, and her self-inflicted quarantine on the mattress from hell had worked. To think, had she believed less in the homeopathic healing powers of spicy chicken noodle soup and more in the over-the-counter cold medicine, she'd have awakened blissfully happy in Mike's arms.

"Ugh." She groaned and winced at her creaky back. She was groggy, stuffy, and only breathing out of one defunct nostril. She was officially a mouth-breather.

She was definitely the furthest thing from the sexy temptress of last night.

It was probably best Mike didn't see her looking like hell on a stick.

An unmistakable whimper sounded outside her door.

"Aw, Blue." She grumbled, then released a rare sneeze-cough combo. "I'm coming."

She swung her feet over the edge of the rock-hard mattress at a glacial pace, cracking her back before padding over to the door where Blue was sitting—almost—patiently with his tail wagging and slapping against the wood floor.

"I know. I'm a bad fur mom. I'm totally slacking. You need to go do your morning business, and we both need to eat if I'm going to be able to take care of the both us." She mussed his hair and picked up her stride slightly. "It's not your fault, I feel like shit."

With Blue outside, Zora made her way to the bathroom to grab the medicine Mike bought. She filled the tiny cup with the purple liquid and downed it before heading back to her dream kitchen. She was going to try every method under the sun to cure her grossness.

It was code blue now—a medical and life emergency.

Monday was here, and she needed to heal herself if she was going to get going on her pages for Leanne. Nobody wanted contaminated food, not even on paper.

Zora opened up the refrigerator and stared blankly inside. Then the cough started up again—a productive cough complete with a gurgling phlegm sound. *Ew.* Whatever she made, it needed to be spicier—with alcohol. Maybe she could burn and sweat the cold out of her pores. Or, puke it out.

She shook her head, utterly disgusted with herself.

She closed the fridge and grabbed a giant beer mug. Her phone vibrated across the counter. Oli's face smiled on screen.

"Hey," she answered in a croak as she brought the phone to her ear.

"Why are you whispering?" The hope in Oli's voice echoed against Zora's ear. "Is Mike still lying beside you?" The woman had Spidey senses like nobody's business.

"Um, no." *Unfortunately.* "I'm in this gorgeous kitchen about to throw something together so I can buckle down and take a whack at this book. I would ask how your shoot went this morning, but I'm still kind of mad at you."

Zora slouched against the counter and wished Oli could see her pursed lips and eyes rolling eyes. "Oh, and since when are you Team Mike?" Zora asked.

Oli sighed loudly. "First tell me why you sound like Darth Vader, then tell me what I did."

Zora didn't miss how Oli sidestepped talk about Mike. Maybe she *was* secretly rooting for her and Mike to be together. That was even more incentive not to tell her about last night. Not yet, at least.

Not until I figure out what it means.

It had been the best sex of her life. Not that she'd had much experience other than Mike. Was this thing between them going anywhere, though? Did he want it to? It was hard to tell. After they'd bared their souls about her mom and Lucas, they'd never discussed what they wanted from each other. She knew Mike wasn't hard up for sex. He could have a different woman every day of the week if he wanted. Is that what he wanted with Zora? Just sex?

Zora expelled a thunderous cough that could shatter glass, and unsuccessfully cleared her throat before filling Oli in on the abridged story of Saturday night—The Disaster Date Edition.

She started with the most important factor. "I went out with Andre."

Oli gasped. "Shut up."

"Yes. Not only did the date suck, that fool sent me a dick pic as a parting gift. Not a good one, either. Can you believe it? You don't even want to know how pissed I was." Zora pinched the bridge of her nose. "This is so your fault."

"Oh. My. Gosh. I would have given anything to see your

face." Oli's laughter grew from a quiet, sporadic gasp to an all-out cackle in Zora's ear. When she came up for air, there were still traces of her giggles. "Yay! Your first dick pic. You're growing up so fast!"

"Indeed, disgusting phallic images in my phone are real knee-slappers. I'm so honored." The sarcasm in her tone leveled out, and Zora could feel one of many topic changes coming.

"Okay, well, welcome to dating, but on another note, since you asked…" she purred into the line. "Girl, I can't even tell you how amazing the shoot was. I got like four hundred frames. The bride is beyond gorgeous." She sucked her teeth. "Now I'm sitting here on the bed waiting for them to download. So, where's Mike?"

Zora let her head fall back as she sighed. "Work. Where else?" She realized she was still at the kitchen island with an empty mug, unsure of what to put in it.

Must be nice to be so busy," Oli said. "Right now I'm on YouTube. There's some sick shit on here."

"What kind of videos are you watching?" Zora was afraid of the answer.

"Larva boob, black syphilis, and, now, blue waffles. Let's just say that I won't be eating for a while."

"I'm not even going to ask why you look at that crap."

"The killer part is, I couldn't even tell you how I fell down this nasty rabbit hole. I was looking up charcoal toothpaste." The line went silent for a second before crackling back to life. "Um…am I on speaker?"

Zora pulled a bottle of vodka down from a cupboard. "Yep. I need both hands. I'm about to bum-rush this cold. For the record, the Internet knows you're a perv. I'm guessing blue waffles have nothing to do with food, so *don't* send me links."

Zora peeked out the window to the backyard to check on

Blue. "As you now know, I saw more than I bargained for this weekend, and I'm not up to it today." She gagged at the memory as she walked back to the refrigerator.

Her phone chimed.

"Too late. Already sent."

Zora gathered the Bloody Mary mix, Tabasco sauce, chili powder, jalapenos, and paprika into the sag of her pajama shirt, using it as a makeshift bag. She turned toward the counter, mid-giggle. "Oli—" she managed to squeak out. Then she looked up.

Good heavens!

Mike.

Zora tried to look away but, shoot, she was only human. She was staring at a long, lean torso and golden-bronze washboard abs that converged into a downward arrow.

Mike was only wearing a pair of plaid pajama bottoms they were the sexiest cotton garment she had ever seen. They hung low on his hips and hung on his morning wood. Then she remembered, and cursed herself, for not staying in bed with a gorgeous naked sleeper.

The next time she succumbed to Mike's bedroom magic, she wanted it to be in the light of day without whooping cough. Although, the sight of Mike lit up by the morning sun felt spiritual in a way—like an unanswered prayer she wasn't fully aware she'd put out into the universe.

Lord, have mercy. Mike, how are you gonna do me this way?

His face was alight with mischief. A warm, rich, throaty laugh rumbled out of him.

"Good…morning." Zora licked her lips then instantly felt a warm flush creeping from her neck to her cheeks.

She clenched her shirt hem between her fingers. Thank goodness, she hadn't dropped the ingredients. She was already mortified. On top of ogling Mike like a dog in heat, she realized her purple ruffle-butt underwear were on full display.

The giggles were bubbling up inside of her at the comedy of errors happening between them. There were new levels of awkward between them daily. She was ready to crawl up in a hole and die of embarrassment. She'd just rolled out of bed without doing anything to herself because she thought it was just her and Blue. There was no telling what kind of rabid animal she looked like.

"Morning." His voice was deep and gravelly. Sexy. He stepped closer to her with a little twinkle in his eyes.

Just act like everything is cool.

"What... are you doing here?" she asked, still holding her shirt, cringing on the inside. God, she wanted to run and hide.

Don't die. Don't die. Don't die.

"I live here," Mike said, far too amused by her level of discomfort. Though, something else lingered in his eyes. Annoyance? Anger?

Is he mad at me? Possibly, regretting last night?

God, maybe it was just sex for him.

"Right." She nodded, trying to even her breathing.

What are you thinking?

Zora felt the crease between her brows deepen as she scooted closer to the counter to comb through her thoughts. The weight of his stare was heavy on her back.

Just say it, already. What are you thinking?

It's not like he hadn't seen every inch of her naked skin the night before, but for some reason, she felt self-conscious. She knew this kind of run-in could happen, but did it have to happen now, when she looked and felt like shit?

Ugh.

Since he was apparently refusing to relieve her worries, Zora had to fill the silence.

She flitted a glance at him then jerked it back to her counter full of spicy condiments.

"Yes. Thank you. I'm aware you live here." She lowered her shirt enough to allow a jalapeno to roll onto the counter. "I meant, don't you need to be at work? It's Monday."

"I heard coughing. I was going to see if I could get you anything...but it looks like you've got it covered." Mike inched into the kitchen and scrutinized all the stuff she put on the countertop. A smile played on his lips. "Bloody Mary?"

Make up your mind. Are you mad, playful...psycho?

"For the cold and this crazy cough, which is getting worse by the second."

He nodded and lifted his chin like he was putting all the pieces together. In his eyes, she could see the clouds dissipating.

"That's why I left your room." She bit her lip and lowered her head. Out of her periphery she saw his shoulders loosen.

"I woke up with this tickle in my throat, and I couldn't stop coughing. I figured you had to work today, so I slept in the guest room. When I woke up, I thought you were gone."

Mike propped himself against the island sink and squared his body to her, leaning in to trace the curve of her cheek with the pad of his thumb. Her skin seared beneath his touch.

"I was fully planning to sneak back in when the coughing stopped," she babbled.

"Oh, yeah?" He flashed her a disarmingly hot lopsided grin. His voice sounded like honey.

She couldn't help but laugh. "Did I mention how much I hate your rocky guest bed? It's like sleeping on the sidewalk."

He stepped close to her and pressed his lips into her hair. Electricity shot through her. Suddenly, she was hyperaware of her surroundings, and of him in the space. He was too close. For a second, her heart stopped, and a chill flurried down her spine. She swallowed against the dryness in her throat.

He nodded to the drink fixings before swerving his eyes to Zora's very bare legs. There was heat in those sparkly green eyes, which he made no effort to avert.

There was also the panty situation.

"The rest of your pajamas are still in my room," he said.

"Oh, shit." A very high-pitched, nosy voice cut through the magic. "Okay, Mike. You have some *game*. It's really about to go down."

Shit. "Shit."

Zora literally forgot Oli was still on speakerphone. She and Mike burst into laughter. "I thought you'd hung up!" Zora wailed.

So much for keeping things between her and Mike a secret.

"And miss all this? Nope," Oli said.

Zora lifted her eyes to find Mike staring at her phone. His brows were furrowed as he scrutinized the image on the screen. "Hey, Oli. This, uh, picture you sent is…interesting."

The words "blue waffles" came racing back to Zora's mind. "Oh, no."

"Oh, yes," Mike and Oli said in unison.

She scurried to Mike's side, her gaze darting over his shoulder. "What the heck is that?"

Mike twisted the phone and they both cocked their heads, squinting to see the screen from different angles.

"What is wrong with you two?" he asked. "Is this what you do when guys aren't around? It's just gross."

"My eyes… Quick, show me something cute, or funny." Zora squeezed her eyes shut, shaking her head. "If one more person shows me disgusting alien genitalia, I'm going to throw up. I need to erase the image from my mental hard drive."

He lowered his chin and pressed the red end-call button. "I

don't know about cute or funny, but I might be able to help you find some other images to keep your mind busy."

At this, Zora arched a brow at him. "Oh, yeah?"

There were so many other battles worth fighting, but this thing between her and Mike, it didn't feel like one of them. Whether she was ready or not, Zora was open, and not thinking about blue waffles at all.

CHAPTER 22

MIKE

Without taking his eyes off of Zora, Mike traded places with her, so she was leaning on the island. He reached past her and picked up the fruit basket from the center and moved it to the other counter before making his way back to her. He planted his hands at the sides of her waist. "I think I might know another way to help you get over that cold."

Zora's eyes lit up a brilliant shade of hazel. She leaned back against the granite and peered up at him.

"I've heard having sex once or twice a day boosts your immune system." He squinted, nodding as he scrutinized every inch of her skin from the warm blushed curves of her cheek, down to the round peaks of her breasts, then to her bare legs. He licked his lips and lifted her up onto the island.

She squeezed her thighs tight around him, and Mike released a groan.

"I'm pretty sure it's weekly, but who's counting? I'd do *anything*," she rasped, "to feel better."

With methodical precision, he scooted her back on the countertop. "I love these, by the way." He fingered the lace of her purple ruffled panties before leaning in to kiss her. As he slipped his tongue into the warm wetness of her mouth, she moaned. Savoring the sound, he lowered her back onto the cool granite surface.

"How is it possible I've been here for barely three days and I've been on my back for two of them?" Zora asked.

"Should we go for a record?" Mike bent over until he was eye-level with her sexy ruffled underwear. Gently, he slid the fabric to the side and licked his lips.

As Zora lifted her legs and set her feet on his shoulders, he blew a cool breath into the meeting of her thighs.

She visibly trembled as she squeezed her ass and lifted her pelvis.

Before she could move, Mike dipped his tongue into her blazing flesh, circling and laving her sweet pink bud. She trembled, but he remained steadfast in satisfying her.

"Mike," she rasped.

"Are you sweating, yet?" He asked, sucking harder. *I am.*

"Yes. Yes. Yes." She panted, her chest rising and falling as she gripped the edge of the counter.

Fuck. How is it that I want her even more?

He curled his tongue upward, finding her clit. He alternated, sucking then licking, and when she was drenched and teetering on the edge, Mike got to his feet and lowered his pajama bottoms. He freed himself as he watched her squirming with need. He flitted a glance toward his room.

"Don't worry. I'm on the pill and I've been tested." Her legs hung open as she writhed on the counter, moaning. She arched her back, letting her shirt slide up to her neck. Rubbing her breasts, she narrowed her gaze. "I want you. Right here."

Mike's shoulders loosened and he let his head hang back,

feeling his cock grow harder as he circled the tip in his hand. "I'm good, too."

Holy fuck.

It was one thing to have sex with latex as a buffer, but this was raw contact and emotions igniting in a completely mind-consuming friction. He grew even harder at the steamy image in his mind.

"Please," she licked her lips and it was almost enough to tip him over the edge.

Without a second thought, Mike pressed the tip of his cock at the juncture of her thighs then pried her knees farther apart as he penetrated her. All at once, a hot, knee-weakening, blaze of lust and need washed over him. She was wet and slick, and the way she met his every move with an equally hard and fast push, he was coming apart.

He glided his hand beneath her and pulled her body up to his, seeking and finding her lips. The kiss was slow, soft, and steeped with everything he should have told her over the years.

I want you.

I miss you.

I need you.

I…love you.

He deepened the kiss.

"You're the only one I ever wanted." It was why he'd spent so many years searching and coming up empty. He'd buried himself in meaningless sex with temporary women who never lasted. Deep down, Mike never thought he'd have her again. "I need you, Zo," he mouthed into the kiss.

"I need you, too."

They moved to a steady rhythm, feeling and tasting the good thing they'd found again. As Zora shuddered against him, Mike held Zora, intent on never letting her go. He just needed to find a way to help her see how amazing they were together.

For him, this wasn't just for a month while she waited for her house to be built. It wasn't because of Patton Place with its termites and wood rot. This was it for him.

He was all in.

An hour later, Mike finished cleaning the kitchen and took a long shower. He'd meant it to be quick, but as the spray hit him and the scent of Zora's coconut body wash lingered in the air, he got to thinking about the way she'd stepped naked out of the shower at Patton Place. The past few days had been the best kind of whirlwind. It was more than he'd expected. Still, he knew he wanted more.

As he stepped out into the steamy air onto the bathmat, he dabbed the towel over his arms and chest then tied it around his waist. It was on his way to his bedroom, that an idea hit him. He knocked on the guestroom door and peeked in on Zora.

"Hey."

Blue, who was asleep on the floor by her feet, popped his head up for a second then laid back down. Mike smiled and eyed Zora in a pair of slim cut jeans and a loose orange sleeveless blouse. She was applying makeup in a small hand-held mirror and looked up at him over the top.

"What's up?"

He drummed his fingers on the wooden frame. "I uh, called in for the day. There isn't much happening I can't get done from home tonight, so I was wondering what your plans were?"

Calm down. We can't have sex every minute of the day.

"I need to…" She hesitated, opening her mouth then closing it just as fast. There was something she wasn't saying.

Mike swallowed, feeling the sting of rejection. *She does have a life without you.* "It's cool if you have something to do. I can just—"

"No." She stopped him with a tender glance, her head tilted, her eyes imploring. "I just need to get going with my cooking plan, but I'm good. What's up? What did you need?"

He centered himself in the doorframe, his shoulders lifting slightly. Just like that, the clouds around his mood passed and he was lighter, freer. He hated that she had the power to sway his mood. Why was he acting like a teenager with nothing better to do than wait around for Zora to give him some attention?

Running his hands over his hair, he straightened his posture and lifted a brow. "It's nothing, really. I was just going to see if you wanted to go somewhere with me. There's something I want to show you," he muttered, doing his best to downplay his nerves riding on edge. *Say yes.*

This was his chance to take her somewhere and show her what life would be like together—just the two of them enjoying each other's company, focusing on each other and not the time passing.

"Uh-huh. What did you have in mind?" she asked, giving him a slow, appraising once-over.

For a second, he'd forgotten he was wearing nothing but a towel tucked around his waist. A warm flush washed over his wet body and heat seared through him.

"Let me make myself clear. I would never say no to anything your eyes are suggesting, but I actually have sort of a surprise for you."

At this, excitement lit her eyes. She ogled him like he was

southern fried steak she wanted to sop up with a biscuit and gravy.

"I'm not gonna lie," she said. "I just want to rip that towel off and take you right here on this carpet, but that can wait. I'm swooning over the fact that you have a surprise for me." She batted her lashes and winked.

Mike wouldn't deny it, the sex between them was amazing. Still, he hated the idea of it being the thing on which they built the foundation of their relationship. There was so much for him to prove. While he wasn't exactly sure he knew how to go about it, he was for damn sure going to try.

Yes, he wanted her body, but only if it came with her mind and soul.

Right now, the ball was in her court but, he was pretty certain the surprise he'd planned would bring it back to his.

CHAPTER 23

ZORA

Zora sat in the passenger seat of Mike's car biting back a grin as they zigzagged through traffic.

"So. Where in the heck are you taking me?" she asked, studying his gorgeous profile.

"You'll see. Patience, grasshopper."

Technically, Zora knew the term had originally come from *Kung Fu,* a seventies movie, but she didn't Mike crap for it. He was probably thinking about *Karate Kid, but he was still as close as possible to perfect in her book.*

Maybe it was due to the rose-colored glasses after getting the best sex of her life, but Mike really was eye candy. His sparkling green eyes, delicious full lips, and the way the sunlight danced on his caramel skin—it was almost too much to look at directly.

How is he even a real person?

People were supposed to be flawed and quirky. Zora knew it was impossible for Mike to be practically perfect in every way, but for her, he was. He still did gentlemanly things like opening doors, saving the last piece of chicken for her, and planning syrupy-sweet surprises.

Who even does these things anymore?

Maybe her standards were too high...or too low. Zora had dated a few men over the years, and they'd ranged from douchebags who didn't offer to pay on dates to a narcissist who sent dick pics after boring her to sleep. Mike being incredibly sweet and chivalrous *on top of* holding the record for finding her g-spot the fastest and curing her cold with his healing stick.

She was still congested, but she hadn't coughed once since their last hoorah on the kitchen counter.

Zora looked at him longingly. She was lost in the shape of his lips, and her resolve waning.

"What are you over there thinking about?" Mike asked.

"Never mind what I'm thinking about. Where are you taking me?"

He shook his head and trained his eyes on the road, but Zora noticed his half-grin.

She feigned annoyance and turned her eyes on the blur of cars driving past her window on the freeway. The sexual tension between them was like nothing she'd ever knew existed. It was palpable, and she was pretty sure it was written all over her face. If she could physically live with him inside her, she would do it in a heartbeat.

"It's practically noon on a Monday. What *big* event is going on? Can't you at least give me a hint?" She meant it to sound hopeful, but it came out seductive and breathy somehow. All she needed were the waggling brows.

"How about you get your mind out of the gutter? You do realize every emotion you have shows on your face, right?"

She giggled. *Yes.*

"It's all right. I feel it too, but we cannot live on sex alone."

Busted. Zora laughed out loud. "A woman can dream." She

could feel the heat on her cheeks. She was blushing. "Whatever. *A* hint." *Preferably, before I spontaneously combust.*

"Let's just say, you won't be disappointed."

And she most certainly was not.

After he parked, they walked a couple of blocks while she studied every building and sign for clues. As soon as they turned into the Hollywood district, she knew exactly where they were headed.

"Oh my gosh. What are we seeing?" She bounced.

His eyes lit up "That's the surprise..."

As they reached the corner of Sandy and 41st, the ornate façade of the Hollywood Theatre came into view with its half-arches and spindly pillars that were right out of a Rococo architectural design handbook. Every time Zora had been there, she spent as much time gazing at the gorgeous exterior as she did watching movies.

This time, it was the massive marquee that caught her eye.

One by one she read the names. "*The Breakfast Club, Less Than Zero, Howard the Duck, Flashdance...*" Her eyes darted frantically from title to title.

"It's a marathon," Mike said, jerking her from her thoughts.

Zora's mouth was still agape as she continued. "Are you serious?" She kept reading. "*Footloose, Karate Kid, Goonies*—oh, my God, I love *Goonies*—*E.T.*..." she squealed. "I think I'm short-circuiting. "Yes! *Short Circuit!* 'Johnny Five alive!' and *Back to the Future*. I had the biggest crush on Michael J. Fox."

The last title on the right side of the marquee was *Some Kind of Wonderful.*

Oli called it when they were cooking at Cuisinette.

I'm Keith, and Mike is my Watts.

She blinked and wondered if she had been taking him for granted all this time. Did Mike love her and only realize it once she was in pursuit of someone else? Even if Andre was a douche, was he the reason this whole thing between her and Mike rekindled from a spark to a blazing flame?

The texts from the night of her date with Andre came flooding back. Specifically, back to the lie among Mike's truths.

I was not at the silent disco last Friday.

He was there.

He saw the kiss and he *thought he was about to lose me.*

Zora's eyes widened. *We are in* Some Kind of Wonderful.

Overwhelmed and amazed at the level of thoughtfulness and this new realization, she turned and threw herself into his arms in a scramble of urgent hugs and kisses. All over his face, she smothered pecks on his lips and his nose and both cheeks and eyelids.

"I can't believe you did this! This is so amazing." She brushed her lips over his again, closing her eyes, slowing down the kiss. No one had ever done anything like this for her before. She couldn't make sense of his thoughtful gesture, but for now she didn't want to. She didn't need to. Whether she was his Keith and he was her Watts, or it was just sex for him, she didn't care. Maybe they were really good friends with benefits, but this moment felt good and right. She didn't want to ruin it by overthinking and overanalyzing.

She could get lost in her worries later.

"So, get this..." Mike started between peppered kisses. "Jason calls me this morning and says his firm wants to hire me."

Zora raised a questioning brow at him, but he waved it away.

"You know how stubborn he is. Anyway, when I didn't bite, he abruptly changed the subject and told me he had tickets to an eighties movie marathon at the Hollywood. Apparently, his plans changed, so he said if I wanted them, I could pick them up at the box office."

"I've been basically Google-stalking people online for weeks for these tickets," Zora said. "They were going for like a thousand a piece on StubBox, and Jason just gave them to you?"

Mike kissed her again, this time more urgently, and Zora could barely stand upright.

Through the kiss, she asked, "Are they seats *way* in the back?" *Like the freaky seats in the back?*

She could feel Mike's lips curl into a smile. A low rumble escaped him. "Your mind is so filthy, but I love it. Had no idea you were such a freak."

Two trailers in before *Some Kind of Wonderful* started, they were seated and stocked with popcorn, Junior Mints, and peanut M&Ms when Zora felt her phone vibrate against her thigh. It wasn't a text message. It was an Instagram notification —a new post from Sophia.

With Mike looking over her shoulder, she tapped on it, and a picture illuminated the screen. A white piña colada with a pineapple slice and a vibrant pink cocktail umbrella sat on a glass table beside Sophia and Everett's clasped hands. It was cute and romantic, really. One problem: At the top right corner of the picture, almost cropped out, was a jade and gold Fabergé egg cradled on a cherry wood stand—uncannily similar to the one-of-a-kind one that belonged to Sophia's mother, Helen. The last time Zora checked, the woman lived in Las Vegas, nowhere near Bali.

"Ohh." Zora narrowed her gaze and shook her head. "When was the last time you talked to Ev and Sophia?"

Mike cocked his head and furrowed his heavy brows. "What?"

"When was the last time you talked to them? I'm serious."

"Um. Let's see." He leaned his head back and drummed his fingers on his thighs. "I think it was the Friday they left. Why?"

"Look at this," she pointed to the egg, which was usually in the center of the glass table in Helen's formal dining room, based on all the pictures Sophia and her mom shared. Now, it was pushed off to the side, in an unsuccessful attempt to move it out of the picture.

Liars.

"Is that Sophia's mother's Fabergé egg?" Mike asked.

Zora nodded. "They are up to no good. What are they doing? Why would they lie about going to Bali? I mean, they could have come back early and had nowhere to stay with Patton Place going through repairs, but it just doesn't add up. Why didn't they call us?"

Mike paused, seemingly caught up in his thoughts. "And why haven't we heard anything more about the fumigation *or* the repairs? Hold on a sec. The phone number didn't work, but I think I still have the email from the pest control company."

Mike searched through his messages on his phone, and Zora began putting together the pieces to the puzzle in her head. She was just getting her mind wrapped around the big picture when the lights in the main auditorium went down and the 50-foot screen brightened.

The movie was starting, but this was just the beginning.

She was left with nothing but darkness, the feel of Mike's warm hand in hers, and the smell of popcorn and conspiracy brewing.

CHAPTER 24

MIKE

Two movies later, Mike and Zora had barely stepped foot out onto the curb in front of the brilliantly lit Hollywood Theatre when Zora began to vent.

"We're totally being set up." Her eyes were wide and she kept running her fingers through her short hair and shaking her head.

She was still bent out of shape over the egg in the picture. Not that Mike wasn't right there with her, feeling outraged and slightly duped by his best friend, but he was more annoyed than anything. This was supposed to be his chance to surprise her and enjoy some quality time. Now she wasn't thinking about the movie marathon or the gesture. Her mind was centrally focused on the idea of a conspiracy by the hands of her family.

"Did you know anything about this?" Her narrowed gaze locked in on him.

Mike threw his hands up. "Nope."

The tension drained from her shoulders, but there was still

fire in her eyes. By the way she stared off into the distance shaking her head, he knew she was stewing.

"Okay, so let me get this straight just so I can wrap my mind around this...farce," she said.

Mike sighed. This was classic Zora. Once her mind was set on something, she would gnaw it to the bone. The only way he was going to get her attention back on him was to help her work through her thoughts.

"All right, fine. Let's do it." He tugged her hand until they were on the edge of the curb out of the way of the theater exit. When they were facing each other, she nodded, seemingly waiting for him to help her see the logic.

"Just to play devil's advocate," Mike began. "You think Everett and Sophia lied about the risk to the baby and her needing to be on low activity? Then they faked a vacation to Bali in order to go Vegas and stay with her mother?" He winced at the way the whole thing sounded coming off his tongue. It was sticky and slippery going down that road.

"No..." she trailed off, chewing on her lip. Mike could almost see the wheels turning. She was coming up empty. "I...just...why would they lie?"

Mike didn't believe for a second Everett and Sophia would lie about anything related to the baby. Why would they skip Bali and go to Vegas instead, though?

"Shit." He took a sharp intake of air. "Oh, shit."

"What?"

Now he was chewing on his lip. "What if..."

"What?"

He winced and scrubbed his hands over his face. "If she needed to stay off her feet as much as possible, it was obviously because of stress, right?" Zora nodded. "Sophia has been working herself to the bone planning the wedding and preparing for the baby. What if they decided the wedding was the biggest source of their stress and eloped in Vegas with her family?"

Zora gasped. "Everett wouldn't leave us out. There's no way he would do this without us."

A honking car horn blared beside them on the street, causing both of them to jump. They were both on edge now. Mike was the one who'd come up with this scenario, but even his blood was boiling now. Everett was basically his brother. Would he get married without Mike standing by his side as his best man? They'd promised each other years ago, whoever was stupid enough to find a ball and chain, the other would be dumb enough to help him carry it. It was in stone.

"The way I see it, there's only two possible options." Mike was shaking his head even as he said the words. Everett was his boy. No way in hell he would leave Mike and Zora high and dry on this one. "I know they wouldn't lie about the baby. Not after what Sophia has been through. So, it's either they lied about going to Bali to secretly tie the knot in a quickie Vegas wedding. Or, they lied about the dry rot and termites to get you out of their house and into mine."

Zora's face lit up as she appeared to register the implications of the second option. They could confirm the fake dry rot and termite situation tomorrow, but if getting Zora out of the house was Everett and Sophia's main goal, they were up to more than vacating their lives. They were matchmaking.

Shit.

Given the hand Sophia's family had in setting her up with Everett, Mike wouldn't put this past them. But this was bigger than Everett and Sophia. It meant, not only was Sophia, Everett, and her family involved, Olivia was also in on it, since Zora's party at the silent disco. He just needed to prove it.

He squinted his eyes and ran the tip of his tongue over his top lip.

"Do me a favor," he glanced up at Zora from his phone. "Call Olivia and ask her if I was at the Silent Disco."

"Why?"

He scrolled through his messages back to the one Olivia sent two and half weeks ago, responding to him after he and Kate arrived at the party. He flipped the screen around and set it in Zora's hand.

Mike watched as a crease between Zora's brows appeared. Her eyes were glowing stars in the blue hombre sky.

"That was the night she set me up with Andre. She was really pushing hard for him, too." Her lips pursed, and she folded her arms, lightly tapping her foot, likely retracing her steps before and after the party.

This made complete sense. The blue dress. That wasn't Zora. The impromptu party, the man, they were all Olivia's doing.

Oli never told Zora about inviting Mike and let him walk in on her tongue tied with another man. His blood boiled just remembering how he felt when he'd walked right into Olivia's trap. She knew it would make him jealous as hell, and it worked like a charm. The way Everett, Sophia, and Olivia spoke in hushed tones and scurried away when Mike entered the kitchen on game night only confirmed they were plotting.

Come to think about it, Olivia was the one who suggested they play Two Truths and a Lie.

Did she really have family in town? Was that really the reason Zora wasn't able to stay at her place? Her line of questioning in the kitchen basically confirmed the whole family was in on getting Mike and Zora together. Olivia knew their history and how abruptly it was over before it began, but she also knew the fire was still there just waiting to be reignited.

Apparently, everyone knew except for him and Zora.

He cocked his head to the side, wondering who else might be involved.

Did Jason really have other plans? Is it too much of a coincidence he just so happened to have a pair of eighties movie marathon tickets?

He glanced down at Zora. "Has Olivia mentioned the family who's supposed to be visiting her, or the repairs at Patton Place? What about the party? Did she even mention she invited me?" Mike's questions were coming rapid-fire now. He needed to get to the bottom of this quickly.

"She said you weren't invited." Zora's mouth fell open. She and Mike were obviously on the same page now.

"I can't believe this shit," Mike said.

Zora had a look of realization on her face when she spoke again. "They all did this. They didn't think we'd make it back to each other on our own."

It was the truth of the matter, dispelling all the lies they'd been telling themselves—love would find a way, even if it required a helping hand. Or, in their case, hands.

The more Mike imagined all the people coming together for such an elaborate ruse, the more amused he became. They were on his team. Maybe this was just the push they'd needed.

"Tell you what. How about we go home, get into some comfortable pajamas, and finish this marathon on the sofa? Maybe you can cook—"

"Shit." Zora's eyes went wild. "Shit. Shit. Shit. What time is it?" She started frantically digging into her purse for her phone.

"It's almost a quarter to eight. What's wrong?"

"I'm supposed to be cooking, preparing. Leanne said she wanted what I had in by Tuesday, which is tomorrow. So, I've basically got the rest of the night to come up with something brilliant. Shit!" She threw her phone back in her purse, squeezed her eyes shut, and began wringing her fingers. She let her head hang back. "I just knew it."

Mike gently cupped his hands over her shoulders. "Whoa. It's okay. We've got more or less four hours until it's officially tomorrow. I think we can put something together. It's basically a progress report, right? This isn't the final stuff she needs."

"No, but, dammit. I knew it. In my gut, I knew this would happen. I should have said no and stayed home when you asked. This is exactly what I was afraid of. Being around you—"

"Don't."

Mike's heartbeat raced and his muscles tensed. His nerves were raw, pulsing on a wave of adrenaline. "I won't let you minimize how great this day has been. I've loved spending every minute with you and I know you're worried about the cookbook, but don't let's this be your excuse to pump the brakes."

Zora sighed. Mike could see her worries and panic washing over her.

"I'm here, Zo. I'll help you because that's what people do when they care about each other. They roll up their sleeves and dig in. Please, I'm begging you. Don't shut me out again."

Zora swallowed then tilted her head from side to side, seemingly weighing her options. "Well…okay, fine, but let's hurry. I can't afford to screw this up."

Mike breathed a sigh of relief.

Neither can I.

CHAPTER 25

ZORA

Zora gathered the recipes she already had and piled them on the table then she just stared at all of it before slumping onto the barstool. She was hopeless. It wasn't the ideas she struggled with. In no time at all, she could come up with a million recipes. Assembling them in arbitrary categories to go with a theme and a *niche*? That was where she got lost. Apparently, it was also the point where Mike stepped in for the rescue.

"Here's the thing. You've got a lot of good stuff, but it's all over the place," he said.

With a sigh, Zora grimaced. "I know. I don't know what to do because I thought I had it figured out. CreOlé was going to be my theme—creole and Mexican food fusion. Then, just to be safe, I did a web search for the name, and it was already taken. The worst part is, it's just some website with a whole bunch of jibber-jabber about nothing."

Mike bobbed his head. "Okay. That's fine. So, it wasn't another cookbook then?"

"No."

"Then we're good. The theme is still original. All we need is another name—just something as a placeholder. It doesn't' have to be the final title." He pressed his forefinger to his lip for a second. "How about...Creole que sí? Like creo que sí, 'I think so.' Or, Mexicreo. Or Mexcreo. Anything, so we can get started."

Zora was still pouting. This was supposed to be the beginning of her empire, but she sat up straight anyway. "I like those."

"Good, now we know the theme and the 'niche.'" He air-quoted the word. "The way I see it, every good cookbook should have something for each meal of the day. Plus, some snacks and drinks. She didn't say she wanted everything, so we have time. Why don't we focus on *one* meal—the first meal of the day—breakfast?"

With Mike in charge, delegating, working the logistics, and analyzing everything she did, Zora narrowed the recipes down to three blended breakfast meals to send to Leanne in the morning: a pan-fried churro French toast with banana pudding dipping sauce and pecan sprinkles; huevos Sardou con salsa y sémola; and pan-seared shrimp and chorizo in an aioli rémoulade sauce with cinnamon sweet potatoes and vine-ripened strawberries.

After she typed them up, she whipped out the pots and pans and got to the business of cooking.

She couldn't believe how fast everything was coming together. Soon, the house was warm with tangy, spicy, and sweet scents tangoing in the air. She and Mike were doing a dance of their own, rotating and twirling around each other, filling every space of the kitchen as they moved. They were communicating without saying a word.

Thank you.

I've got your back.

I couldn't have done this without you.

Try as she might, Zora couldn't fight the smile toying at her lips. *This.* They were *just being* with one another without having to say a word. It was what she imagined the good stuff was about. They were impossibly close, touching and laughing so comfortably, and it warmed her heart. This was home and happiness to her. She couldn't imagine ever letting it go.

Just for a second, she wondered if that was how Mom felt about Joseph at the beginning.

Zora was busy perfecting her poach on the Sardou part of her huevos Sardou—delicately pouring the creamed spinach and hollandaise sauce over the eggs—when Mike cleared his throat. He was still chopping away at the onions, tomatoes, and cilantro for the salsa as he spoke.

"You're going to need photos, right?"

"Yeah. I'll probably just take some with my phone for now." She hated the tinge of bitterness in her tone. God, she didn't want to lose him…or herself.

He squeezed a lime, letting the juice drip into his mixture then looked up at Zora. "Personally, I think we should get Olivia over here to take some professional pics to send."

She stopped everything she was doing and met Mike's mischievous gaze with a lifted brow. *Oh, you are sneaky, Mike Kennedy.* "I know exactly what you're doing."

He moved a few inches from his side of the counter over to Zora. It was barely noticeable, but she saw the slight curl of his lips. "Divide and conquer."

It was all he said, but she was definitely reading between the lines. Without Oli's co-conspirators around, Mike and Zora could play good cop-bad cop on her and get all the information they needed. It wouldn't be hard to break her since Zora knew the telltale signs she was lying. She'd start out with pursed lips and a furrowed brow and ease her way into a light tug of her earlobe. If she was really telling a whopper, there was the extra-dramatic, full-body yawn-stretch.

Oh, I can't wait to call Oli on her shit.

Between Andre and the love intervention, Zora was ready for some payback.

On the phone, she played her part—dramatic, crestfallen, woe-is-me complete with sniffles and a sizeable gulp over the faux-lump in her throat. She begged Oli to come because it was a "911 girlfriend emergency."

When she got off the line, Mike was smiling widely.

It was going to be so good.

As soon as the doorbell rang, Zora wrung her fingers and took a few breaths as Mike eased into the living room toward the door. She cracked her neck and shook out her shoulders before she hunched over the sink and let her head hang dramatically. For good measure, she quivered her lips then quickly stopped. *Overkill.* She needed to be subtle.

It was showtime.

She heard Mike open the door. "She's in the kitchen—straight back through the living room and to the left," he said loud enough for Zora to hear.

Slowly Zora lifted her head, her eyelids were low and hope-fully giving off the *I'm helplessly doomed without you* look she was aiming for.

As soon as Oli came into view, it was obvious she'd been sleeping and the call had scared her. She was out of breath, her hair was wild, and she was in flannel pajama bottoms with a tank and her camera bag slung over her shoulder. She came flying past the couch and threw the bag onto the floor as she reached the island.

"I'm here!" Her eyes flew through the air frantically, like she wasn't quite sure what to do with them.

She's crying? Shit. Zora might have crossed the line.

Zora straightened slightly and scanned the counter, trying to see it from Oli's perspective. Her reaction *might* have had something to do with the curated mess in front of her. Aside from Zora's doe eyes and the flour expertly dusted across her cheeks (courtesy of Mike) for dramatic effect, she *was* barely standing upright against the kitchen counter. She was sort of hunched over in what she now knew looked like agony.

"I can't do this." Zora threw her face into her hands unsure how to fix the situation. "I don't know what I'm doing. I'm—"

Before she could finish her thespian-worthy monologue, Oli was at her side. "I'm here now. We're going to get you through this. Let me just see what we're working with."

She scanned the counter. Three beautifully dressed breakfast plates lined the granite. They looked mouth-watering, colorful and camera-ready.

Oli leaned in closer, scrutinizing the dishes. "I can't see what you're missing here. This all looks great. In fact, it's making me pretty hungry."

Time for the switch flip.

"Oh, yeah? I think it's missing a few things." Zora stood up taller and cocked her head. She sort of felt bad about the ruse, but Oli *did* have it coming.

She stared, waiting for Oli to turn around. For a prop, she picked up the measuring spoons. "Let's see. If we want it to taste like love, I guess it needs a few teaspoons of misdirection. I don't know, like maybe a fake fumigation and alleged dry rot…definitely, a tablespoon of secrets you keep from your best friend." Zora cocked her head and flashed Oli a pointed glare.

"Uh…" Oli looked at her like she was crazy.

Nope, you don't get to play innocent.

Zora slowly edged around the island until she was standing shoulder-to-shoulder with Mike. Both of them had their arms folded, and their eyes shot daggers at Oli.

"Oh, and a cup of family meddling. That's always the best flavor to go with a gallon of lies." Zora lifted a brow and shook her head. "Don't look so surprised. We're not as dumb as you think we are. We know about the little plan you and my brother and Sophia put together to hook us up. Go ahead, try to lie about it. I *dare* you."

Pursed lips. *Check.*

Furrowed brow. *Double-check.*

"I...I don't know what you're talking about."

There was the light tug of the earlobe.

"You are in rare form tonight. I'm just waiting for the dramatic yawn-stretch because I know you're about to conjure up some whopper of a lie. Let's not waste each other's time. Just tell us the truth."

Oli's shoulders slumped and she closed her eyes. "Fine. What do you want to know?"

Before Zora could start, Mike jumped in with his burning question, which was not exactly the direction she hoped they would go, but she guessed it was at least a start.

"Is Patton Place really infested with termites and dry rot, or not?"

"No," she muttered.

Well, that was easier than I thought it would be. My turn.

"Okay. Do you really have family in town staying at your place, or did you just want me to stay with Mike?" Zora asked.

To this question, Oli met her eyes. "You know I would let you stay with me. I wouldn't have cared if you had to sleep on the couch or the floor or the ceiling, but this was bigger than you crashing at my spot. To answer your question, yes. My cousin was in town for two days over a weekend, so technically it wasn't a lie."

"Then why are Sophia and Everett in Las Vegas? Did they...elope?"

A laugh escaped Oli's lips and she held onto the sink, her shoulders rising and falling as she shook her head. "No," she said adamantly. "They would never do that to you guys."

"Then, why?" Mike asked.

"If it was going to be believable, Everett and Sophia couldn't stay home, so they decided to go stay with her mom and do a little staycation. They couldn't give you Patton Place as an option. We figured we had to eliminate all your other options. We took away Patton Place and my house, first. We knew hotels wouldn't be feasible long-term, so Sophia got her realtor to help you…" She cringed as she let the other shoe drop. "*And* conveniently show you the worst places she could find."

Zora wanted to laugh because Ellen had shown her some pretty heinous places, but this still wasn't a laughing matter. Even though they were getting to the truth, it still felt sly and underhanded, like she and Mike were getting the short end of the stick somehow.

She blinked and looked away. "You guys really went out of your way for this…scheme."

"Don't think of it like that." Oli's voice was softer and pleading. "We love you guys, and we just want you to stop getting in your own way."

Mike unfolded his arms and glanced over at Zora, then ran his warm hand down the nape of her neck. "Zo, they meant well."

But it still didn't feel right.

Why am I so mad?

Zora bit her lip a little too hard. "So then you did lie about inviting Mike to the silent disco. Is that why you were pushing so hard for me to be with Andre that night? That's pretty fucked up. You wanted him to see me kissing another man. You wanted Mike to be hurt."

The accusation lulled in the air like a thick, oily haze. It was sticky, and it felt wrong to do this to her best friend, but Zora needed to understand the root of this thing. *What were they all hoping would happen?*

"I wanted you to remember what you guys had!" Oli shouted in a burst of emotion. Her hands were shaking, and her face was flushed.

She inhaled and began again a little more gently. "We all wanted you guys to get out of your own way and recognize you have something special. That shit doesn't just come along every day, and you guys were taking it for granted. So, if that makes me a bad friend for wanting the best for you, for loving you too much, then so be it. I love you, Zo. Both of you. And I know how much you love each other."

Is it that simple?

It all sounded sweet and lovely, but was it realistic? Yes, Zora loved simply being with Mike. Every second they spent together was proof they worked well as a team, but where was the family circus going to be when her house was built and Mike went about his merry way? What was going to happen when everything went sideways?

I guess I'll find out. Fuck it.

CHAPTER 26

MIKE

By Thursday afternoon, Mike was seriously considering skywriting his thanks to Everett, Sophia, and Olivia from Portland to Las Vegas. Every night since Olivia spilled the beans about their impromptu intervention, Zora had slept in Mike's bed. She staked her claim on the right side, but always managed to ease her way into the middle to find him rock-hard and ready for her.

When they'd confronted Olivia, Mike thought Zora was going to be pissed, but to his surprise and sheer gratitude, shedding light only seemed to open her heart and knock down her guards. Being together was beginning to feel less like a charade and more like fate working to realign the stars.

Mike couldn't be happier.

It was what he'd always wanted, even though he'd imagined it happening under different circumstances.

He couldn't remember the last time he was completely satisfied. His happiness at home and at work was all because of Zora. The woman was feeding him mind, body, and soul—

heavy emphasis on the *body* part. Even now, it was lunchtime and he was still stuffed from a hearty breakfast, but he ate the grilled lemon pepper chicken and vegetables for lunch because she'd made it.

"Kendra," he yelled from his office into the lobby. "It's almost one. Any cancellation from Arnold?"

Mike scarfed down the last bite of his chicken, beaming as he tucked the empty Tupperware container back into the lunch bag Zora packed for him—another little piece of her that stayed with him. He was smiling on the inside. Pride. Zora lit up at the sight of his empty containers. It was like it made her feel good to know he was eating and enjoying food she prepared.

Something about seeing her happy…it thrilled him.

From the hall, Kendra's raspy reply bounced off the walls. "Not yet. Looks like that two-faced dog is going to show his ass today. No call. No show. Tacky."

Mike laughed as he adjusted his chair and logged back into his computer. "All right. I guess we're nipping this thing in the bud today."

"Damn right, we are."

Mike leaned back in his chair and rocked as he lifted his chin. A slow smile tugged at his lips and lightness settled in his chest. He was relaxed. Deep down, he knew it was because of Zora. Things that would usually bother him rolled right off of him. All week, she had reassured him that he was making the right decision about Arnold. As Mike helped her cook, she waded through the pros and cons of doing business with a company which not only lacked genuine concern for Monroe Properties but proved its intent to undermine it.

This was what it felt like to be seen and heard.

"Child, you know he's going to stroll in here and think he's got this shit under wraps, too." Kendra was still thinking out loud from the lobby, laughter bubbling from her. "It'd serve him right if we weren't here if and when he finally decided to show his face."

"Yeah, well, he's got another thing coming this time."

Mike glanced over to his phone on the desk, absently tapping his fingertips together. He halfway wanted Arnold to skip their meeting. Getting off early wasn't the worst idea. He'd get to see Zora sooner.

He refocused on his computer screen for a few seconds only to have the idea snag his thoughts.

What's the harm in a quick text?

It was killing him not to send Zora a message just to let her know he was thinking about her. He swiped his phone off the desk and let his thumbs hover over the keyboard before stopping short.

"No. Let her have some space," he mumbled to himself as he replaced the phone on the desk. He inhaled and blew out a breath, leaning back in the chair with his hands clasped behind his head.

"Where is this guy? Should we just call it, and knock off for the rest of the day?

Mike got to his feet with sigh. "I don't know about you, but I could use a few extra hours of personal time." *To make it home early to Zora….*

"You won't hear any complaints from me," Kendra said.

Naturally, that's when Arnold decided to strut into the building.

As much as Mike wanted to rush home to Zora, he wanted to make this business decision face to face. Zora's confidence in him and his abilities to make a great partner, in business and in life, meant the world to him. Whether she'd said it directly or not, unknowingly, the examples she gave when they talked about going into business with Arnold lent themselves to the spark growing between him and Zora. Good partnerships needed to be based in loyalty and for the long-term, she said. It was about what they could both bring to the table and why it was better because of each team player. Even more, it couldn't be based on conditions and contingencies. It needed to be a choice that made both parties feel lucky to have found the other.

She was right. On so many levels. He felt lucky as hell. He wanted to prove himself to be the kind of partner both Zora and Everett would choose in business. Maybe he was reading too deeply into, but he wanted to be the partner Zora wanted in love.

Mike gathered the files as Kendra showed an unapologetically late Mr. Arnold into the conference room.

Despite being over thirty minutes late, he walked in squinting with a hard smile and a dismissive nod. He had salt-and-pepper hair with a heavy side-part, steely blue eyes, pock-marked jowls, and a dishonest politician's gray suit complete with an ugly matching tie and pocket-square.

"Sorry about the time. Got caught up in business meetings. You know how these things go." He winked and laughed a fake, underhanded cackle that belied his pompous, nose-in-the-air demeanor. He must have felt that the deal was all wrapped up, and this meeting was simply a minor detail to be checked off his list of menial things to do for the day.

Oh, this is going to be entertaining. Thirty minutes late. You're lucky I don't want to prolong this any more than I have to.

Mike took wide steps around the table, allowing his arms to swing as he walked. "So glad you could make it," he said, extending his hand for a strong handshake as he leaned in. "Forgive me, but I have one of those *business* meetings myself in half an hour, so if you don't mind…" He held his hand out to the table, motioning for Arnold to be seated in the chair closest to the exit.

"Ah, yes. Sure, sure," he said, sounding put out by the leading gesture. By his grimace, Mike could tell he assumed he'd be the one running the show.

Here goes nothing.

When Mike was seated across from Arnold, he shifted in the chair and resumed an easy-going manner while looking him directly in the eye. "Don't take this the wrong way, Mr. Arnold, but in preparation for our meeting today, or last week, I did some research on Arnold Investments. Just a requisite review… checks and balances." He tapped his fingertips together and met Arnold's gaze. His expression had gone from exaggerated casualness to pinched.

Don't look so surprised.

"I gotta be honest here," Arnold began. "I don't think it's your place to be completing any reviews on my company. The name on the sign out there is 'Monroe.' I've been working with Everett and his family for all these years because of loyalty."

Is that what we're calling it?

Mike's top lip curled and laughter bubbled up inside him. His posture was strong—shoulders back, chest out, chin high. *This is too good.* "With all due respect, Mr. Arnold, due diligence is exactly what I was hired to do. I know all about loyalty, which is why *I've* been with this company since Everett took over and he grew it to what it is today—a competitive, profitable enterprise, forecasted to double its market value in the next two quarters. It is precisely because I'm looking out for Monroe Properties that it has achieved these milestones ethically and legally."

In his chair, Arnold leaned back and drummed his fingers on the table. "And may I ask what your 'diligence' resulted in?"

"Indeed." Mike gave a half-shrug. It was light-hearted teasing, but Mike enjoyed himself, nonetheless. His muscles relaxed, and he spoke boisterously,. "As it turns out I discovered you also met with Easton Investments with the intent to sell the Chessington building to them."

Arnold's eyes went wide. Apparently, he wasn't aware the information had leaked. Mike would have to give Kendra and her friend at Arnold Investments a special gift of thanks once this was all over and done with.

On a deep inhale, Arnold shook his head and paled with shock as he attempted to explain the information away. "Let's be honest, here. At the end of the day, this is just part of business. I wanted to make sure I was getting the best bang for my buck." A self-righteous smirk appeared on his face. "You can't fault me for that, now can you?"

I most certainly can.

Inside, Mike was cringing. He hated the expression *bang for your buck*. It sounded exactly like what Arnold was doing: trying to fuck them for a dollar. But Monroe Properties was not hanging out on a street corner dangling its goods for the first taker. Monroe Properties didn't need *his* buck.

"Trust me, I know exactly what you're talking about, sir." Mike lifted his chin and breathed an even sigh. "But, given this new information, it's my duty to inform you Monroe Properties will no longer be pursuing any business ventures with Arnold Investments. As such, we are formally withdrawing our bid for the Chessington building. On behalf of the partners and myself, we thank you for your consideration and wish you the best in your future endeavors."

In the back of his mind, Zora's face flashed before him. Her eyes sparkled as she gave him the thumbs-up for doing the right thing. Mike was riding high on a feeling of lightness and he couldn't wait to get home to tell Zora all about his day.

It hadn't been the easiest thing, though.

He watched as Arnold's mouth fell open, but then he stilled Mike in place with his beady eyes.

Ready for this whole scene to come to an end, Mike stood and extended his hand—finality drenched in the gesture. Arnold was slow to take it, and when he did, the handshake was weak and lingered for a moment too long as he met Mike's eyes. The stare was meaningful. Like he knew something Mike didn't.

Arnold went poker-faced, gathering his belongings as he ambled toward the door, but Mike couldn't dismiss the pregnant pause and the blank expression plastered on his weathered face.

Sure enough, when he reached for the door handle, he pivoted back to Mike. "One more thing. Just a heads up, I've been doing a little digging, too. Seems Baker & Bronson is entertaining the addition of a certain promising attorney who makes it his business to oversee the checks and balances of his current employer. I don't know about you, but it makes me wonder what both of those company's policies are regarding loyalty." One side of his mouth pulled up in a wicked grin. "Just a thought."

With his bomb drop, he tapped his head with his hand then saluted to the merits of one-upmanship.

Fuck.

Mike blinked, watching his form fade into the distance as he rounded the corner back to the lobby. A muscle in Mike's jaw twitched. The thought of Arnold telling Everett about the interest from Baker & Bronson was sobering. What would Zora think after everything they were building based on honesty and trust?

What am I going to do?

He pinched the bridge of his nose.

"Kendra, I'm working from home for the rest of the day."

Enough of keeping up this charade.

Whether Everett was ready or not, Mike was going to put it all out there and ask his best friend to make it official—he was going to ask to be made partner.

CHAPTER 27

ZORA

"Okay. I see you and Mike are all coupled up." Oli hummed through the thin dressing room wall between them. "Girl, I am not mad at you, though. Domestic goddess is definitely a good look for you. Packing his lunch and your cute little movie nights… I'll bet the sex is next level—"

"I'm going to stop you right there," Zora rolled her eyes even though Oli couldn't see her. "Can we maybe not tell the whole world what's going on in my life? In case you hadn't noticed, we are not the only people in here." There was a low grumble to the last words as she tried and failed to reason with her best friend.

They'd spent the entire morning in Mike's kitchen shooting pictures of the finished lunch dishes for the cookbook before eating way too much of the finished product then deciding to work it off with some minor retail therapy. At the time, catching up with Oli seemed like a good idea. Now that Oli was putting all of her business out on Front Street for any- and everyone to hear, Zora was questioning her own logic.

The sound of Oli sucking her teeth echoed through the room. "Oh, I noticed. I just don't care. It's not like anybody in here knows who we're talking about."

"Whatever. Just come out because…ugh. I can't wear this."

Zora unlatched the door, walked out, and centered herself in the wall-length mirror then winced at her reflection. It was just dinner with Mike. Why did she have to get all dolled up? The man had seen her looking like death on a stick, coughing and hacking away in frumpy pajamas…and with no clothes at all. A frilly red dress wasn't going to make any difference— even if did sort of make her ass look like an Olympic gymnast's.

"Yes. That is going to make *all* the difference." Oli came out of her stall looking fierce in a deep purple bandage number that highlighted her perky boobs and fit like a second skin. "If you let me get my hands on your hair, and with a little bit of make-up…" she trailed off, but Zora filled in the blanks.

She could have him eating out of the palm of her hands.

That's surely what would have come next, but that's where Oli was wrong. There was no *could* about it. He'd already eaten —chocolate syrup, honey, and caramel drizzle—off the palms of her hands and other body parts. They were thoroughly enjoying every sweet second with each other. Even though she knew it was going to come back to bite her in the end, the whole throwing caution to the wind thing was doing wonders for both her libido and her complexion.

"I see you thinking about it," Oli said.

Zora looked at her flushed, smitten expression in the mirror and dragged her hands slowly over the svelte curves of her body, remembering Mike's warm deft hands on her this morn-ing. Their skin was pressed firmly together. A slow, excruci-ating burn had pricked, pulsed and teased…

A breath hitched in her throat.

Still hung up on the memory, Zora grazed her teeth over the tip of her thumb.

"Mmm. Mmm. Mmm. Now I know it's good."

Zora rolled her eyes. "Shut up," she said, trying and failing to bite back a shit-eating grin. She'd barely noticed that Oli stopped talking. Then, she looked up and past their reflections in the mirror.

She saw a mass of loose, sunny blonde curls, and YouTube tutorial-perfect makeup attached to a dancer's sculpted body.

Kate.

Of all the T.J. Maxx dressings rooms, in all the world, she walks into mine.

Of course, she couldn't be the type to smile awkwardly and keep walking because Zora didn't have that kind of luck—any, apparently.

"Hi," Kate said, biting her bottom lip as she scrutinized Zora's reflection in the mirror. "I wasn't eavesdropping or anything. I just heard you guys talking, and I couldn't help but overhear that you and Mike are together now."

Wow. She doesn't beat around the bush.

Zora smiled nervously and gave a noncommittal nod.

What do you really want me to say here? Yes, we're going at it like rabbits? I'm happier than I remember ever being? I'm not going to lie.

Kate gave a half-smile and lowered her chin to her chest before meeting Zora's eyes in the mirror again. They were standing a few inches apart, close enough for Zora to smell her light floral perfume, but it was as if Kate couldn't meet her gaze without the mirror as a buffer.

"I'm…really happy for you guys," Kate said in an even and soft tone. Zora wanted to find some kind of fault in her words, some hidden double meaning, if only to feel validated in feeling defensive, but it wasn't there. Kate was genuine, and her voice was filled with the emotion.

Silently, Zora scanned the half dozen or so hangers full of yoga pants and sport bras in Kate's manicured hands. The woman was perfect—physically and, probably, mentally. She didn't seem to have any screws loose or active vendettas. Apparently, they were going to engage in mature conversation without one of them going for the jugular or clawing for hair.

"Thanks," Zora said.

But, there was something still niggling at Zora. Why did things even end between Mike and Kate? One second they'd been good, and then, just like that, it was over. Clean break. No explanations. Not that Zora should question it, but why not Kate? If this gorgeous woman wasn't enough for him... *Why am I?*

"I just..." Kate swallowed, and the sight of her glistening eyes in the reflection rattled something loose in Zora. Kate was hurt, and here Zora was picking out dresses for a date with the same man who'd caused her pain, thinking she was lucky somehow. All these years, Zora had front row seats to the show —Mike and his magic revolving door of women.

Dammit.

It was like coming inside from the darkness, and her eyes slowly adjusted to the light. Realization flooded in from every direction.

She wasn't lucky.

She was just next in line to be dismissed.

In that moment, Zora couldn't breathe. Her throat closed, and her heartbeat raced. It sounded like a sledgehammer slamming against steel. She blinked and blinked, but she wasn't seeing clearly.

"Zo?" Oli's face came flying into her line of vision, magnified and blurred. Her voice was too loud. "You good? Oh shit, you don't look so good. Let me grab my purse."

As soon as Oli ran off, Zora stumbled backwards into the wall.

"Whoa," Kate mumbled as she steadied Zora against the wall, helping to lower her to the floor. She tilted her head and studied Zora for a second. "I think she's dehydrated. How much water did you drink today?"

"N-not much," Zora managed. She was still shell-shocked. Why was Kate here?

Why is she helping me?

Everything about Kate was soft and real. The wild strands of hair in her face and her pale blue eyes reminded Zora of the calm of the ocean. She seemed genuinely nice and thoughtful. If she didn't need to keep her distance based solely on Kate's status as an ex, Zora would totally be friends with this woman.

"I didn't get much sleep," Zora added and immediately wished she could slurp the words back in.

I'll bet the sex is next level.

Kate had definitely heard every word.

Gah, I'm such an asshole.

"It's fine. I'm fine," Zora said, the words drawing together into a jumbled mess. She struggled to get to her feet, wobbling as she did. "Uh…thank you for your help." She cleared her throat in an attempt to be more poised than she felt. "We have to be going."

Zora eyed Oli hoping she would catch the hint, but Oli cocked her head and the crease between her brows deepened.

As one of my oldest, dearest friends, why can't you for once read my mind? I'm fucking losing it over here.

Oli bobbed her head and puckered her bottom lip in a knowing smirk. "So you're wearing this out of the store, or did you want to take it off first and maybe pay for it? I don't know…maybe let the cashier put it in a cute plastic bag for you? I won't do crime because I, for one, cannot do the time."

Breathe. Do not kill your best friend.

Zora refused to fall apart with Kate sitting courtside. There was no way in hell she was going to ask Kate what happened between her and Mike.

Annoyed, Zora flashed Oli a death stare before turning to Kate. "It was nice seeing you, and thanks for your help." Still in the dress, she lifted her chin and pulled back her shoulders as she calmly walked into her dressing room, picked up her clothes, shoes, and purse, and padded barefoot past Oli. "I'll meet you at the register."

Zora yanked the tag off the red dress and handed it to the cashier along with her credit card. "I'll still take a bag, though, for my clothes."

While the guy rang her up, Oli bypassed the other five people waiting and made her way to the register with Zora. "We're together." She flashed a quick smile at the cashier and set her dress on the counter before meeting Zora's glare. "I'll Venmo you or something, but, are we going to talk about what happened back there in the dressing room, or what?"

"Can we just get out of this store?" Kate could be checking out at any minute.

Apparently, the answer was no.

Judging by Oli's smirk, the chances of her letting this one slide for now was slim to none. *Fine.*

"It's a sign."

"That what? You need to drink more water or that I don't have a hot man waiting for me at home and I'm still getting this dress because it's $9.99? You don't just pass up a deal like this."

Zora sighed. "Agreed. But how are Kate and I here at the exact same time? Were we looking at the same woman? Explain why Mike would end things with her. She's perfect." She put her credit card back into her wallet.

"Um, no. You of all people should know you don't judge a

book by its cover. All that…" She fanned her open hands in front of her face in a circular washing motion. "It's decoration. A good trip to Ulta or Sephora will do it for any woman, but what's going on in her noggin, that's a completely different story. She could be a crazed lunatic or a jealous psycho. Who knows?"

The cashier breathed loudly and both of their eyes shot to him.

"If you could just sign here, you're all set." He pointed to the signature pad with the stylus strung to a long cord.

Zora signed and pressed the okay button. "Do you know why they broke up?" Zora asked Oli. "With the whole setup and everything, you must know something."

"Ahem."

Again, Zora and Oli were interrupted by the cashier.

His shoulders slumped and his head sort of hung to the side like she was the customer he'd dreaded all day but knew was coming in one form or another. "Would you like your receipt by email or printed?"

"Lord have mercy." Zora jolted around and tapped the stylus on the email button then waited for the screen to clear back to the landing page. She could feel her face screw into a twisted grimace when she turned back to him. "Is there anything else?"

The guy flashed a tight smile and shook his head as he pushed a button to illuminate his register number two sign.

Together, Zora and Oli walked out of the automatic doors into the cool afternoon air. Really, her anger was misdirected. She was irritated Oli wouldn't say more. Angry with Mike for making her feel so insecure. She was most angry with herself for allowing things between her and Mike to escalate so quickly to the point she was already losing herself. He was all she thought about. This was exactly what she hadn't wanted.

She was more than this thing between them.

Zora lifted a questioning brow at Oli, still waiting for her answer. Childishly, she refused to speak first, but the instant Oli opened her mouth, a loud ping sounded in the air.

"It's not me. That's your phone," Oli rested her hands on her hips and waited expectantly while Zora scrolled through to the message. "Well? Who was that?"

"The builder. My house is going to be finished earlier than they thought. My closing date got moved up to April 10th."

If Zora hadn't attuned herself with the signs of fate before, she did now. She should be ecstatic. She was getting exactly what she wanted. A house. Independence. Space. Staying with Mike was always temporary, but somehow the idea of moving out and adding space between them felt final, like an ending. This small change in direction made her feel like they were on a downhill slope.

Now, more than ever, she needed to know what happened with Mike and Kate. Zora's future with him depended on it.

CHAPTER 28

MIKE

M ike scrubbed his hands over his face as an emptiness settled in the pit of his stomach.

"Look who it is!" Everett's cheerful voice bellowed and thundered throughout the cab of Mike's car.

"Hey. How's it going out there? Is the water nice?" It was a shitty dig and Mike knew it. Everett and Sophia were no more telling the truth about being in Bali than he was about Arnold and declining the Chessington building purchase. Still, it hardened his chest a bit about asking for what he deserved.

It was now or never.

"Listen, Ev. I don't mean to call in the middle of your trip, but I need to give you the rundown on the meeting with Arnold. I, uh…didn't go through with the deal."

The resulting silence went straight to Mike's chest as he waited. Then it thickened until he heard Everett exhale his frustrations.

"I see."

"I know I should have called you first, but Kendra and I did some digging after Arnold delayed the meeting by a week. We found out he had Easton Investments on the calendar the same day. He used our offer to hedge his bet and see if they would beat it, but they must not have been able to match because he showed up today."

Everett sighed, but Mike kept going.

"I was sure he would cancel, but he came. Late, but he was there, smug and pompous like he had this thing in the bag. I just...I knew it wasn't the best purchase for the company. I couldn't in good conscience let the company build such a risky partnership."

Mike dug his nails into the leather of his seat while he leaned his head back against the headrest. Everett's silence was killing him. When Ev didn't immediately jump in, Mike felt compelled to fill the silence.

"I had Monroe Properties' best interest in mind. Anyway, I've already found a few other buildings for you to consider that make good business sense as far as the numbers go. The owners are well-respected among their peers. I'm hoping you're okay with this decision and that...you'll consider me for partner."

Mike was holding his breath.

Come on, Ev. Say something.

Half-heartedly, Mike imagined Everett jumping at the chance and telling him he only needed to make it official, but it didn't go that way.

"Mike." Everett sighed. "I have to tell you, I'm kind of pissed off that you overrode my decision without even consulting me. I don't just...I don't know if I want a partner who makes unilateral decisions that could affect the company's future."

A long hesitation dug along the fault lines of their friendship and shook Mike to the core.

The heat level in the car seemed to rise. It smothered Mike.

His heartbeat was sluggish as he pushed up his sleeves and pinched the bridge of his nose. "This guy was supposed to be loyal to your family and he's out there giving other people a chance to undercut you? It's wrong."

"You're supposed to be loyal to my family. Mike, you *are* my family, and you didn't even think twice about doing what you thought was best without checking with me. What kind of partner does that? What kind of *friend* does that?"

Fuck.

Everett was right. Mike should have called him. He'd had days before he met with Arnold the second time, and not once did it cross his mind to reach out to his best friend.

"You're right. I know, and I'm so sorry. I should have called you. In the back of my mind, I didn't want to add to your worries. I thought I was doing you a favor, looking out for you." *Catching you before you fell.*

He closed his eyes and immediately, Lucas' face came to mind. He was scared and falling, reaching for Mike and he couldn't save him. This was the same thing all over again. It had been ever since. He was always busy trying to rescue someone, save someone.

Until now, Mike didn't realize he was the one hurting them.

Tears welled in his eyes as he bit back the pain.

"I'm so sorry," he said.

"I know." Everett's voice was softer now, even. "Listen, man. I'm coming home early. We'll be back on the third. Let me…think about what you said, and we'll talk then." Mike couldn't dismiss the sadness in his tone, like he was betrayed.

He was so caught up in his end goal he didn't care who he hurt to get there.

Mike walked into the house half an hour later with a bouquet of roses and a decent offer from Jason's law firm, but he was deflated. He didn't want to leave Everett any more than he wanted to make a lateral move. What was he really working toward?

"Anybody home?" he called from the door as he hung his keys on the hook. "Something smells good."

"Back here."

At the sound of Zora's heartwarming voice, he sighed with relief. This was what he wanted, to come home to the woman who made everything better. His house felt like a home with her in it: warm with the savory scent of home cooking, busy with the sounds of love.

"Where's Blue?" he asked.

"He's playing in the backyard. Just fed him."

Zora walked out from the hallway toward the kitchen, and he stopped in the foyer. As good as she cooked, there were simply no words for how good she looked. She was startlingly attractive with her full pout and tapered pixie cut…and that dress.

She was barefoot with a sexy little red dress on. It had tiny straps holding up a thin fabric that did nothing to hide the swell of her breasts.

Warmth flooded his insides, and suddenly he felt over-heated. Mike loosened his tie and let the ends hang around his neck. He might have been burning up, but, God, he couldn't take his eyes off her hardened nipples.

"Aren't you a sight for sore eyes?" He tugged his lip between his teeth and shook his head as she broke into a smile. He was hoping the smile was for him, but he suspected she'd noticed the roses.

She flashed him an empathetic puppy dog look. "It didn't go well."

"No, it actually went well with Arnold. I just got off the phone with your brother, though. It seems he doesn't want a partner who makes decisions without talking to him first."

Zora rolled her eyes. "Give him a little while. He knows how good you are. He's just stubborn and doesn't want to say yes too fast to any idea he didn't come up with. Anyway, stop worrying. You're here with me now."

"Yes." Mike smiled and warmth filtered through him.

"Hi," she purred.

He closed the distance between them and slipped his hands around her waist. "Hi yourself." Brushing his lips over hers, he squeezed her against his chest. "I missed you."

"Missed you too."

Mike pulled away and tilted his head as he narrowed his gaze. It wasn't what she said, but *how* she said it that gave him pause. It was as if she was being careful not to add the "I." Like she didn't want to own it. It was the way you'd say it to a friend.

"Anything eventful happen today?" He was fishing and praying she'd take the bait.

Her brows waggled playfully. "Nope."

Mike broke into a smile. "With that look on your face, I find that hard to believe," he said, but when he looked past her, he finally noticed the dining room. His brows knitted together. A mix of shock and appreciation laced his tone. "You did this?"

The table was covered with a white sheet in lieu of a table-cloth. Two plates were set one across from the other with all the silverware, linens, and glasses. In the center, two candles were lit, giving it an intimate, romantic ambiance.

"Are these for me?" She bounced on her heels and his stomach did a little flip. She was looking at him with that adorably sweet, half smile. For a brief moment, he caught a glimpse of the girl he'd known once and the woman he was falling head over heels for.

She gave him a wistful glance as her warm eyes crinkled around the corners and lit up.

"Yes."

"They're perfect. Thank you."

A shiver coursed through him and his face grew hot. He blinked, stepping out of his trance to guide her by the hand into the dining room. The delicate curve of her neck seemed to glow in the light of the chandelier.

But then she pivoted to him.

"I was actually hoping we could talk?" She batted her lashes at him.

Here we go. What is going on with this day?

Mike craned his neck back. "Do I even want to know what this is about?"

Zora swayed into the kitchen and lifted herself up onto her tiptoes, opening the cabinet above the refrigerator. Mike had no clue how she knew that's where he kept the vases, but he sure was enjoying the view. It appeared that she was just about to ungracefully climb onto the counter, when he leaned in behind her.

"Uh, I think I can get it," she said, but Mike ignored her and extended his arm to clutch his hand around the vase and pull it down.

His mouth was no farther than an inch from her ear. "Here you go." He could feel the curve of her behind firm against his growing hard-on.

She exhaled. "You're not playing fair."

"As the saying goes, 'All is fair in...'" he trailed off, but he didn't miss the questions in Zora's eyes when she turned to meet his gaze. When he didn't finish his sentence, she edged past him to the sink.

He heard the thud as she set the vase in the sink basin and turned on the faucet. The awkwardness between them was back, and Mike hated it. He hated not being able to see her face. He swallowed and straightened his shoulders skimming through things that might be bothering her. She was on track for her book deadline and he hadn't even told her about his conversation with Everett. So what was it? She'd spent the day doing a photoshoot and shopping with Olivia, and…

"How was your day with Olivia?" He asked.

Mike ground his teeth and felt the tightening of his jaw as he exhaled. Something happened. Whatever Zora needed to talk about, he was sure Olivia had something to do with it.

"Fine."

Yeah, I'm sure.

Deciding to help, Mike swiveled around and stood beside her at the sink. He removed the plastic from the roses and pulled a knife from the drawer, gripping the stems with his left hand and cutting the twisted wire ties with his right.

"You're sure? Your day with Olivia doesn't have anything to do with what you want to talk to me about?"

She flitted a glance up to meet his eyes then quickly lowered her head. "Yeah. It's fine. By the way, thanks again for these. It's really sweet of you, but you don't have to buy me stuff. Just letting me stay here is thanks enough." She sounded stilted and measured.

"I've got you. This is thick and thin right here." He tapped his chest then pointed to Zora. "You know I'm here for you."

She paused for a moment. "Hmm, let's see if that's the case." Mike could hear the smile in her voice. "First champagne, then roses. It's only natural that jewelry be the next—"

"Shit." Mike sliced his finger. He dropped the flowers and let the water run over the cut, but Zora took over. She moved the vase and grabbed for paper towels, wrapped it around his finger, and squeezed.

"Band-aids?"

"My bathroom. Medicine cabinet. Top shelf."

In seconds, Zora was gone and back with the whole box.

She removed a bandage and set it on the edge of the sink. Seemingly in savior mode, she took Mike's hand without saying a word and carefully unraveled the paper towel. "Ouch. You did get yourself pretty good, but it looks like you just missed needing stitches."

Dabbing at the cut, she peeked up at him with a laugh biting at her lip. "Hold it just like this," she instructed, straightening his finger. Her eyes were laser focused on the open wound. Her dainty hands caressed his fingers, leaving a trail of heat where their skin touched. As she adhered the bandage with precision detail, the smile reached up to her eyes. "Is this how you act every time a woman mentions jewelry in idle conversation?"

A full grin spread across his face. He couldn't help but laugh, too. One second he was "helping" with the roses, and the next he was on the verge of an emergency room visit. It sucked. He didn't mind the part where a beautiful woman fussed over him, though. She was gentle and attentive.

Beautiful? Stunning, actually.

"You don't just use the "J-word" so casually like that." He laughed. "Next time I'll just stick with a gift card."

A small giggle escaped Zora's lips.

"Thank you for this." He held up his wounded middle finger, dramatically limping over to the table and taking his seat.

After Zora expertly arranged the flowers and placed them on the table, she plated the food from the stovetop and poured the champagne. Over dinner, their conversation consisted of eighties movie references and Olivia's brilliant photoshoot of Zora's lunch dishes for the book.

He was half finished with his salmon when Zora determined it was a good time to change the subject to serious matters.

"Do you know what love is?" she asked.

Mike almost spit out a mouthful of wine on her. He sputtered as he spoke. "Uh, yeah. That's a really random question, though. That's what you want to talk about?"

"I'm just asking because I need a favor."

He leaned back in his chair and crossed his arms over his chest, studying Zora's face. He couldn't read her expression. Rather than jump to conclusions, he jutted out his chin, urging her to continue.

"I was wondering if just for tonight, we could play a game of All Truth, No Lies?"

CHAPTER 29

ZORA

Zora bit back a laugh as Mike squirmed in his chair.

"Relax. It shouldn't be hard to tell the truth if you're not walking around all day telling lies. I'm just...trying to get to the bottom of something. That's all. Let's call it...research."

"For your cookbook?"

No. "Yes."

"Funny. That did not alleviate my fears at all. How are love and truth related to food?" He laughed. "I have a better idea. Why don't you tell me what it is that you're trying to get to the bottom of? Wouldn't that be easier? C'mon, McFly."

She pressed her palm to her chest in mock surprise. "You did not just go *Back to the Future* on me."

"I did."

"I love the fact you're finally using movie references properly, but can you do this for me, please?" She pouted and batted her lashes. "It's important."

Mike stared at her for a long minute then shrugged. "Fine. Ask away."

Zora perked up in her seat and bit into an asparagus tip. "Now. We'll alternate, but I'll go first. It's really more like Twenty Questions, but we don't have to do twenty," she said it quickly, to avoid any pending objections. Without pausing to give him the chance, she lifted one brow. "Have you ever been in love?"

The question was out there lolling in the air, and she was breathless, waiting.

At least she'd find out now if he'd loved Kate.

He threw his hands up in the air. "See? This is what I'm talking about. I'm gonna need more champagne if we're going this route—and possibly a honey bun. Salmon is not going to cut it, no matter how well you seasoned it."

Zora burst out laughing and shook her head as she got her feet. When she returned from the kitchen, she topped off his glass and tossed him two honey buns from the pantry. "I gave you an extra one since I know you've got mixed emotions about this." She winked. "A little sweetener."

He took a ginormous bite of the honey bun and slouched against the back of the chair, seeming to finally consider the question. "You're killing me, woman." He sighed and smiled, his cheek bulging as he chewed. "Yes. I have been in love."

Zora nodded, her brows raised, urging him to continue.

"Just once, but it didn't work out. Don't ask the name or when it was, but know that it was real."

Uh. Don't do me like that.

A strained smile formed around the edges of his mouth. He had this far away, unseeing look in his eyes like he was back there with this mystery woman, and it was killing Zora. She hoped to gain some insight about what Mike thought about love, but his response was so personal and heartfelt. She had no details, but she was jealous of this lucky woman who made Mike travel in time to be with her. The idea that he still longed for someone, it jarred something loose inside of Zora. Sadness? Jealousy? She swallowed hard over the lump in her throat.

"Wow. Do you…still love her?" *Is it Kate?*

Mike snapped out of wherever his thoughts took him. His eyes were arresting, his mouth distracting as he glanced at her. Zora's heart tripped around in her chest as her pulse quickened.

Somehow, she knew she should be focusing on spilling the beans about moving out a month earlier than planned, but at the moment, all she could think about was the possibility Kate was the woman he loved. If so, *why* had they broken up?

He slowly shook his head with a reprimanding *tsk, tsk* and smiled that disarming smile. It left a warm tightening in her stomach. "Don't go trying to ask follow up questions. If you want specifics, ask specific questions. You're not slick, Zo."

"Okay, fine." Zora threw up her hands playfully. "Ask your question, then."

He made big work of squinting his eyes and pressing his pinky finger to his pursed lips. "Zo…did you hook up with—"

"Nope. Nope. Nope." She wagged her finger side to side between them. "All the questions have to be related to love. Nice try, though. A for effort. Go again."

"Zora Marie Monroe, I'm flipping it on you. What are your deal-breakers…" he asked, adding, "…in love?"

She hadn't expected the question, but besides the obvious ones, like cheating and beating, she really only had one. The one thing she was afraid of when it came to relationships was losing herself. Changing for someone other than herself meant…*changing everything that makes me, me*. It was why she wasn't gung ho about falling for guys. It occurred to her just then, that maybe it was why she was always drawn to Mike. He never once asked her to be anyone other than herself.

"My deal-breaker—singular—is a guy who wants me to

change for him," she said. Her brows lifted. *Bam! Mic drop.* "Back to you. Since you've clearly been nose deep in it, define love. Oh, and by the way, middle names do not intimidate me, Michael Dwayne Kennedy."

She stood and began gathering their empty plates. He fell in line with the wine glasses and honey bun wrappers, stopping to blow out the candles.

"I've got the dishes, if you want to put the food in the fridge." He rolled up his sleeves and pushed the stopper into the drain.

A wave of heat washed over her as she took in the strong lines of his broad shoulders and forearms. His sunbaked skin flexed with each movement as he turned on the faucet and poured in dishwashing liquid. She just stood there staring in amazement.

As delicious as his body was to look at, this went beyond physical. The man was going to do the dishes. By. Hand. It didn't matter they'd made only a few dishes dirty. He was doing it without being asked and without complaint.

Holy shit. What a turn-on.

Dishes—well chores—definitely felt like a component of love. Most of the married women she knew complained about their husbands boycotting the household duties, leaving clothes all over the floor, and basically wanting a trophy for taking out the trash. Partnership or respect, in some sort of way, felt like it should be part of the good stuff.

Then again, this *was* his house.

She shook the thought from her mind and realized Mike was stalling.

"Go on, I'm listening," she urged him to continue with his answer as she opened the lower cabinets, pulled out two Tupperware containers, and began placing the leftover salmon and asparagus into them.

"I hope you realize people have been trying to define love for centuries and they still haven't got it down to a science." He dunked a plate and wiped in circles with the sponge. "The way I see it, it's more of a feeling than any particular word. There's no checklist."

Damn.

"To *me* it's about the way the person makes you feel, like the best version of yourself. You get to be there for them in good and bad times because you want to and vice versa. It's so many little things, instead of some grand gesture like in your movies." He tipped his head to her. "Not everyone is going to hold up a boom box or give you diamond earrings to prove they love you. It's having a shitty day and she's the only person you want to see—the only person who makes you forget all about the hard things. It's listening, sharing, talking, and laughing. It's comfortable and easy. It's feeling like you belong. Does that make sense? I know I'm babbling."

He laughed, a loud guttural laugh from the belly and continued. "I know I already said this, but love feels like a choice because you get to choose to be there for your person and it sort of feels like an honor that you get to."

Choose to be there for your person...

More than anything, if she had a choice, Zora would always choose Mike. "Yeah, I know what you mean."

But would he choose me?

Zora finished putting the food in the fridge and now she was propped against the stainless-steel door in utter awe. God, she wanted Mike's version of love. Everett and Sophia had it, and they couldn't explain it to her. Grandma Babs described love as a gift, but she didn't give many details. But the way Mike explained it? She was speechless. She wanted someone to choose *her* like that.

Mike peeked over his shoulder at her. "Too deep?"

Her heart did a little lurch and she scrubbed her fingers over her face and through her hair.

How am I going to explain this to him?

She was breathless. Her mouth was wide open and she literally could not close it. He took her breath away. "No. That was so beautiful, Mike," she hummed. Her brows traveled somewhere near her hairline. "I'm so jealous over here."

This got an adorable giggle out of him and satisfaction bloomed in Zora's belly because she was the one who caused it.

"We're going to dial this back. A lot." Mike rinsed the last fork and set it on the drying rack. He turned and positioned himself against the sink with one foot up against the cabinet door. He had an easy posture and a beaming smile as he gave her a slow once-over from head to toe and up again until his gaze settled on hers.

Have mercy. She wanted to run her teeth over his bottom lip.

"You like to see me squirm, so I'm going to return the favor. I'm not talking about hookups, but sex is part of love, so tell me, how many times have you made love?"

Zora did not squirm or nervously bite her lip. To her credit, she did not bite his either. Like Mike she undressed him with her eyes then centered a confident gaze on him. By his definition, there was no question in her mind.

"Once."

CHAPTER 30

MIKE

Once.

Mike repeated Zora's answer in his mind and it rocked him to his core. He was holding his breath. She'd only *made love* once while he'd been with dozens of women. Although, only once did it mean anything to him, either.

He badly wanted to know if he was her definitive once—if their one night a million moons ago had meant as much to her as it did to him. Maybe it was just this morning or last week, any of the times that had left him yearning for only her touch.

Still, he couldn't bring himself to ask for fear of what her answer might be. He didn't know if he could take it if he wasn't to her once.

Mike pushed himself off the counter and raked his hands through his hair. He was in a hurry to get out of the room. The walls had never felt so close. He had never been so aware of his heart's rebellion against his mind. He didn't think he could bear any other truth.

He weaved out of the kitchen into the dining room and

toward his bedroom, stopping just at the door. "It's Friday. Movie, couch, popcorn, ten minutes?" He lifted a brow in question. "We'll finish the game?" He meant to turn and walk away then, but every nerve ending in his body tingled and his pulse quickened. His heartbeat pounded in his chest.

Just say it.

Zora was still leaned against the refrigerator staring at him, waiting. Her eyes pinned him in place.

When he spoke, his voice was gravelly and foreign to his own ears. "I…love you, Zora."

He was still holding his breath, not believing what he'd just said. In the back of his mind, he'd imagined saying the words somewhere romantic and candlelit with their hands clasped and a ring burning in the breast pocket of his suit jacket. Somehow, this was so much better. He was living with the woman who starred in his dreams. She was everything he could ever want in a woman and more. A long time ago, she took up residence in his heart and never left. Defining what the word love meant to him only helped him realize what exactly it was he'd been feeling all these years.

"I…" Zora's mouth opened and closed. Her eyes were impossibly wide as a slow smile grew on her face. The blush on her cheeks deepened. "I…I love you, too." The words came out slow and carefully, like she needed him to hear her clearly.

He'd heard her loud and clear, because warmth flooded his insides and he was riding on a tide of pure elation.

The way she eyed him without moving, Mike was back there in the cellar. He remembered it clear as if it were yesterday, how she looked at him as she clutched the thin fabric of his shirt. She was trembling and shaken, shame glistened in her eyes. He'd wanted to tell her then.

They'd made love.

Or, at least that's what Mike thought it was until she'd sat up rigidly, breathing heavily. Her hair was down to her shoulders then, and the rays of sun had drawn streaks of gold through her ebony curls and highlighted glowing circles over her bare shoulders. When the light hit her eyes, he noticed the tears welled in them.

"Are you all right?" he'd asked stupidly, but she only nodded unconvincingly, and at the time, he couldn't yet figure what it meant. He wasn't sure whether they'd been tears of the same joy he felt or sadness over her mother. He suspected it was a mix of both. They were sharing their highest high and her lowest low, but he was grateful that he got to be there for her. In some small way, he'd saved her from something. He didn't know what at the time, but maybe being together had sealed a tiny fracture in her broken heart.

It was love then.

And it was the same love now.

Mike's heated gaze took in the sight of Zora's silken brown skin and the happy tears in her eyes now. Regret bloomed in his chest as his cock hardened. All these years, and he'd never once told her how he felt.

His heart ached to be near her, and this time he wasn't going to let her go. He rushed to Zora and covered her lips with his. The kiss was urgent and hurried, steeped in all the promises he would make to her as soon as he could find the strength to tear his lips away.

"I love you, Zora Marie Monroe," he said again, just to taste it on his tongue. "I want us to have this every day. I want to be with you, live with you, and share my life with you. If you cook, I'll clean. I'll be your taste-tester," he said excitedly in between kisses. "There's no joy in my life without you in it."

He lifted her into his arms and she straddled her legs around his waist, peppering kisses all over his face.

"I don't know how I could say no to you doing the dishes."

She bit her bottom lip and he felt giddy. His spirits soared, and excitement raced through him. Then, just in case he wasn't one hundred percent sure how Zora felt about him, she sealed it.

She bent her mouth to his ear and whispered, "I want to make love to you again."

CHAPTER 31

ZORA

Zora had just placed the charcuterie board of assorted brie, dried fruit, and snack bites on the table when she heard the click of the key turn in the lock.

"Surprise!"

Zora and Mike flashed wide smiles as they strained to hold the "Welcome Home" banner above their heads. Blue shot toward the front door. They'd spent the last few hours in the amazingly unfumigated, termite- and wood rot-free living room of Patton Place getting ready for Everett and Sophia's return.

She squealed as they came into the arch of the hallway. She dropped her end of the banner and went in for hugs. Blue went crazy. His tail wagged as he jumped up onto Everett.

"I'm so glad you guys are back. I missed you so much." Zora's eyes playfully narrowed, and she met Sophia's sheepish smile.

Sophia winced and squinted one eye shut. "Yeah...about that..."

"It's all good. We know matchmaking and meddling runs in

your crazy family," Zora teased Sophia. "How is my little niece or nephew?" She rubbed Sophia's round belly thinking how much she couldn't wait to bury her face in a sweet, soft baby belly and blow raspberry bubbles just to hear the baby coo and giggle.

"Growing at an uncomfortable rate." Sophia absently rested her hands on her hips and blew out a labored breath. "Tired."

A wave of emotions washed over Zora. She hadn't been aware just how much, but now, having Everett and Sophia back, she realized just how much she'd missed them. It was relief that they were home safe and hadn't eloped without her there to bear witness to the life they were building. They hadn't shut her out. She still got to be a part of all of it.

Zora and Mike switched, and she hugged her brother while Mike folded his arms gently around Sophia, careful of the bump.

Mike's expression softened. "How are you and the baby doing?"

"Welp. He or she's still in there." Sophia shrugged.

"Hey, Ev." Zora squeezed him into a bear hug complete with a grizzly grunt, but she pulled apart just in time to see him glare at Mike.

"Um…what was that?"

"Hey." His tone was level and too even.

She'd expected the same jovial reception she'd gotten when she spoke to him on the phone. Maybe even for him to be giddy and gloating after getting the setup over on her, but, nope. Nothing. He was noticeably quiet as he lugged his and Sophia's bags into the foyer.

"Seriously, that's all you're going to say? You guys have been gone for like almost a month—after a rather shifty lie, mind you—and all you've got to say is 'hey?'" Zora folded her arms, cocked her head, and lifted a perfectly arched brow at him.

Everett sighed and continued lining their bags along the wall. Clearly, he was going to be childish and clam up, so Zora turned to Sophia.

"What's up with him? Why is he all bent out of shape now?" She reached down to muss Blue's fur. He seemed to sense the tension.

"Well…" Her eyes darted to Everett's which were wide with warning.

Zora flicked a glance between them, then over to Mike, who had slinked back into the living room and sat on the couch with his elbows on his knees, fingers steepled beneath his chin. After seeing the *I'll just stay over here out of the way* look on Mike's face, Zora registered the annoying reality of the situation.

Un-be-lievable.

"You have got to be fucking kidding me. Are you two really going to act childish, like you haven't been friends forever or lied to each other before?"

"Stay out of it, Zo?" Everett's deep, nerve-shredding bass pinballed off the walls.

"No. I will not stay out of it."

Everett cracked his neck as if settling in for the long haul.

"This is about shady-ass Harrison Arnold, who you know is a straight-up pompous, out-for-himself clown. You're going to let him come between you and Mike, who has been your best friend since day one and who always has your back?" Zora was fuming. Heat rushed up from her neck to her cheeks. She was shaking she was so pissed. "You need to check yourself, Ev."

She watched as he set a suitcase down without saying a word and locked the front door before turning on his heel back toward the living room where Sophia and Mike were seated for the show. This was classic Everett—stubborn and hard-headed with his silent treatments and superiority complex. He always thought he was right. *Ugh*. Zora knew this was Mike's battle, but her brother had gotten way too high up on his judgmental horse and she planned to bring him back down to earth.

"You think because Babs left you in charge, you're the only one who knows anything?" Zora inhaled and held her palm in the air because, Lord, she was seeing red.

This conversation had been a long time coming.

"FYI I still own fifty percent of Monroe Properties. Maybe it didn't occur to you that Mike *did* consult an owner of the company before he did what was best for it, and for us. *I* told him Arnold wasn't someone we should partner with. *I* agreed with him that declining the deal was in the best interest of *our* company. *You're* the only one who makes unilateral decisions around here." Zora folded her arms and stared pointedly at her brother.

The corners of Everett's mouth tugged downward as he bobbed his head. "Got it. Zora's in charge."

Typical. Way to deflect.

"Nope. I'm not going to let you make this about me. Why don't you just say what you have to say instead of being a dick about it?"

She watched as he cracked his neck again, and she could see the thin, tight lines forming around his mouth. He nodded, not in agreement with her, but seemingly adding it all up in his head and preparing for his eventual and delayed comeback. He never was any good with the zingers.

"Yeah, stand there and brood while you conjure up something to be mad about. Real nice, Ev. Mike blew up a freaking dozen balloons and helped me make that damn banner. We come here to welcome you guys back, and this is how you treat us?" She shook her head. "Asshole."

"*I'm* the asshole?" Everett asked, stupidly with a confused grin plastered on his face. "Are you sure you're not talking to Mike?"

"Yes, you. Don't drag him into this."

Zora grabbed her purse and stalked over to take Mike's hand before turning back to her brother. "You really are a piece of work. Just so you know, I hate the person you're becoming."

She was halfway down the hall when she swiveled around and took her last shot. "Oh, and just in case you were wondering…your little setup worked. Mike and I are together. I'm so glad you asked how things have been going around here."

The angry tears welled up in her eyes and she could only shake her head to keep from falling apart.

"Stay, Blue," she commanded.

As she reached the door, Mike pulled her to him. "I can't let you do this. This is your brother, your family. I'm not going to stand in the way. Everett and I will talk about it soon, but I don't want you getting stuck in the middle of all of this." With the pads of his thumbs, he wiped away her tears and softly brushed his lips against hers.

"I love you," she whispered, squeezing her eyes closed to keep the tears at bay. "You're my family, too."

"I love you, too. Now let's go back in there. I'll just…keep my mouth shut." He pulled his bottom lip between his teeth and a lopsided grin tugged at the corners of his mouth.

With her hand in his, she turned and let him lead her back into the living room where Everett was helping Sophia remove her jacket and shoes.

"If you want to keep arguing, you can just go," Everett said without turning to look at them. "This is exactly why we left. She doesn't need this kind of stress."

Stubbornly, Zora refused to look at him either, but she did feel kind of bad. "I'm sorry, Soph." *Not you, Ev.* As she dropped Mike's hand, she made her way over to the hors d'oeuvres.

"Why don't you have a little something to eat? I made those parmesan-crusted chicken bites you like, and there's cheese, grapes, dried apricots…all for you."

A wide grin spread across Sophia's face. "You know the way to my heart is definitely through my stomach."

For twenty minutes, there was peace in Patton Place. They talked about Everett and Sophia's not-so-secret trip to Vegas where they visited her mom most of the time, but Everett splurged for a week on The Strip. Sophia's eyes lit up as she talked about their poolside days and casino nights, shopping and eating at five-star restaurants. She insisted the trip actually did help her decompress from life's worries until Everett heard about the deal on the Chessington building going bust.

At this point in the story, Zora scooted closer to Mike and set a hand on his thigh in warning not to comment. But, of course, Everett couldn't leave well enough alone.

"You know, last week after I talked to Mike, I got another phone call," he said.

Zora bit the inside of her cheek and tilted her head slightly as she listened. Her nerves were jittery and she could feel the fire lighting her fuse. Instead of asking who the call was from like she figured her brother was baiting her to do, she winded her hand in circles urging him to keep the story moving.

"From what I understand, though he might be a 'pompous, out-for-himself clown' as you put it, Arnold kept his feelers out for me, and I'm glad he did. It seems my best friend and your… roommate?" His brows lifted in question as he glared at Zora then turned his stare on Mike. "He went and found himself another job offer at Baker & Bronson with his good friend, Jason. Is that right Mike? Did I cover all the high points?"

Zora swallowed and sat up straighter. "What?" She slid Mike a guarded look, her heartbeat slowing to a hollow thud. "You took it?"

She'd known about the offer, but not in a million years did she ever think Mike would take it.

"Yeah, while you were urging him to cancel the deal because Arnold had the nerve to consider another offer on the table, your boy was hedging his own bets." A smug smirk twisted Everett's face. "If I wouldn't make him partner, he was just going to leave anyway and weasel his way to the top at another company. He's got all his bases covered."

Zora sat completely still as she let her brother's words sink in. For the briefest second, she looked at Mike. She was shaking her head. His green eyes were dark and pleading.

What. The. Fuck?

Mike was saying something, but she didn't hear a word he said. In the moment, her heartbeat pounded in her ears and she couldn't catch her breath. She was under water and the only other sound was the soft whoosh of her breath hitching and tearing itself out of her.

Suddenly, her mind waded through her conversations with Mike and skidded to a halt on one they'd had last Monday. That morning in the hallway, she'd been so blinded by the sight of him in a towel she brushed right over it.

Jason calls me this morning and says his firm wants to hire me.

She had naively let her guard down and let go when she should have been holding on with all of her might. This was exactly what she was worried about—being with a man who never stopped thinking about himself long enough to appreciate what was right in front of him. No matter how hard she tried, it seemed she was bound to fall to the same fate of the Monroe women before her: staying too long at the party.

How could I be so stupid? How could I not see this coming?

Zora knew all about ambition and drive, wanting more, wanting to be valued as an equal. She didn't fault Mike for challenging himself. The same force pushed her when it came to her cookbook and making a future for herself. It was okay not to want to be dependent. What wasn't okay was lying about it, even if it was by omission. He had every opportunity to tell her the truth, but he'd let her find out like this.

She was blindsided. She'd opened up to him and let him all the way in, but Mike didn't trust her enough to do the same.

Tears pricked at Zora's eyes and she chewed on her bottom lip, heat crawling up her neck as she figured her next move. She could feel the wall erecting around her heart, closing up again, when Mike's voice broke through the fog.

"You have to believe me. I was never going to take it. I was just—"

"Just what?" Her sharp and shaky voice shot through the silence. Rage swept over her. Her temples throbbed. Her body locked up. "Making sure all your ducks were in a row? Forgetting what it means to be loyal? Leaving me out of the loop? You were never going to give Ev the chance to really think about it. You were too busy working on your own backup plan."

"No. It wasn't like that."

"It sounds exactly like that."

He was no different than Harrison Arnold. No different than Joseph.

Mike was going to replace them just like Joseph replaced Mom. Eva Monroe had stayed with him and lost everything that made her amazing. She lost her greatest gift: her life. If Zora stayed with Mike, she'd inevitably lose herself, too.

"I can't do this," she said.

Mike recoiled. His moss green eyes went round before he scrubbed his hands over his face and shook his head. "No. Jason did make an offer, but I never asked him to," he reasoned as if saying so would make it all better and they could go back to the way things were five minutes earlier. "Yes. I do want to be working toward something bigger, a new challenge, but not if means losing you again. Zo, I can't lose you again."

His brows snapped together and he bent down in front of Zora, begging, urging her to listen to reason, to not let the good thing they had go so easily, but she already knew better.

"You know something?" Her voice was even and she could feel heat burning at her cheeks. "I got caught up in the same dream, but that's all it is, a dream. That's all it ever was. This… you and me, was only temporary. We were playing house, but none it was real."

She got to her feet and smoothed her clothes, tugging her jacket tight before meeting Mike's gaze.

"We're all wrong for each other. It's time I let go of the memory of what we had once." Zora swiped at her tears and walked toward the door. She needed to get out the house and the closed, tight space.

Space.

She didn't have a plan, but at least Zora knew her first step. She needed to get out of Mike's house.

CHAPTER 32

MIKE

Mike didn't think twice about running after Zora. He wasn't going to let her let go again. If he had to, he would hold on for the both of them. And that's just what he did. He begged her for hours and held her tight in his arms through the night.

The next morning, Mike's eyes shot open at the sound of a car door closing, and he didn't have to move to know.

Zora was gone.

His heart was in his throat and his chest tightened because he knew it was for good this time. Still, fear twisted in his gut as he searched the house. He walked from room to room calling her name. His voice was agonizing to his own ears as he slammed doors and circled the perimeter of the house.

But everything was gone.

The porch light was still on. The road was shrouded in a thick mist, and in the stillness, he could hear crickets chirping. Mike was out front of his house still on his hands and knees on the wet paved walkway unsure whether it was night or day. He sat back on his legs, his chest tightening as he watched the reflection of the sky in a puddle.

One by one, raindrops fell to the same beat of the lawn sprinkler, perfuming the air with the scent of wet grass and pine trees.

"You all right over there? Can I help you with anything?" A male voice snapped Mike out of his revelry as he searched for the source.

"Yeah. Yes, I'm okay." His eyes followed the voice over to the house on his right. He didn't live in one of those master-planned communities where all the houses looked exactly alike. The build was also contemporary, but his neighbor's house looked a little more lived-in with a sofa set out on the curb and a red wagon on the front lawn.

Mike was struggling to get to his feet when he noticed an older man in worn jeans and a flannel tucked in at his protruding waistline. Despite the drizzle and the sprinklers, he wore only sturdy boots and a beat-up Vietnam Veteran cap with its embroidered insignia on the front panel.

He'd met him once briefly but couldn't recall his name at the moment. It was mostly during comings and goings that Mike saw the man, but he'd never stopped to talk to him before.

"I just…" Mike couldn't bring himself to speak about what was really happening.

Leaves crunched underfoot as he walked the few steps over to his neighbor's dusty pickup truck. Up close, the man's features, normally hidden under his cap, came into view. Tawny, pockmarked skin and kind sunny brown eyes beamed back at Mike. He had gnarled knuckles, a staunch capable frame, and he looked like one of those guys who'd never shied away from getting his hands dirty a day in his life. If there was a job to be done, you wouldn't have to ask this guy twice.

"Did you lose something?" he asked in a hearty, downhome voice.

The irony was not lost on Mike, and a small laugh escaped him. He *had* lost something…or, rather, *someone*. He couldn't help wondering, when he was searching on the wet pavement and in the shallow puddles, did he look lost? He guessed on his knees was where he needed to be—with his hands pressed together in prayer if he wanted Zora back.

Vaguely, he noticed the truck's motor was still running. "I don't want to keep you."

"Oh, it's all right. I'm just letting the oil work its way through its veins." The man jutted his chin to the truck.

Mike peeked up at the weathered cap. "Uh…thank you for your service, sir."

"Oh…well, you're welcome, but…" He waved his hand in the air as he dipped his chin, pushing the topic away. "I did my duty to this great country a long time ago." He stopped himself there, and there seemed a question was weaving its way through his mind.

Mike tilted his head, his ears ready for whatever wisdom he might impart.

"What did you do?" his neighbor asked.

Mike stared blankly. "I'm sorry. I don't know what you mean."

"What happened with your lady friend? I mostly keep to myself unless my daughter and my grandson come to visit, but I look out for my neighbors, whether they've asked me to or not. The way I see it, if she's not out here with you, she left. Good women don't leave unless we've fouled up somehow. So, what did you do?"

A nervous smile quirked at Mike's lips.

"Is it really that obvious?"

"At the end of the day, we're just different than they are," his neighbor said. "They know right off the bat what they want and go after it, full force. We, on the other hand, tend to take our time figuring out what we want and put off going after it until we've lost it." Crinkles formed around the edges of his eyes as he smiled. "I've seen the other ones you brought around, and they didn't have you on your hands and knees. If it doesn't feel like you're dying a slow, torturous death on the inside, she's not worth all the trouble."

Mike matched his neighbor's raucous laugh because there was no denying the man was right.

"When it's real love, the person who makes you feel like you're dying is the only one who can make you feel like you're finally living. Don't let her get away, Son."

Mike released a chest full of air, nodded rapidly, and shook his neighbor's rough hand with both of his, assuring him he planned to heed his advice. On the inside, he felt butterflies that seemed to be hopped up on meth. Anxiety swirled around him, and his stomach knotted as fear twisted his gut.

It wasn't a question of *if* he was going to try to get Zora back, but *how.*

If he was going to do this, it wasn't going to be some weak profession of his love and empty promises. Where were the dramatics in that? *When* he groveled for her, he needed to be on his knees. He needed to dig in and get his hands dirty.

Or maybe, hold up a boom box and find a pair diamond earrings.

CHAPTER 33

ZORA

Bright, and far too early, Zora stood on the curb taking in the site of her new home. She was at the final walk-through armed with an inspection checklist and a decades-long dream of home ownership. She'd attended these pre-closing walks a few dozen times with Monroe Properties when Grandma Babs was teaching her and Everett the ropes, but this was different. Buying this house meant Zora was driving her own life.

Even if at the moment, she'd rather let someone else take the wheel.

"If you see anything at all—a crack, unfinished paint—anything, not to worry," Steven, the builder superintendent said. "That can all be fixed. I want you to just rip off a piece of this blue tape and stick it right on."

Does it work for hearts too?

The world felt like it was spinning, and all she could think about was the hollow ache in her chest. The past two weeks back at Patton Place had broken her. Every night without Mike felt like she was drowning in grief. Her body was leaden, and her insides were shredded. Now, she was just...numb.

Why couldn't broken hearts be fixed so easily?

"Okay, great," she said.

Steven might have been a middle-aged guy with far too much energy so early in the morning, but, apparently, he was in tune with people. He patted a gentle hand on Zora's shoulder and looked into her eyes. He must have noticed her splotchy skin and puffy face and seen the sadness, but he was decent enough not to mention it.

His tone was soothing when he spoke to her. "Still tired? I know it's early, *but...*" Just that quickly, the chipper singsong tone was back in his voice. "I can have Paula bring down a cup of coffee if you want. That might get the wake-up train going."

Zora forced a smile. "Yeah, I'm just...still sleepy." A nervous laugh escaped her. "It's fine. I'm fine."

She imagined her spastic nerves were showing all over her face. As far back as she could remember, she'd wanted to buy a new home with money she'd earned herself. Now she was actually doing it. She should have been bouncing off the freshly painted walls with pride and contagious joy. Her chin should be high at the idea of uplifting the legacy of generations of Monroe women, but Zora couldn't get past the bitter sweetness that overshadowed her milestone.

Here was this amazing house just waiting for her, but all she wanted was go back home. Mike's home.

"All righty, then. Let's get to it," Steven said.

She wandered into the first of two spare bedrooms on the first floor, one of which she planned to use as her office. The thought blew her mind, and for a moment, she wondered what her mom and Grandma Babs would think if they saw her. How proud would they be to see her going from neighborhood lemonade stands to published author with a house she'd purchased outright.

Pride filled her, and she blinked away the tears welling in her eyes.

"It's amazing isn't it?" Steven asked. "Nothing like buying your first home. It's humbling."

Yes, it is.

Zora tossed an easy smile at Steven who was standing at the door before turning back to the window.

"I love it." Zora stood in the center of the room for a moment and just breathed. Outside, the day was clear, and the trees seemed to be dancing with the daylight to the tune of birds chirping. If she was going do the work of getting over Mike, she couldn't think of a better place to do it. The house was quiet and soothing to her wayward soul.

It was going to be work settling in, though. Every vision she had of herself traipsing through the house cooking, reading, or sprawled out on her sofa watching movies reminded her of Mike. In every scenario, she wanted him sitting right there with her.

If only she could trust him.

She couldn't, though. He'd proven himself a coward and a liar, and she couldn't go down the same road her mother went.

"You know, this model is one of my favorites," Steven said. "I really love the window seat option. It's perfect for a reading corner or if you just want to sit and have your morning coffee while you watch the sun come up and contemplate all of life's mysteries." Steven sighed, but it was exactly what Zora had been imagining.

She had no clue how she'd ended up back here, broken-hearted and grasping for light in the darkness. Ever since that day back in Grandma Babs's cellar when she'd let Mike go, she had hoped that if they did find their way back to each other, it would be for good—the whole, "if you love something, set it free" theory. Love would find a way. If he came back to her, it meant they were supposed to be together.

Hope was a dangerous thing.

Now, more than ever, she knew those hopes were only to be relegated to fairytales.

It wasn't real.

It was time to grow up. Zora wasn't going to lose herself. She wasn't going to give up. Even if it meant going it alone.

"Sounds amazing," she said.

It did.

Over the rest of the walk-through, Zora went about opening and closing doors and drawers, turning on faucets, and flipping light switches throughout the house. She checked every window, flushed toilets, and even let the chill from the refrigerator wash a calming cool over her face. The beautiful, spacious, and clean house was going be her reprieve from the outside world. She imagined good, restless sleep in a too-big bed, cooking meals for one, and one day becoming the independent grown-up she'd always dreamt of being.

The only problem with growing up was letting go of childhood dreams.

CHAPTER 34

MIKE

Seventeen days.

Exactly. Mike was counting the days, the hours, the minutes, the seconds, and even the breaths since Zora left him. All of his messages and calls went straight to voicemail. He didn't dare go back to Patton Place since his relationship with Everett was still on thin ice. He'd even tried Olivia, but she made it plain she was Team Zora, and it was no use trying to convince her that despite his actions, he was too.

"Kendra," Mike called from his office. *For now, at least.*

She edged into the doorway and sagged against the frame, pressing her hand to her heart as if it pained her to see him. "Yes," she said, her tone soft and low with way too much pity drizzled over it.

"Can you not?"

"Not, what sweetheart?"

Mike swiveled in his chair to face her and there it was. The mirror reflecting back at him. "Listen, I'm good. I know you've probably been asked not to say anything about me and Zora, but I know you know, so you can stop treating me like I might crumble into a million pieces." He shrugged and tossed his hands up as he leaned back against the chair, clasping them behind his head. "Honestly, yes, I'm hurt, but she doesn't want me, so I have to move on, too. I'm just going to keep my head down and do the job I was hired to do, but, honestly, I don't even know if Ev is going to keep me around much longer."

Kendra tossed a glance over her shoulder before edging all the way into the room. Quietly, conspiratorially she shut the door behind her. "What's the plan?" she asked in a hushed tone.

"What plan? I just told you I'm going to keep working until he gives me the boot, I guess. Then I'll figure out what my other options are."

She sucked her teeth loudly.

"Okay, I heard that."

With her hands planted on her hips, she twisted her mouth into a smirk. "Mmm. Mmm. Mmm." That sound was motherly and filled with attitude. It was a telltale sign that Mike was in for some schooling and quite possibly a neck roll-eye roll combo.

Mike sighed and sunk into the seat. "What? Ev's barely strung together two words for me. It's not like things are exactly working in my favor. I asked him if he wants me to quit, but...nothing. He won't even talk to me."

A finger wagged in front of his face and he lifted his chin to see a "shame on you" look on Kendra's face.

"Michael. Dwayne. Kennedy. Here I thought you were growing up and finally growing a pair. Come to find out you ain't shit. You ain't gon' be shit. You ain't about shit."

Seriously?

Mike cocked his head in disbelief because he hadn't been on the receiving end of this kind of scolding since his mother stayed at his place a couple of years ago and found his porn stash. It was shocking and downright embarrassing, but his mother had nothing on this woman.

"Dang, Kendra."

"Don't 'dang' me. If I recall correctly, you and I sat down at that conference room table together, and you told me you were in love."

He scrubbed a hand over his face because this was some bullshit. He didn't have time for I-told-you-sos.

Kendra's brows were raised, daring Mike to refute a word she'd said. She waited, and when she seemed satisfied that he let her have the floor, she continued. "I distinctly remember you saying Zora was your only chance at love…" The words hung out there in the air, loaded and heavy as she tilted her ear to him.

Before he spoke, he waited for a second to make sure she wasn't going to jump down his throat again. "May I?" he asked tentatively, flashing her questioning eyes.

When he saw her slight nod, he paused and pressed his fingers together in a steeple beneath his chin.

"I said it, but I also said the only family I've ever known, my best friend, and my job were at risk. All of my chips are in, and by the looks of things, obviously the bet didn't pay off."

"So that's it?"

Mike sighed and let his head rest against the chair. "Unless you have another idea… I've been wracking my brain trying to figure out how to get to her, but so far, I've been coming up empty." He blew out a frustrated breath because he wanted to be with Zora as much as Kendra apparently wanted them to be. "I'm going to do *something*. I just don't know what yet."

"Welp…it's April. Spring *is* the time for change and new beginnings," she said.

His mind went straight to flowers, strolls in the park, and bike rides—all things he could do with Zora, but, none of them were grand enough. Whatever the brilliant plan was, it had to be on a big scale with a lot of heart. It couldn't be about him and proving himself. It had to be about Zora. He wanted to prove he'd changed and that he was worthy of a new beginning with her.

"Yep," he agreed.

For a minute, Mike thought he'd finally appealed to Kendra's senses. She was sort of standing there, staring past him, unseeing. Then, she just snapped to, shook her head, and turned on her heel toward the door. She stopped only to flick Mike on the side of the head.

"Think. She's not going to sit around waiting on you to get your shit together forever." With that, she swung the door open and whipped through it, letting the handle slam into the wall with a loud crack.

If he hadn't been before, Mike was officially awake.

By the end of the workday, he was mentally exhausted. Somehow, he'd managed to do the bare minimum work-wise, but he *was* tired of wracking his brain then finally searching "grand gestures to win back the love of your life" on the Internet and still coming up empty-handed. Mike finally conceded that his crisis might not be solvable.

Desperate times would indeed call for desperate measures.

F orty-five minutes later, he stood on the dock at the marina with his phone pressed to his ear and wind whipping through his clothes.

"Tell someone to put down the boarding ramp," he instructed over the phone.

"What are we getting into tonight?" Jason answered.

Muffled movement sounded in Mike's ear, then he noticed

Jason above him on the deck.

"Oh, shit. You're here. Hold on a sec." Jason ended the call, but Mike could still hear him as he yelled for someone to set up the ramp.

It only took a few minutes, but once Mike was onboard, he made quick work of loosening his tie and losing his jacket and shoes. He sat on the lounger and stretched his legs out in front of him, but he wasn't relaxed.

"All right, brother, you want to tell me what's happening? Are you here to reconsider the position with Baker & Bronson because the offer still stands."

Mike sighed. "No. I'm still passing on that, but thank you." He inhaled and began again. "You're gonna love this...I need your help."

Jason turned and scooted to the edge of his seat. "Holy shit. It's that bad?"

Despite the pity party vibe, Mike smiled. "I know."

"Okay, then. Lay it on me. What do you need?"

For the next fifteen minutes, Mike recapped everything that had transpired between him and Zora since her party at the silent disco up until she left him two and half weeks ago. He told Jason about sleeping in the guestroom on that hard ass mattress because he couldn't sleep in his own bed anymore without her. He told him about the high points of his conversation with Kendra and how Everett had basically ghosted him from his life. He even told him that he was one hundred percent sure he was in love with Zora.

Somewhere in the middle of the recap, it hit him.

Mike ran a finger over his top lip, and the corners of his mouth tugged upward. "J? Do you still have that connection with the Hollywood Theatre?"

"Yeah, why? You think of something?"

"Mm-hmm."

CHAPTER 35

ZORA

"Hey, y'all."

Zora let herself in at Patton Place, dropping her purse and keys on the entry table. When she looked up, she noticed all the house lights were turned on and one of Sophia's shoes was scattered on the floor.

"Um…" She cocked her head back to peek into the formal dining room at her right then to the left into the office. "Blue?"

What the heck are these fools doing?

"Guys?"

She took a couple of steps and paused again. Her heartbeat sped up as she flitted her gaze around the room. She hated the way worry knocked around in her chest. It was enough to send her mind whirling into worst-case scenarios. All she could think about was Sophia lying on the floor somewhere holding her belly. For the sake of her poor antsy heart, Zora took a deep breath to calm herself.

"See, this is how people get ulcers and wrinkles. Don't jump to conclusions…" she mumbled to herself as she blew out a breath, but it didn't keep her mind from wading into memories of her mother on the bathroom floor. She'd always thought that if she'd gotten there a few minutes sooner, things might be different.

Once more, she peered down the hallway toward the kitchen, biting her the tip of her nail.

"Shit. Soph—"

Above her, Zora heard the creak of floorboards and her eyes shot up, relief flooding her insides.

"Zo, is that you?" Ev called.

What's he doing here on a Thursday in the middle of the day?

"Yeah, I'm back. I'm just stopping by to check on Soph and the baby."

There was silence for a bit followed by footsteps at the stairs. Zora inched closer to the rail as her brother and Sophia appeared at the landing. As soon as she took in Everett's disheveled boxers and tee and Sophia's teensy terrycloth robe straining at her bare middle, she was more than a little embarrassed.

Shit. Shit. Shit. Shit. Shit. "Uh…I'll just come back."

Zora whipped around and grabbed her stuff off the table and headed toward the door, but Everett was on her heels.

"Hold it. Hold it. Wait," he said, grabbing her shoulder and turning her around.

"I'm sorry." Zora squeezed her eyes closed, wincing. "I didn't realize you guys were—" She cut herself off, completely mortified that she'd interrupted their afternoon delight. Which she was sure was already a difficult task given the size of Sophia's baby bump.

Ew, don't think about your brother having sex.

Zora shook her head trying to knock the thought loose.

When she'd thought about paying them a visit, she figured it would be some girl talk while she helped Sophia with her hospital bag. Maybe she'd have a glass of wine to celebrate finally submitting the cookbook, and *casually* bring up Mike. *So much for that.*

"It's fine. You know you're always welcome in this house, but what are you doing here, Zo?" Everett asked. "You have a brand-new house of your own."

"Yeah, I just told you I was checking on Soph and the baby." Her shoulders were practically up to her ears as she held up her palms. *Can't a girl visit her pregnant sister-to-be…again?*

Everett held her by the shoulders at arm's length as he scrutinized her.

"What?" she asked, unsure whether she really wanted to know what he was thinking.

At that moment, Sophia chose to edge her way into the mix. "Zo?"

"Yesss?" Zora dragged the word out. She noticed the way both of them were angled toward her. Their heads were cocked and lowered, studying her as if they were weighing the consequences of going down a particular road.

Then, a wide, smile spread over Sophia's face and she pointed a finger at Zora. "Ooh. I know what you're doing!" she accused.

"Just what exactly do you think you know?"

"I know, too. I was just thinking that," Everett added.

Zora, who'd had just about enough of the deranged situation wiggled free from her brother's arms and walked around them, marching toward the kitchen. They shuffled behind her still oohing and ahhing about something or other.

"Something is really wrong with you two. I'm not doing anything but trying to be a good sister and aunt and coming to check on you. You've been under a lot of stress, so I'm worried about you." She threw her hands up and twirled around to shoot them an eyeroll before plopping down on a barstool. "So, sue me."

The conspiracy theorists planted themselves in front of Zora, crossing their arms. Sophia did not avoid direct eye contact. In fact, she picked up on Everett's cue and pointed a pudgy finger near Zora's face.

"Three visits in one week," she said, her lips twisting into a smirk. "I'm still doing the same as I was yesterday. Nothing's changed. So, either you've become a hypochondriac overnight, or, I suspect you're really spending all your time here to avoid something at home...or something *not* at home."

She eyed Zora over the top of her brows, smugly.

No harm in plausible deniability.

"You're crazy. Both of you. Now it's a crime to visit my family three times in a week? Would it be better if I only came once or twice? Would that make me less crazy?"

Sophia and Everett shared a meaningful glance, and then they nodded.

"Bingo." Sophia tap a finger to the tip of her nose.

"Mm-hmm. Deflection. You said she'd deny it," Everett murmured.

Zora could not believe what they were saying. Not that it wasn't true, but they were talking about her like she wasn't even there. "I'm sitting right here," she pouted.

"Good. Maybe you'll get your head out of the clouds and stop acting like nothing bothers you," Everett said.

"Shut up, Ev." Zora averted gaze and swiveled around, propping her elbows up on the granite island. At this point, it did seem rather stupid to keep denying it. *I mean, if I can't talk to my family about Mike then who can I talk to?*

Sophia waddled around the counter, apparently pleased with her interrogation tactics. *She was good.* She pulled a loaf of bread out of the stainless-steel breadbox, and peeked over at Zora. A half-smile toyed at her lips. "You hungry?"

Zora released a heavy sigh and propped her head up on a fist. "Yeah. What are you cooking?"

Everett inched past Sophia, grazing the small of her back with a gentle hand as he popped into the pantry. They were so adorable and loving toward each other. What they had was exactly what Zora wanted with Mike. The uncomplicated easiness of a loving touch, the rock-solid team ready for whatever the world threw at them... They were the kids of the eighties movies grown up. *After* the hot guy waited outside the church leaning on a candy apple-red corvette. *After* Baby was firmly and freely out of the corner. After the music and the big finale kiss.

Zora knew love was about making a life after the grand gesture. *In Some Kind of Wonderful,* even after Keith arranged that incredible evening, Amanda Jones figured out she didn't want to "be with someone for the wrong reasons" anymore. Zora smiled because, deep down, she knew that she didn't want to be without Mike for the wrong reasons. Mike was her Watts.

Sophia's giggle snapped Zora out of her trance. "What?"

"Oh, nothing. I just said I'm not cooking. I'm making peanut butter and jelly sandwiches. Want one?"

"Yeah. I'll have one. Extra jelly, though."

Everett cleared his throat and Zora could tell they were over there sharing some inside joke about her. "You're cheesing hard over there," he said.

"Whatever, Ev." Zora adjusted herself in the seat and attempted to be preoccupied by a document sitting on the counter. Then, she actually read it. "Is this about the Chessington building?"

He slid a cup of milk and a plate with a diagonally cut sandwich across the island to her then took an enormous bite out of his own PB&J. A glob of jelly appeared in the corner of his mouth.

"You'll never believe what I found out," he said, swiping at the glob with his tongue. "In a strange twist of events, turns out old Arnold *is* a shyster."

"What, it just sounds better when you say it? Mike and I already told you that. What clued you in?" Sensibly, she stopped giving Everett crap and took a bite of her sandwich. The rich goodness made her feel like a kid again.

God, why did I ever stop eating PB&J?

"For what it's worth..." He took another bite and began talking with a giant bulge sticking out of his cheek. "I knew you guys were right, but I didn't like the way you went about. That's neither here nor there, though. I'd ordered some structural and environmental reports before I left and I must've forgotten to have them forwarded to Mike, so I just got them."

She nodded.

"Low and behold, Chessington is a fucking shitshow. Arnold used substandard building materials. It's going to take millions in remediation to meet code, so we pretty much lucked out."

Zora closed her eyes and inhaled, shaking her head. Everett couldn't really be so obtuse. "No. You do *not* get to attribute this to luck unless you count yourself lucky for having Mike around. Ev, he saved you...us. Do you know what that janky building and your precious pride could have done to Monroe Properties and Babs's dream? Ugh."

Everett ran his hands over his hair. "I know."

"I don't think you do," Zora said. "This has nothing to do with me and Mike. Kendra told me he declined the offer from Baker & Bronson. He should be *your* partner. Period. No ifs, ands, or buts about it, Ev. He's family, and he cares about the company. Sometimes more than you and I."

Even as she said the words, she believed them. She believed in Mike and she knew he was a good man. She didn't believe herself for ever doubting him.

Why didn't I believe him?

When she looked up, she didn't know how long she'd been in her head, but Everett and Sophia were both staring at her. Her truth was reflected on their faces.

Tears stung at her eyes.

"What should I do?" Zora asked. Her voice sounded weak. Her belly was tied up in knots and there was dullness in her chest weighing her down. *What have I done?*

Everett walked around the island and hugged her, pulling her in tight to his chest. "I'm going to make this right. I was being stubborn, but I was always going to do it. He deserves the partnership. As far as you go—" Everett loosened his arms and pulled back to look at Zora—"this is something you have to do by yourself."

"What if I lose myself? I don't want to end up like Mom."

"Is that what you think happened? You think she lost herself in Joseph and that's why she killed herself?"

Zora opened her mouth, but nothing came out. She felt her eyebrows squish together as she nodded to her big brother. Her chest tightened and she felt like she was overheating. She couldn't find the right words. *Wasn't that what happened?* She'd built all of her dreams and goals around that truth and trying to avoid the same mistakes.

Everett's expression was blank at first. Then it turned pensive. "Aw, Zo. I'm so sorry. I thought Babs talked you about it—"

"About what?"

He smiled and shook his head. He released a heavy sigh. "Mom was sick, Zo. I mean, yes, Joseph was a narcissistic bastard who didn't appreciate her, and he violated her as a woman, but she loved him when she was herself."

"What do you mean, when she was herself?"

"They didn't really get a chance to diagnose her because she accused the doctors of being out to get her, but her mental capacity was breaking down slowly. It was like she'd lost the connection between emotion and thought. She didn't have sympathy or heartfelt responses. She looked, talked, and walked like Mom, but she wasn't herself. She would go on these walks for hours at a time and come back the next day."

Zora's tears began to fall freely as she listened to her brother dispel everything she thought she'd known about her mother.

"All those books she used to read, she'd be holding them upside down just staring at the page—lost in her head somewhere. When she'd sleep, I'd sneak in there and tap on her head, begging the real mom to come out. She was inappropriate and withdrawn. She had no feelings. All her personal relationships suffered because she was stuck in a delusional fantasy. Zo, when we lost her, it was because she was a fragment of a person. Her mind was split."

Zora's shoulders shook as sobs trembled through her body.

"You're never going to be like her, so don't let *her* illness affect *your* future. If you want to be with Mike, go be with him."

She hugged her brother a little tighter then. She didn't want to be alone for the wrong reasons.

CHAPTER 36

MIKE

Mike walked off the elevator into the lobby of Monroe Properties that Friday with a plan. Yesterday he'd drafted most of the lease agreements and the deeds for the two higher priced downtown purchases. On the way to work today, he'd even stopped at the county building to file them. Pretty much everything he needed to get done for the week was complete, save for a few documents to review, but that wouldn't take long. He needed the free time and clear head space. Big gestures required big chunks of time to plan them.

"Morning, Kendra." Mike slipped past her without meeting her inevitably pity-filled eyes and quickly closed the door to his office behind him.

He dropped is messenger bag on the desk, took off his blazer, and pushed up his sleeves before fishing his phone out of his pocket. Safari was still open on the Hollywood Theatre homepage which listed its upcoming events. Slowly, he scrolled down and found Saturday, May 16th.

A tidal wave of relief washed over him at the words "closed for private event."

"*Yes*," he whispered and pumped his fist into the air. He pressed the phone to his chest and closed his eyes and let his head fall back. "Thank you, J. Yes."

Having the location checked off of his to-do list set the rest of the plan in motion. Now, he just needed to get to the details. Then, the hard part—getting Zora to show up. He spent the next half hour flipping between Amazon and The Movie Store, filling his carts with everything he needed to take his surprise over the top.

He'd barely pressed "purchase" when his door flew open, and he nearly jumped out of his skin.

"Shit! Dammit, Kendra. Are you trying to give me a fuc… freaking heart attack?" he exclaimed.

"Why are you so jumpy?" Kendra asked. "Are you doing something you're not supposed to be?"

Mike scrubbed his hand over his face and blew out a breath. "No. Now what can I help you with?" He hadn't meant to sound so edgy.

Kendra studied him for a second—too perceptive, as usual. "Uh-huh. Just so you know, I don't believe you for one second." Her right hand immediately found its home on her hip. A scowl twisted her face.

I prefer the pity face.

"Thank you, Sherlock. Did you come in here for a reason, or is interrogating me going to be part of your daily agenda?"

Just to extend his discomfort, she let the silence linger before she spoke again.

Mike shifted in his chair, tapping his fingers together and flashing her an "any day now" look.

"Everett wants to see you in his office," she said, finally. Her lips pursed and her eyes narrowed.

Shit. The man hasn't even looked at me, and now he wants to see me in his office?

"He does? About what? I already emailed him the filed deed confirmations."

Kendra shrugged, which didn't ring true. There wasn't a thing going on in this company, or the office, she didn't make it her business to know.

"Okay, well if you aren't going to tell me, can you please go mad-dog someone else?" Mike got to his feet. He locked his monitor and checked his desk as Kendra backed out of the door, still glaring. He shook his head, but he couldn't bite back his grin. He loved her crazy ass. She reminded him of women in his own family, and Babs, too.

As he stepped out of the office, he peeked over to Kendra's desk, but she wasn't there.

Hmm. Maybe she went to the restroom.

He shrugged it off and ambled toward Everett's corner office. As the glassed-in room came into view, Mike slowed his pace. He'd expected to see his best friend sitting pensively behind his computer, but Everett wasn't alone. Sneaky Kendra had joined him. Sophia, Olivia, and Jason were also standing behind Everett. They were all huddled close together.

Mike's first thought was that it was some kind of bogus attempt at an intervention. One person was missing from the bunch, though. *Has something happened to Zora?*

Mike's heartbeat sped up, and his throat tightened. He took a deep breath, but the fear bubbling up inside him didn't subside. He swallowed and inhaled as he turned into the doorway.

"Is she okay?"

He couldn't fill his lungs. The way his chest was rising and falling so rapidly, he thought he might black out.

Sophia was the first to address him. "Calm down. Zora's

fine. We're here for something else." She smiled, and Mike's airways opened slightly.

"*Told you* he loved her," Olivia said and elbowed Jason, who was sidled up to her. Mike guessed he was more than happy to be there.

Interesting.

Mike pinched the bridge of his nose and felt the heat crawl up his neck to his cheeks. "Shit. That's embarrassing," he said, entering the room and walking up to the desk to face his friends and family.

"Welp, at least we know how you really feel. Not that *I* didn't already know." Kendra rolled her eyes, but a grin replaced her annoyed expression. "We're here for *you*, silly. You, my little grasshopper, deserve everything that's coming to you."

"Uh...should I be afraid? She's dangerous." Mike's laugh was contagious. Giggles spread through the room.

Everett stood then. His expression was blank, but the way he failed to blink, his silence spoke volumes. He lowered his chin for a couple of seconds before meeting Mike's gaze again.

"Look, I know I should have trusted you. I was wrong, and I'm sorry. You've never done anything but help me uplift this company and my family's name. You're not only the best friend a man could ask for, but you're everything I want in a business partner." He paused briefly. "If you still want it, Zora and I both agree, we'd love for you to be equal partners with us at Monroe Properties."

Mike opened his mouth then closed it almost immediately. He smiled instead.

It was everything he'd been working toward. Still, some of the joy was lost because the only person he wanted to tell and celebrate with was the one person who wanted nothing more to do with him.

"Thank you," he said. "I don't know what to say."

"Say yes, fool," Kendra quipped, and again laughter filled the room.

"Yes," Mike said firmly this time.

In a matter of seconds, a delicious-looking chocolate cake with fancy decorations appeared and everyone blew party horns. Sophia presented a giant congratulatory greeting card on the table. It was filled with well wishes and anecdotal accounts of Mike's drive and ambition. It was signed by everyone, including Zora.

"Aw man. This is awesome, guys. Thank you so much."

"No thank you, my friend. There's just one more order of business. Let's make this official." Everett placed a partnership agreement on the desk.

It took Mike only a few minutes to review the details of the document. When he deemed it accurate and fair, he signed it to the tune of champagne popping and more horns blaring as he shook his best friend's hand.

"Now that that's done how about we toast?" Jason crowed.

Sophia, Olivia, and Kendra passed out champagne flutes. They were beaming, but Mike hadn't missed the tinge of sadness in their expressions. He felt it, too. They didn't have to say anything for him to know the whole celebration was over-shadowed by Zora's absence. She was the one who had supported Mike's decisions and lobbied the merits of making Mike a partner to her brother. She should have been there with them now.

Everett seemed to sense it, too. He raised his glass and centered his focus on Mike. "To my best friend, business part-ner, and brother. I think every one of us here today are on the same page, and I say that with your best interests in mind." He paused and pressed a fist to his lips. "What have you been in your office ordering from Amazon, what does it have to do with the Hollywood Theatre, and how are you going to use it to get Zora back?"

Mike released a deep, guttural, raucous laugh.

Damn, Kendra.

He knew she'd been snooping...probably looking at his screen. He wouldn't put it past her to hack his computer to snoop on him. The FBI and CIA had nothing on that woman. Put her in a room with moneybags Jason, shady-ass Olivia, and meddling Sophia...*shit.*

"You got me." He held up his hands. His body was shaking as he tried to catch his breath. He bit his tongue until the laughter was just a tickle in the back of his throat. "No, for real. though. I'm glad you asked because I'm going to need all of your help. Here's the plan..."

CHAPTER 37

ZORA

Since Patton Place was out of the question, Zora was set to spend the day watching TV—alone—in her very quiet, very unfurnished, practically empty new house. Then, Oli texted and shocked the hell out of her with an invite to do a cake-baking class at Cuisinette. If that wasn't surprising enough, Sophia was in, too.

"Umm…are we going to talk about why we're here when Oli swore up and down that she would never step foot back in this place?" Zora squinted her eyes and pressed her lips flat, noting Oli's averted gaze and earlobe tug.

"Uh—"

"Don't. Just stop. This question is to Sophia, since I already know you're about to tell a whopper of a lie." Zora shook her head. "Can't even look at me can you, Oli?"

Sophia's voice cracked. She was unnaturally quiet as her eyes darted around the room. "The, um…chocolate chip cake," she said too quickly. Her eyes were wide. "Yes. Oli said 'chocolate chip cake with whipped chocolate buttercream,' and I was like, 'yes, please.'" A small giggle escaped her lips, but the smile that followed was about as weak as her answer.

To avoid the heat of Zora's stare lasering through her she poured a dozen or so chocolate chips into her hand and stuffed them in her mouth.

"I know you're pregnant and all, but I'm going to need you to stop eating all of the ingredients before we start." At the risk of getting her hand gnawed off, Zora slowly pushed the tiny glass bowl away from Sophia.

"Look, if they don't want me taste-testing, then they shouldn't have put all of these mouth-watering treats out in front of a woman with a sweet tooth and an appetite for two. We still have like fifteen minutes before the class starts." Sophia pouted. "I'm hungry. All this talk about cake. I want some so badly." The last word came out as a whine.

Zora took one look at her protruding bottom lip and her round belly resting on the counter and felt bad. Given the intensity of Sophia's cravings, Zora decided not to ask any more questions about why they were at Cuisinette.

"Whatever, at least we're here, and I'm out the house," she said to a sullen-faced Sophia who looked like she was going through chocolate withdrawal.

"Aww, want me to go see what I have in my purse?" Zora asked.

"Nope. Got her covered." Out of the pocket of her neon pink apron, Oli slipped Sophia a few almonds she'd taken from the pantry. "It's not chocolate, but they are honey-roasted."

Apparently, sugar in any form would suffice. Sophia *wasn't* too good to bite. She snatched them out of Oli's hand and shoveled them into her mouth like it was her last meal.

For a moment, Zora looked around and compared the gorgeous and vibrant commercial kitchen to Mike's. This place didn't have a leg to stand on. Now that she'd cooked in her dream kitchen, Cuisinette didn't quite have the same stand-out appeal it used to. It felt stark and cold, and the colors were too busy. She missed the warmth and familiarity of his space, of knowing her way around, and the overall level of comfort she'd felt with him in the next room.

"Anywho…" Oli cocked her head. "When am I getting an invite to this new house? You've been holed up in there, probably cooking yourself crazy and sulking."

"I have not."

Both Oli and Sophia shot her a suspicious look.

"Fine. Let me get some furniture first."

She and Sophia watched as Oli popped one of Sophia's chocolate chips into her mouth and shrugged.

"Well, I hope you've at least had a chance to unpack your party clothes. We're getting together next Saturday to celebrate Mike's promotion," Sophia said. She held up her chocolate-stained hand. "Before you try to deny it, Zo, we know you want to be there."

She did.

Zora slouched against the counter with a sigh. "I do. It's just…it's going to be so awkward. I'm so jealous that everyone else is all hunky-dory with him. Meanwhile, I'm the odd woman out. He probably doesn't even want to talk to me, let alone see my face."

Now Zora grabbed a small handful of Sophia's chocolate chips and shoveled them into her mouth. When she looked up, they were both staring at her.

"What? Oli did it and she didn't get in trouble."

"You're serious with that shit?" Oli asked, but Sophia rephrased for the sake of argument.

"What she's trying to say is, who cares about the chocolate? We can go refill in the pantry. I'm still trying to figure out why you think it's going to be awkward with Mike.

Weren't *you* the one who walked out, the one who didn't trust *him*?"

Zora drew a breath before releasing it and throwing her hands up. "Exactly," she huffed. "I'm the one who ended it, so how stupid and wishy-washy am I going to look trying to weasel my way back in?"

Ugh. So stupid.

She dropped her head into her hands and grunted as she replayed the scene of Everett and Sophia's welcome back party. They'd been so happy planning it and setting it up. Then she's accused him of lying, but what had he really lied about? Her mind treaded slowly into the memory of their last night at his house—making love—and she'd cried in the darkness because she'd known it was over.

Everett's voice echoed in the back of her mind.

Go be with him.

"I wouldn't even know where to begin. I don't know what to say to him. 'Sorry' just feels so…inadequate," Zora muttered.

Sophia and Oli looked like they wanted to start in on her, but that's when the instructor clanked her whisk against her mixing bowl to gain the attention of the class. "Welcome. I see some of you are already psyched about the chocolate chips." She shot Sophia a pointed stare, but Oli and Zora shared her discomfort since they'd helped.

Sophia flashed the instructor a tight smile and rubbed her belly. *Major guilt trip.*

"Welp, let's get started." The woman's cheeks flushed. Apparently, no one wanted to be the one to reprimand a pregnant woman for inhaling chocolate. "Our ovens are already preheated to three hundred twenty-five degrees. Grease and flour the three six-inch cake rounds in front of you, and line them with parchment."

All around the room, there was movement and clanking

pans as everyone followed the instructions. Oli seemed very excited by the flour and coconut oil—her healthy substitute. Zora was all finished and waiting for the next step, so she decided to help Sophia.

"You begin by extending an olive branch," Sophia whispered in Zora's ear. "Help us celebrate his promotion next weekend."

Zora sighed as she lined the last pan with parchment.

"And for the record, sorry is never inadequate. It's just a starting point."

"I know." Zora bit her lip. "I just feel so stupid for letting him go. Again."

Her throat was thick with emotion, and the hollow ache in her chest echoed in her ears.

"Now, take your mixing bowl and whisk in the flour, baking powder, and salt until they're well combined." The woman's eyes darted around the room then landed on Zora, who looked back at her like a deer in headlights.

Umm…

"Did you have a question, or maybe need me to go back a step?" she asked.

Zora felt her brows pinch together as she shook her head. But then she realized, the instructor wasn't talking to her. As Zora turned, she saw that the woman was looking at Sophia.

"Are you okay, Soph?"

She was holding her belly and her eyes were wide. For a split, second Zora wasn't breathing.

"Shit, what is it? What's wrong? Talk to me, Soph."

And then…poof.

All over Zora's black leather booties, Sophia's pink ballet flats, and Oli's platform sneakers. A white plume of flour, baking powder, and salt. She'd dropped the mixing bowl and doubled over, holding her stomach with both hands.

"Ow!" Sophia winced and a flash of horror darkened her eyes.

"No. It can't be," Zora muttered. "You're only five months along."

That's when the tears began to stream down Sophia's worry-stricken face and Zora remembered. The stillborn Sophia had delivered. This baby, her niece or nephew, was supposed to be Sophia's rainbow baby.

"What do you feel? Is it a contraction?"

Sophia nodded. "I think so."

She sobbed and crumpled to the floor, her shoulders trembling. It was too early. The baby needed every second in the womb to build strength and grow. The baby needed its mother. Sophia didn't have to say it, but Zora was scared, too.

"No. No, we're not going to sit here and do nothing." Zora wrapped Sophia's arm over her shoulder and lifted her to her feet. "Oli go grab our stuff. Call my brother and tell him we're headed to the emergency room at Legacy."

Everett was already waiting at the entrance when they pulled up at the front of the hospital. His eyes were bloodshot, and he looked scared beyond belief, but Zora could tell he was trying to be strong for Sophia. He'd already checked her in and completed all the necessary paperwork, but he was quiet.

"Don't worry, baby. I'm here. We're going to make it through this together," he said, wrapping her hand in his.

In a blur of movement and calls for help, Sophia was whisked off in a wheelchair, leaving Zora and Oli out of breath and shaking with fear. Since Sophia was past twenty weeks, they took her up to labor and delivery where a whirlwind of nurses took over until the doctor arrived and the tests began.

Oli took a seat in the waiting area, but Zora couldn't sit. She paced the length of the hall skittishly. Her nerves were frayed. She kept shaking her head and worrying that it was her fault.

Everything—the building purchase, Mike's promotion, Mike and Everett fighting, she and Mike—it had stressed Sophia out.

"She can't lose the baby."

She was talking to herself, but she hoped God could hear her plea.

Zora slouched against the wall and an agony-filled wail tore through her chest and escaped her lips. She couldn't quite catch her breath. Sob after sob came out of her. Her chest felt like it might swallow her whole. Just thinking about Sophia losing the baby was too much to handle. Even she'd thought it was avoidance, going over to Patton Place every day, but it had been more. This baby meant a new chance at a family. It wasn't just a light in the darkness for Sophia, but for her and for Everett, too. They were growing their small family, rebuilding, and planting new roots, and Zora got to be a part of it.

In that moment, Mike came rushing through the door. A war between heartache and anguish played on his face.

"Hey…" He was out of breath. His eyes darted all around, but he pulled Zora into his arms and wrapped them tightly around her.

Her heart hammered against her chest. The fact that there was no hesitation in his action meant everything to her. "Hi."

"I'm here. What do we know?" he asked, pulling back to search her face.

"She just…she was holding her stomach," Zora cried as she proceeded to fill him in on everything that had happened so far. "What if she's losing the baby?"

"Don't talk like that. It's going to be fine. The baby's going to be fine. We're all here for her." His reaction worried Zora, though. She saw it in the slight twitch of his brows and the breath he held.

Zora laid her head on his chest, and just for a moment,

breathed him in. He smelled of mint and rain and endless daydreams. She leaned into the warm, familiar feel of him.

For once, she wanted to be the one who calmed his fears.

As he stepped back and ran his hands over his hair, she pushed off the wall, wiped away her tears, and framed his face in her hands. "I'm so glad you're here and I'm sorry about everything."

Mike nodded and lowered his forehead to touch hers. "I love you," he whispered. "Nothing is ever going to change that." Then he tipped her chin up and brushed his lips ever so softly over hers.

Oh, the butterflies are back. How I've missed you.

He felt like coming home again after a long time away— bliss in the middle of this chaos. She wanted the kiss to last forever, but before she could tell him that she loved him, he pulled apart. She reluctantly opened her eyes to see him flick his eyes to Everett who was beelining straight for them.

Zora tensed, turning to square her body to her brother's. Her antsy pulse vibrated over her skin as she surveyed his face for any signs of trouble. There were none.

"They were contractions, but it's Braxton Hicks," he explained. Relief smoothed the lines of his forehead and he broke out into a victorious smile, his arms wide open. "Turns out it's normal, but she just needs to take it easy."

"Was it because she was stressed out?" Zora asked tentatively, unsure she really wanted to know the answer. Still, she knew she needed to know in order to avoid any further instances until the baby was due.

A flush crept across Everett's cheeks and he cleared his throat. "Uh…"

"What? What is it?" Mike asked.

Zora tilted her head, weighing her brother's reaction. "What are you not telling us?"

Everett rubbed the back of his neck. His voice was weak, and his gaze averted when he began to explain. "Well…the doctor said it can come from increased activity of the mother or baby. Most of the time it's dehydration, but…" His voice cracked and he swallowed before letting the words race out of his mouth almost low enough to be a whisper. "It could be too much sex."

He winced and Zora and Mike exchanged a meaningful glance before darting their eyes back to Everett.

"Wait." Zora's shoulders shook as she bit back a grin. "This is too good," she said way too loudly. Just then, Oli turned the corner from the waiting area.

"What's too good? I want to laugh, too."

Zora held up a single finger as she tried to compose herself. Giggles sputtered free from her lips.

Mike started to fill Oli in, but Zora held up a palm.

"No, please let me tell it." She lifted her chin and cleared her throat. "What my dear brother is trying to say is that these two have been shacked up in the house doing it nonstop like rabbits. Did I tell you guys I walked in on them doing kinky stuff the other day?"

Mike and Oli doubled over with laughter while Everett simply smiled and nodded his head, letting them have joy at his expense.

"Go ahead. Get it all out, but at least *I'm* getting some," he said, arching a brow at Oli and shooting the same *too bad I can't say the same for you* look at Mike and Zora. "Mmm-hmm."

Zora, finally able to breathe, shook her head at him. "That's a shame you can't keep it in your pants. Sent the woman into early contractions… Mmm, mmm, mmm!"

At that, a wave of laughter rumbled through all of them.

They were raucous and giggling, but the crazy day had a way of putting everything into perspective for Zora. There was so much love and good times to be shared, and she didn't want to take any of it for granted. Yes, there was still a lot that needed to be said between her and Mike, and she would say them soon, but she realized life was too short to miss out on the good stuff.

Babies and weddings.

I love yous and I love you toos.

Publishing cookbooks and making partner.

She wanted to be there for them all.

CHAPTER 38

ZORA

Zora rubbed her arms as she looked up at the gleaming lights of the Hollywood Theatre. It wasn't the ideal location for a confession, but at least it was nostalgic. She just wished it didn't feel so awkward to be back here. She and Oli had taken two shots of tequila before they'd left the house, and still Zora's nerves were frazzled. Between the dry mouth and heart palpitations, she didn't know if she'd be able to go through with her plan. It was one thing to tell the love of your life how you felt. It was a completely different animal to do it with people watching, waiting, and judging.

What if he doesn't want me back?

A shiver pulsed over her chilled skin, but it still didn't extinguish the hot fear coursing through her veins.

She'd given Mike a full week to reach out since the day at the hospital, and...nothing. Not a word. Crickets. How could she come to a life-altering revelation and then simply try to force it back into the proverbial toothpaste tube? She couldn't. It was out. She loved Mike—like gut-wrenching, scream it from the rooftops, happily lose herself in the best of ways love. He might be content to be patient, but there was no way in hell she was going to let another second go by without putting all of her cards on the table.

So what if he was surrounded by a room full of people the whole time? Sure, it was his party, and no one else, not even Oli, was privy to her plan, which she'd suddenly realized was half-hatched and more than a little terrifying.

She cleared her throat, ready to get to the bottom of things so she could get the show on the road. "Tell me again why we're here?" She was fidgeting again, but by now she'd already given up on trying to temper it. "It doesn't make sense. This is where we're celebrating *Mike* making partner? He doesn't even like movies that much."

Oli shrugged.

There was no eighties movie marathon this time. Best-case scenario: there'd be a lot of fast talking followed by slow kisses. Worst-case scenario: Zora would be going home horny, humiliated, and hungover.

Great. Just great.

Her fingers and toes were tingling, and it had nothing to do with the chill in the air. She couldn't stand still with all the butterflies racing in her stomach.

A gust of wind ruffled the layers of the wine-colored chiffon maxi skirt Zora paired with a Kings of Leon tee. She pulled her black leather jacket tight against the evening chill. "Ooh, Lord it's cold. Let's get inside," she said, pressing her hands at her billowing skirt as they rushed through the door.

They hurried inside where they were surrounded by the pink walls and muted chandelier lights of the theater lobby. Zora noticed Oli's eyes dart expectantly over to the concession stand. Then, she looked down the hall, toward each of the theater doors then finally, back to Zora.

"You guys came here once, right?" She tapped her fingers against her lip. "I, uh…I'm not sure why he picked this pla—"

"Wait." Zora paused while she scrutinized her best friend for the telltale signs of a lie. There was no ear tug. No pursed lips. "Hmm. So, Mike picked the place?"

Why would he want to come back here to celebrate?

Oli bit her bottom lip and shifted from foot to foot before meeting Zora's gaze. Her expression looked haunted, and her silence was unnatural.

Zora planted a hand on her hip and cocked her head. Nerves or not, this was an interesting development. "Am I supposed to believe this is *just* a night for celebration and not some deranged plot to get me here? Come on, why are we really here?" She dipped her chin and stared at Oli from beneath her brows.

Guilty as ever, Oli averted her smoky gaze.

And there it was, the pursed lips first, followed by the infamous earlobe tug.

"Fine. I'll just ask him myself." Zora fished out her phone and began tapping out a rapid-fire message. She bit back a shit-eating grin. She was bursting with excitement at the prospect of exposing whatever this setup was that she'd just stumbled into. She couldn't afford a wrench in her plan, and she wasn't about to waste a perfectly fabulous outfit and fierce makeup on a prank.

As soon as she finished typing, the three little irritating dots popped up on the screen. She was anxiously waiting, but, of course, they just sat there, rotating and laughing at her.

"If you're not going to tell me what's going on, then at least tell me who's in on it." Zora said. By now, her nerves were getting the best of her. She was liable to end up with either an ulcer or a full-on panic attack.

She released a heavy sigh.

Oli grinned, glanced at her phone, and abruptly moved toward the concession stand.

Zora scurried behind her. "What was that all about? Why'd you check the time?"

"Hi. I'm here for Michael Kennedy's event," Oli said to the concession attendant, who quickly directed her to the last room on the right. She turned on her heel and moved with purpose toward the room. Oli decided to put Zora out of her misery a little.

"Everett, Sophia, Jason, and Kendra are here." She ticked off names on her fingers. "I think Kara, Steph, Remi, and Lexi might show, and a bunch of Mike's frat brothers, law school friends, and some people Jason invited."

"That's an interesting bunch." Confusion bled into Zora's tone. *Come on tequila, kick in. I need you.*

Oli stopped and turned around. Zora narrowly missed crashing into her.

"Oh, yeah. Everett reached out to Mike's parents, too. Mike's dad won't make it, but his mom said she was going to try."

Um…no pressure. Breathe. It's going to be fine.

Zora scoped out the emergency exits and tried to fill her lungs, but why should they listen to her and keep her breathing? Her heart was knocking around in her chest like a crazy pinball.

The corners of Zora's mouth pulled down, and she nodded. "So, this is going to be…legit." *This is not an ideal time to ask him to be with me forever. Deep breaths.*

Oli pivoted and continued down the hall.

Zora inhaled and slowly released the air as she wrapped her arms behind her back and wringed her fingers together. She slowly trailed Oli. Her fight or flight instincts kicked in. At the moment, flight felt like the best option.

When they came to a stop outside the door, Oli flitted a glance at Zora as she gripped the handle. "You good?"

Well, at least it was a party. *There's got to be booze. I'm going to need way more liquid courage.*

Mother or not, a whole room full of people or not, she was doing this now…or never.

Zora's phone pinged, nearly giving her a heart attack. Mike had responded with his two truths and a lie. Right away, she knew which ones were true. She bit back a grin and typed out a response. Her thumb hovered over the small green vertical arrow. There was no doubt in her mind what she needed to do next.

> **Zora:** #1 is the lie. You suck at lying. First off, if you ever plan on beating me at this game, the two truths should not be glaringly obvious. Lol. Your turn.
> 1. I miss you like crazy.
> 2. I'm hopelessly in love with you.
> 3. I'm at the happiest place on earth.
>
> Where are you?

Zora pressed send, and almost instantly, the phone pinged again. Her smile was too wide to suppress, but she couldn't look at the screen, otherwise she might lose her nerve. She took too deep breaths and met Oli's searching gaze.

"Okay. I assume you guys are still acting like freaking two-year-olds, playing games, and you've made your choice. Are you ready to put the phone away before you ruin the whole night?" Oli flashed her a pointed look, but her tone was more playful than pissed. "You do know you're about to see him in like a nanosecond, right?"

Zora's shoulders were drawn back and her chin was held high. She wasn't telling herself any lies anymore. She didn't want to hold him at arm's length. Finally, she wanted to tell him how she felt, and let the cards fall where they might. Zora knew exactly where her heart lay. Yes, she'd lost a little, but she'd found a happier version of herself when she was with Mike.

"I'm ready now," Zora said.

CHAPTER 39

MIKE

"She's coming in now."

Mike cracked his neck and shook out his arms. A few more minutes of discomfort in exchange for happiness for the rest of his days... His nerves were all over the place, and his heart was pummeling his chest, but he couldn't imagine what his life would be like without Zora in it.

Through the curtains, somewhere in the auditorium, he heard shushing wash over the crowd.

"Oh, good. Zora, you're here. They're about to start." It sounded like Sophia, but he couldn't be sure without seeing. Mike stiffened.

"Your seat is up front," someone else said.

Then Zora's voice.

"Is this a surprise?" she asked, her volume growing louder as she seemed to approach the front row. "Why didn't anyone tell me? We were standing in the middle of the lobby. He totally could've seen us."

A giggle bubbled up inside of Mike. His palms were sweaty,

and he felt like at any minute he might faint, but it was going to be worth it.

Zora was worth it.

Through the small cracks in the curtains, Mike noticed the house lights dim. He took a deep breath and clapped his hands together. He exited stage right and waited in the wings for his cue. *Showtime.*

Slowly, the theater drapes parted. The spotlight shined on a life-sized cardboard cutout of Phoebe Cates fresh out of the water with slicked back hair and the infamous teensy red bikini from *Fast Times at Ridgemont High.*

"Hold it for a few more beats," Mike said into the headpiece. His eyes were fixed on Zora. Sophia and Oli were on either side of her, but she was right where he needed her to be, dead center in the front row—his main focus.

She was a sight for sore eyes, but tonight, she was different. Her outfit wasn't as drastic as the tight blue dress she'd worn to the silent disco, but she'd dressed for the occasion. She looked chic and cool with her own bohemian flare in a long skirt and leather jacket, but it wasn't just the clothes. Her dark pixie cut was layered and fringed to frame the delicate curves of her face, and she had deep wine-stained lips.

It was still her, only, more mature somehow.

Mike licked his lips.

His friend Eric's voice hummed in his ear. "You still want us to hold it?"

"Uh, yeah." He snapped out of his trance. "Almost. Give me a few more seconds." He was still watching Zora, waiting for a reaction. He couldn't take his eyes off of her.

She slouched back, and her feet hooked around the chair legs as she studied the single cardboard cutout on stage. Her eyes twinkled—sparkled— with an almost child-like glee. She seemed alight with some kind of renewed joy and zeal for life.

The corners of Mike's mouth quirked up. "Cue the music. Spotlight two."

On the stage, the upbeat drums of *Walking on Sunshine* by Katrina and the Waves filled the air. As the horns blared, the light glinted off a Michael J. Fox cutout from *The Secret of My Success,* and Zora's mouth fell open.

It was the exact reaction he was hoping for.

Mike now had a full-blown smile as he watched the corners of her eyes crinkle and recognition brighten her face.

"Go," he instructed.

By the first hook, spotlights had already lit up a *Pretty in Pink* Molly Ringwald, a *Short Circuit* Johnny Five, a *Flashdance* Jennifer Beal, *Howard the Duck,* and one of Mike's personal favorites Ralph Macchio, *The Karate Kid.*

As soon as the hook ended, the music scratched, the auditorium went silent and dark, and Mike got into position. He stood behind another cardboard cutout. Dressed in a full flight suit with a bomber jacket and aviator sunglasses, he tightened his grip around the mic.

"You never close your eyes…" he sang. Light flooded the stage. In his deepest baritone, he belted out the first lines of The Righteous Brothers' *You've Lost that Loving Feeling.*

Zora jolted upright and slapped her hand over her mouth. Affection glowed in her eyes as she sized him up in all of his Maverick splendor.

It was embarrassing as all heck, but to see the smile dancing on her lips, Mike would do it a million times again. He tipped the glasses down onto the bridge of his nose, pointed at her, and winked.

To his sheer pleasure, Zora pressed her hand to her heart and threw her head back in laughter. It was faint beneath the blare of the music, but it lifted his spirits to know he caused the melodious sound.

Then the entire room began to sing along. "You've lost that loving feeling!" they sang and cheered. They were on their feet dancing.

Mike was positively jubilant as he worked the stage, making his way, one by one to each of the cutouts. Spotlights continued to light up a *Less Than Zero* Robert Downey Jr., *Footloose* Kevin Bacon, *Some Kind of Wonderful* Mary Stuart Masterson, and E.T.

He wasn't finished.

The full cardboard casts of *The Breakfast Club* and *The Goonies* greeted the audience. It was sheer pandemonium as everyone pointed and enjoyed the show.

On the last notes, Mike slipped into the wing and grabbed his final prop. Just as John Cusack was lit up, Mike mirrored him with both hands, and lifted a giant boom box above his head.

"I love you Zora Marie Monroe!" he yelled.

The song was over, but the room buzzed with excitement. Mike observed the crowd reaction. Everyone was on their feet. Everett thrust his fist in the air. Jason looked like a proud papa. Between Sophia's shimmering eyes and Oli's glowing expression, he was sure he'd hit it out of the park.

Zora was still in her seat.

A tidal wave of panic washed over Mike. Doubt crept into his thoughts and worry squeezed his chest.

What if it wasn't enough? Please say I'm not too late.

Suddenly, it was quiet.

Mike set the radio down, pulled off the glasses, and jammed his hands into his pockets. He didn't take his eyes off of her. The show was fun, but he knew he needed to go deeper. He dropped his chin to his chest. "You must have been...nine," he said, pivoting to pace the stage. He didn't stop to see if she was looking, but he sensed her listening. "I was about fourteen, in the eighth grade, about to be a freshman."

His guests settled back into their seats. He was sure they'd noticed Zora's reaction too, or lack of one. Still, he forged ahead.

"Ev and I had been riding bikes at the park up the street. I remember it was blazing hot. We were going to head back to Babs's to cool off and play *Blade Runner*. When we got to the house, though, you were waiting for us on the porch."

For a second, he stopped, stuck in the memory all those years ago. He didn't know it then, but he'd fallen for her that day. It took him all this time to realize she'd climbed into his heart and stayed there.

"Zo, up until that day, you were just Everett's little sister— sweet, but mostly annoying." He chuckled, and laughter rumbled over the audience. "You'd just gotten your hair pressed. You had on this purple dress with ruffles at the bottom and around the collar. You were the most beautiful girl I'd ever seen."

He sighed and finally looked at Zora.

Her eyes swam with tears, but she was staring, unblinking at him. His chest tightened because he couldn't tell whether or not they were happy tears.

"The thing is, I'm certain that was the exact moment I fell in love with you." A collective sigh rumbled over the crowd.

"Mike…" She sounded breathless. Her chest was rising and falling.

"Let me finish," he said. "For years, I kept my distance because I thought it was the right thing to do. I was convinced you deserved someone better. When we got older, as damaged as I felt after losing my brother, I didn't think I could give you unconditional love."

His throat was thick with emotion.

"After being with you over the last month, any doubt I had is gone. I got a chance to see what it was like when we were together, and I know all those years I was just biding my time. I don't ever want to be without you. What I'm trying to say is… I'm ready."

Zora's sobs were faint, but he heard them.

"I'm asking you to love me. Be *with* me. If I have to give up my house and move into yours, I'll do it. Or, we can rent it and buy a new one together. I don't care, I just want to be with you."

His heartbeat raced and a sort of manic energy coursed through him like he had to do something. He wrung his hands —balling them into fists then opening them again. He did this over and again because he wasn't sure what else to do.

His throat was dry, but he swallowed anyway, praying that something he'd said reached her. "Your cookbook will be out soon, but I want you to have a whole library of books full of recipes. I want to be there to taste-test as you make magic in your dream kitchen." He was babbling now and hated the desperation in his emotion-choked tone.

In his ear, the line cracked, and Eric's voice came through. "You're breaking my heart, here. Should I bring it out now?"

I'm bombing.

Mike didn't speak, he only nodded, and within seconds, Eric materialized with a box and an envelope.

"I hope you don't need it," Mike said, "but in case it takes a little something to persuade you, I come bearing gifts." He smiled, bent at the knees, and extended a hand to Zora.

Thankfully, she didn't hesitate to get to her feet. Mike guided her up onto the stage with his free hand and handed her the gifts. It took everything inside him not to pull her into his arms and just hold on.

"What is it?" She peeked up at him. There was a gentle pink blush on her cheeks and Mike couldn't have been happier.

"Why don't you open them up and find out?" He bobbed his eyebrows even though he didn't feel particularly playful.

Zora took the lid off the small red box and retrieved a snow globe. It took her a few seconds, but when she shook it, she seemed to recognize the flurry of glitter and smiling Mickey Mouse-shaped snowflakes twirling in the watery storm.

"I can't take this. It was your brother's."

"I want you to have it." It was a risk, but Mike took a step closer and slid his arm around her waist, pulling her into him. He could feel the warmth coming off her skin. "Zora?"

She dipped her chin and let her forehead rest on his chest. He peppered soft kisses on her hair and gently rubbed his hand along her back.

"I love you so much," he said.

For the briefest moment, Mike thought she was crying again. Her shoulders shook and she leaned into him, tightening her arms around him.

Then, she grunted.

She mumbled something he couldn't quite make out.

"What?" he asked.

She lifted her head and there were traces of tears running down her cheeks, but the corners of her mouth were quirked up in a smile.

"I said, how am I supposed to compete with this...? I don't even know what to say."

"Uh...I don't understand. *Are* we competing because I'm really confused now." Mike said. "You were singing along to the music and enjoying yourself, and now you're laughing hysterically."

Zora shifted out of his arms and pivoted to address the audience. "Look, I had this big plan. I even took two shots of tequila before I left the house to make sure I went through with

it. *Two.* I'm a lightweight, so you know how that's going to go."
She jerked her thumb downward. "Right. Anyway, I got myself
all worked up to do this 'grand gesture' and profess my love to
this, this…overachiever." She laughed nervously.

"Wow." It was the only word he could think of. Mike
couldn't believe his ears.

"Yeah, 'wow,' is right," she said. "I can't compete with this."
She threw her hands up and started to pace the stage.

Raucous laughter fell over the audience.

Whether they'd planned it or not, they were giving them a
show.

"Unbelievable." Mike shook his head and threw his hands
up, too. He angled himself between Zora and the crowd. "Do
you guys see what I'm dealing with here?"

In classic Everett form, he had Mike's back. "I've been
dealing with her for like thirty years! I'm just glad it's someone
else's turn!" he yelled up from the audience.

Mike swiveled around and squared Zora's shoulders to him.
"So, let me get this straight. You're upset that that I made such
a grand gesture?"

"I was singing and dancing, then I thought about how sweet
and heartfelt your gesture was, and I knew I couldn't do
anything to let you know how much I love you," Zora whined.
"I mean, a book dedication just doesn't seem like enough. Plus,
it doesn't release for a few months, and I—"

"Wait…." Mike's heart knocked around in his chest, and a
warm sensation flooded through him. "You dedicated your
book to me?" He felt airy and breathless as he hung on for her
next words. This wasn't something to take lightly. It certainly
wasn't nothing. It was as grand a gesture as there could be.

He searched her bright eyes. She had no clue what this
meant to him.

Zora pulled her bottom lip between her teeth, and the right corner of her mouth hitched up into a slow and sexy half-smile. "Yes," she muttered, sheepishly. Her shoulders caved inward and she blushed a million shades of pink.

"Zo…"

She stole his breath. He ached with need.

A fresh wave of desire slammed into him, and he cupped her face, running the pad of his thumb over the swell of her full bottom lip. Heat seared through him as he scrutinized her. The same desire he was feeling darkened her brown irises. Beneath the flutter of lashes, there was lust glittering in her eyes.

He didn't give a damn that they were in a room full of people.

His body throbbed with an almost dizzying need to be with her. Every inch of him craved her.

Before Zora could say another word, Mike covered her lips with his. The kiss was tender and soft at first. She melted into his arms as he let his lips linger on hers. Electricity coursed through his veins. Then, she slipped her tongue inside his mouth, searching. She tasted of spicy tequila and rich chocolate. It pushed him over the edge, and he thought he might come apart at her touch.

Zora moaned her satisfaction.

Passion took hold of Mike and he deepened the kiss. It suddenly felt urgent and so long overdue. It was filled with promises of a future together—of *their* beginning. As he sucked and licked and laved his tongue in her sweet mouth, her soft moans were his answer.

In that moment, he felt like he was walking on sunshine and drunk with happiness.

Someone whistled in the crowd and cheers and catcalls erupted.

"It's about damn time!" someone called out.

Mike was holding on as tight as he could. He didn't want to let her go, but he felt her smile on his lips. He dropped his hands first, twining their fingers together, but their bodies were still flush and their lips only inches apart.

Her eyes snapped open. There was heat blazing in them. She blinked, stepping out of her trance, and a small laugh fluttered inside him.

"Get your mind out of the gutter," Mike teased.

Despite the audience, they didn't move to step apart. "Well, Mr. Grand Gesture, if you didn't want my mind to be filled with dirty thoughts, you shouldn't have kissed me with that filthy mouth of yours," Zora rasped. "Oh, and wipe that smug grin off your face."

"Uh...you guys do know we're still here, right?" It was Oli, but neither Mike nor Zora even glanced in her direction.

"Quiet, I'm enjoying the show." Jason's deep baritone was filled with a strangely playful and upbeat tone.

"Hold your horses. We're still working on a happily ever after here," Mike called out to the sound of applause.

"Work a little faster," Zora said. "I need a drink."

Mike lowered his voice back to a whisper. "I was just thinking about your two truths. So, you miss me like crazy, huh? And you're hopelessly in love with me?" He couldn't fight the joy dancing in his heart and on his lips.

An ear-to-ear smile spread across Zora's face.

"Then what was the lie?" he asked.

Her brows knitted together, and by her pursed lips, he figured she heard the humor in his voice.

"Well, in a way I am, but clearly I'm not at 'the happiest place on earth,'" she argued.

"Yet..."

"What do you mean 'yet?'"

Mike slipped the envelope she was still holding from her hand and held it out of reach. "First, you didn't tell me whether you wanted to live with me."

"First, tell me. Is this even a celebration for your partnership, or was it all a setup? And, second, I love you, Michael Kennedy. Our address won't change that. It doesn't matter where we live. No place feels like home without you, so let's try them both out, and we'll rent the other." She shrugged. "Now what's in the envelope?"

He slowly lowered it. "Kiss me one more time. Quickly."

The kiss was urgent and filled with yearning.

When they pulled apart, Mike exhaled and squeezed her butt. "This is a celebration of me making partner, your cookbook, our family and friends...oh, and winning at the big gesture." He teased. "Now open it, already."

With a tentative smile, she pried her finger beneath the flap, peeking up at Mike wearily as she slit the length of the envelope, and pulled out a pair of tickets.

"Holy shit. We're going to Disneyland?" She pressed her hand to her heart.

"The way I see it, anywhere we're together is the happiest place on earth."

Elation suffused every one of her features, but, apparently, she wasn't fazed by the sentiment. She turned to the expectant crowd and held the tickets up. "Holy shit! We're going to Disneyland!"

Zora jumped up and down jubilantly. As she ran down to the audience, hugging everyone and celebrating, her words kept playing in Mike's head. *No place feels like home without you.* Deep down Mike knew she was right. Even though she'd said them so freely without thinking, they echoed the song in his heart. It amazed him how one day she'd walked into his life and now he couldn't imagine ever living without her. She was the last thing he thought of before falling asleep and the first thing he thought of when he woke.

All he wanted to do was spend the rest of his life making Zora happy. She was his home.

EPILOGUE

ZORA

I f wading through a sea full of strollers and mouse ears wasn't the best idea of fun, any time after mid-February was indisputably the worst time to go to Disneyland. It was practically June in California, which meant, even after the sun had gone down, it was still blistering hot. Then add in the Memorial holiday tourists and the fact that Zora and Mike's so-called grand gesture trip was hijacked and turned into a couples' getaway.

An uber-pregnant Sophia and Everett had come along. *Who doesn't want their over-protective brother with them on a romantic date?* If they weren't enough, Oli and Jason, who any other time hated each other's guts, decided a weekend in Cali would be "amazing."

Fun.

The night was coming to a close, and Zora had barely gotten to spend any time with Mike.

The day started off as expected. Despite the lines, they rode Pirates of the Caribbean, Matterhorn, Indiana Jones, It's a Small World, and the Jungle Cruise. By midday, Sophia was hungry, her feet were swollen, and she was understandably tired of touring the park's wide array of seating options. So, the guys took off for Splash Mountain and Big Thunder Mountain, while Zora and Oli stayed with Sophia.

The line was so long at Haunted Mansion that by the time they got off, all three women agreed food was in order.

"What time are we meeting the guys?" Zora turned on the flash on her phone's camera and snapped a few pictures of Oli posing with Goofy and Donald Duck. She was wearing a bright yellow Belle shirt to match Jason's blue Beast one.

Zora sighed. The shirt was a blaring reminder that she was missing her other half. Once the couples all decided to join the trip, they'd gotten matching shirts. She was wearing a pale green Princess Tiana shirt to go with Mike's forest green Prince Naveen one, and Sophia and Everett got the cutest Mickey and Minnie set. His said, "Her Mickey," while hers said "His Minnie."

The whole idea was adorable and sweet, but it would've been even sweeter if they actually got to enjoy their princes and mouse.

Sophia who was gnawing on her second turkey leg, mumbled something, snapping Zora out of her revelry, but her mouth was too full.

"What?" Zora asked.

"She said 'eight fifteen.'" Oli was beaming as she moved out of the way for the cute little family behind them to have their pictures taken. She checked her watch. "Yeah, it's only seven forty-five now, so we have a little bit of time, but this is like *the* worst place to meet. The fireworks for that Mickey's Mix Magic spectacular thingy starts at eight thirty, which mean we won't even be able to move, hear, or see anything."

Sophia swallowed. "Why can't we just stay here?" She was still holding the turkey leg, looking like she might clobber someone at any minute. Her eyes lit up and she waggled her brows. "I finally got a good seat, and if you guys love me...I'm praying one of you will go get me a Dole Whip from the Tiki Juice Bar."

She crossed her fingers on both hands and flashed them a puppy-dog pout.

Zora flitted a glance over at the crowds on Main Street lining up for the show before meeting Oli's gaze. They were near the Partners Statue of Walt Disney and Mickey holding hands. They were waiting for the guys to come back from riding Indiana Jones for the third time. *Freaking flash passes.* Then, an idea hit her.

"We have like thirty minutes. It's literally right there." Oli shrugged.

"Okay, fine." Zora knew Sophia was still working on the foodie must-try list she'd downloaded before they came. This one had been right up there at the top with the beignets. At least if she couldn't get on the rides, she could enjoy the food. "We'll be right back, Soph."

Zora and Oli had just reached the entrance to Adventureland when Zora jerked her thumb in the direction of one of the trader shops. "Can we run in here for a sec first? I want to check something out." She bit her bottom lip and veered into a small store with hanging plush animals, pineapple spears, and safari-themed clothing and trinkets.

She searched the aisles, high and low, picking at this and that.

"What exactly are you looking for?" Oli asked. "There are a bunch of souvenir shops on Main Street. I want to get that cute Belle sweatshirt with the rose on the sleeve. Think I should get something for Jason?"

Zora popped up from behind a jewelry display in the next

aisle. "Um, excuse me. Do I detect something brewing between you two?"

"No, you do not. I mean, he's cute and all…" Oli's brows were knitted together, but most notably, her eyes were averted.

"Look at me," Zora said. She had yet to close her mouth. She'd sensed it at Mike's party at the theater, but the denial was strong. "You know what I think?"

"Please keep it to yourself." A grin was plastered on Oli's lying face. "He's not even my type."

"Thick, beefy, defensive lineman types. Please. What I think is all this couple stuff is getting to you. You've got a thing for Jason. Don't try to deny it Olivia Harden. You and I know he is a walking six-foot four slice of creamy deliciousness *and* a walking hard-on, so *do* spare me the *he's not my type* rigmarole."

Oli folded her arms across her chest and gave her weakest impression of being pissed, but Zora saw right through it. She stared for a few more excruciating seconds just to rub it in before selecting two silver rings mounted with tiny green frogs, and beelining for the register.

"What are you even buying?" Feigned annoyance laced Oli's tone. She was standing by the door, tapping her foot and glaring.

Zora was about to respond with something X-rated until she noticed a kid standing next to her in the line. "Don't get all mad at me just because it's obvious you want Indiana Jones to tie you up with his lasso and take you for a ride on his mine cart." She didn't even try to hide her laughter. Although, somewhere into the middle of all that humor, Zora remembered she owed her best friend a little payback for the whole Andre debacle.

As they left the little boutique, Oli shot her a sheepish glance. "So…what do I do?"

"About what?" Zora twisted the top of the small plastic bag and stuffed it in her pocket.

Oli sighed. "I mean, this is new. I've never dated a white guy."

"Why are you looking at me like I would know? Mike has been it for me since forever, but I assume anatomically speaking, it's the same thing with a higher SPF." A pair of pursed lips and sagging shoulders confronted her. "Okay...you're attracted to him, right?"

"Obviously." Oli rolled her eyes. "From how Mike talks about him, I know he doesn't have a problem with women, but has he ever dated a black girl? I mean, a brown skin, 'around the way,' little bit of hood in her black girl?"

Zora stepped into the line in front of the Tiki Juice Bar and turned to her best friend, scrutinizing her for a moment. She'd never heard Oli worried about any man, black, orange, yellow, wealthy, or famous.

This was serious.

"You really do like him." There was tenderness in Zora's voice.

Oli swiped her hair out of her face seemingly unsure, which was an anomaly.

"The way I see it, the only thing that matters is do you think it's mutual?" Zora asked. Just then, they reached the front of the line. "One Dole Whip, please," Zora said.

In less than a minute, the order was ready, and they headed back for the statue where Sophia was waiting for them. Oli didn't backtrack to answer the question. In fact, they didn't say anything else. Zora followed her slow pace, giving Oli a little more time to be in her head.

"Hey. I thought that was you guys. I'd know that walk anywhere," Mike said, walking up beside them and grabbing Zora by the waist. He leaned in, peppering kisses on her neck and up to her cheeks.

Warmth cascaded over her, and she melded her body to his.

She felt light, airy, and playful as she bumped Oli's shoulder, pushing her into Jason. That was the thing about love. Being in it felt so good and so right, it was hard not to want the people closest to her to feel the same overwhelming sense of joy.

Zora slipped her hand into her pocket and fingered the small plastic bag. Her nerves were on fire, and the flames were spreading.

"We were just saying how we couldn't wait for you guys to come back, weren't we?" She winked at her best friend whose eyes went as wide as the rings nestled between Zora's fingers.

"Uh, yeah," Oli muttered.

In her periphery, Zora caught Jason stealing a glance at Oli. The look said everything. Not only was he noticing her, there was something else behind his stony façade. Zora saw past the square jaw, cleft chin, and side-swept blond hair. His face softened, and the hard lines yielded to a mix of appreciation and desire. There was affection gathering in his rain-washed gray eyes as they darted from Oli's mouth down to her décolletage.

When the wind carried her glossy, black mane, he pulled his gaze from her hair to her face.

That's when Zora's stare snagged his attention. A guilty smile tugged at the corners of his mouth, and he pressed a finger to his lips.

Zora flashed him a smug grin that said, *yes, I saw everything, and I may or may not keep your secret.*

Immediately, he stumbled back a few steps.

Mike shot him a meaningful glance before whispering something about redeeming a favor.

Jason sidled up safely at Everett's side. They could both trust that her brother wasn't focused on anything other than his gorgeous fiancée and the teensy bundle in her belly. Zora looked at Everett, who was mumbling something to himself and taking deep breaths.

"Ev, what's up?"

He flipped his wrist to check his watch just as they reached Sophia. "Before I forget—" he jammed his hands into his pants pockets and pulled out a bunch of earpods. He began passing them out to the five of them, then placed a set into his own ears. "Put these on," he instructed.

There were a few extra sets.

"Seriously, Ev, what's going on?" Zora asked. "What are these for, and who are the extra pairs for?"

He blew out a breath and flitted a glance at his watch a second time. "I don't have time to explain. It's eight twenty-four. They're already setting up for the nighttime spectacular. We need to hurry if we're going to make it before it starts."

Zora was now completely confused, but she went along with it, helping Sophia to her feet and following on his heels. Everett was just as much a Disney freak as she was. Maybe he just wanted to get in a few more rides while everyone else was occupied with the show.

They crossed over the main road and down the small green path next to the castle toward Snow White's wishing well. In the day, the place was a shady spot in the center of the park where it was usually quiet and empty. Now though, the grotto glowed in neon shades of iridescent blues, pinks, and purples. Above the statues of Snow White and her dwarfs, string lights lit up the trees like tiny fairies and glittering pixie dust. It was mesmerizing.

Zora beamed when she turned to Mike. "Do you have any coins? I want to make a wish."

Mike dug around in his pocket but came up empty. "Sorry, babe."

"Does anyone have a penn—" Zora was just about to go person to person asking, but then a crackling noise sounded in her ear before a voice she didn't recognize called them all to attention.

"Can everyone hear me okay?"

Zora jolted around and a man was standing with them. He must've seen the questions in her eyes because he gave a small wave and began to explain.

"Some of you don't know me yet, but I'm Will, Kendra's cousin."

And why are you here?

She felt the crease between her brows deepen as she looked around to see if anyone else was as confused as she was. She noticed Everett tense as he intertwined his fingers with Sophia's. Mike stood directly behind Zora, letting his chin rest on her head, apparently also unfazed by the guy's appearance. Oli and Jason were the only ones who were with her outside of the loop.

What was going on?

She lifted her chin and pushed her shoulders back to hear this guy out.

Will's phone glowed to life and he stared at the screen as he spoke. "Can you all hear me? This is sort of like a microphone check." He let out a short bark of laughter, but Zora was still not seeing the humor yet.

As each person nodded, she felt compelled to ask the questions no one else seemed to think were necessary. "Yes, we can all hear you in these things, but what exactly are we doing and what are you here for?"

He shot Everett a surprised glance, but her brother only shrugged.

Zora was just about to go off on him when spotlights began sweeping across the sky. Lasers shot from Sleeping Beauty Castle as fake snow fell to the rhythm of a musical beat. "It's a

Good Time," hummed through the air along with fireworks and a laser slideshow on the buildings.

"It's time," Everett said. He turned to face Sophia as her family walked up behind her. Her mom and aunt with their boyfriends, and Julie and Nico. Then Kendra joined them.

Zora stifled a gasp as Will began reading from his phone.

"We're gathered here today to witness and celebrate the union of John Everett Monroe and Sophia Elizabeth Kent in marriage…"

Zora's mouth flew open and she could barely breathe. She was so happy. Excitement raced through her. She pressed her hand to her heart and leaned against Mike's chest. It all made sense. The couples' trip. The guys going off to ride on their own. The earpods. The Mix Magic Show. And now this random guy joining them. It was all planned and prepared. Will was an officiant there to marry Everett and Sophia.

A sneak wedding.

Tears swam in Zora's eyes as she watched them speedily exchange vows and rings. She felt so fortunate to be a part of such an incredible day.

"You may now kiss the bride," Will said.

Everett wasted no time covering Sophia's lips with his. It seemed heartfelt and gentle but filled with so much promise.

Cries of congratulations filled their ears as the sky continued to light up, and Zora went in for hugs, careful not to squeeze the baby. It was giant reunion of the best kind.

Sophia's eyes sparkled as she turned to all of the people she loved. "I had no idea."

"Me neither, but I'm so happy for you guys!" Zora cried. "I love you so much."

In that moment, as she hugged her new sister and watched Mike embrace her brother, it was Everett's words that played in her head.

If you want to be with Mike, then go be with him.

Zora closed her eyes and blew out a breath. *Now or never.* Fishing the small bag from her pocket, she released Sophia, and counted backwards from ten to calm the butterflies rolling in her stomach. She was staring at Mike, waiting for him to turn around and trying not to have a nervous breakdown.

She cleared her throat and stilled herself as each pair of eyes centered on her. Between her fingers, she rubbed the two rings together.

"Mike—"

"Wait," he said, scraping his hands through his hair before dropping them and shaking them out. "Zo…"

As he lowered himself to one knee, recognition dawned on Zora's face.

His mouth twitched and a disarmingly hot smile danced on his lips.

"Are you literally trying to out-gesture my big gesture again?" Zora asked, but she couldn't bite back the grin tugging at the corners of her mouth.

Mike pulled his bottom lip between his teeth and flashed those glittering green eyes at her. "You're just so impatient. I don't know how I'm ever going to be enough for you, but I'm hoping you'll make me the happiest man alive and marry me."

Zora stuck out her tongue and brightened at their playfulness. "I mean, do you even have rings? I have rings. I actually put a lot of thought into this. They're not from Tiffany's." She held up the two rings with the small green frogs on them. "I think they're—"

"Perfect," Mike said, getting to his feet because obviously they were not the traditional type of couple. He pulled her in tight against him and stared into her teary eyes. "I love you so much. Now will you please marry me and stop embarrassing me?"

"Under one condition."

"Oh." Mike deflated and let his arms hang by his sides. "I'm dying to hear this *one* all-important contingency. Please, don't hold back on account of my bruised ego and shattered heart."

His eyes crinkled at the edges.

Mike electrified her. Her breath and her pulse quickened. Longing whispered through her throbbing body as they slid the rings on each other's fingers.

"Well actually, it's a few conditions."

"I'd expect nothing less from you."

Zora inhaled and listed her conditions. "I'll marry you, Mr. Kennedy, if we get to live in your house and the dream kitchen is mine. Oh, and, no more lies. Only truth from here on out."

"Deal."

Thank you for spending your time with Zora and Mike. If you enjoyed Mixed Emotions, please consider leaving a review.

If you loved the All Mixed Up Series, grab the All Mixed Up series collection BOXSET! Three books all wrapped up in one...

Join me in my reader group. I'd love to chat! That's where I connect with readers most.
Mia Heintzelman Reader Group

Get the ALL MIXED UP SERIES BOXSET Now!

ABOUT MIA HEINTZELMAN

Mia Heintzelman is a graduate of the University of California, Berkeley and the University of Nevada, Las Vegas. She is a Chicago native who always has a book in her purse, loves to pair sweet and spicy tea with fluffy socks, and can't go wrong with polka dots and pearls. She lives in Las Vegas with her husband and two children.

www.ingramcontent.com/pod-product-compliance
Lightning Source LLC
Chambersburg PA
CBHW020334180626
46812CB00001B/203